the quick and the dead

matthew john lee

Published by

MELROSE BOOKS

An Imprint of Melrose Press Limited
St Thomas Place, Ely
Cambridgeshire
CB7 4GG, UK
www.melrosebooks.com

FIRST EDITION

Copyright © Matthew John Lee 2008

The Author asserts his moral right to
be identified as the author of this work

Cover designed by Catherine McIntyre

ISBN 978-1-906050-78-8

Printed and bound in Great Britain by:
Biddles. King's Lynn, Norfolk.

Mixed Sources

Product group from well-managed
forests, controlled sources and
recycled wood or fiber
www.fsc.org Cert no. TT-COC-002303
© 1996 Forest Stewardship Council

FSC

PEFC

PEFC/16-33-293
PEFC - Promoting Sustainable Forest Management

There is a land of the living and a land of the dead, and the bridge is love.

Thornton Wilder

In this world there are foulers, there are followers and there are flowers.

This book is dedicated to Monica.

One of the flowers.

Part 1

Chapter 1

The English Channel
between Calais and Dover

O N A LARGE ship a person can almost forget they are at sea. It is like being on an island with no social ills, where unemployment is a luxury only the wealthy can afford and the less privileged working class possess the cleanest clothes and the widest smiles. The vessel does not sail in rough seas and the weather is always warm and sunny. There is no earth to sustain an ecosystem and no goods are manufactured yet its conspicuous consumption of the finest of products is a source of great pride. All the created pollution is piped away to another world beyond its borders of which the passengers have only a dim awareness. It is a situation with which they are all happy and content.

'On a large ship,' mused Benedict.

But Ben wasn't on a large ship and he wasn't cruising in a part of the world whose climate allowed for days of uninterrupted sunbathing. He leant against the white metal railing, cold and unyielding, which separated his moving island from the grey-green sea below. From a distance it looked calm but up close the effortless rise and fall of this huge mass of water was almost mesmerising. Like a sleeping giant, the soothing rhythm of movement whilst in repose gave evidence of a tremendous latent power. The air was clear, though one could hardly say this was a pleasant day for June. Light grey clouds obstinately refused to move across the sky, though where they were whitest a shaft of sunlight had forced its way through. It lit up a small area of water, which came alive with dancing sparkles. It was one of those sights of nature that had the ability to lighten the soul though there was no sign of this uplifting effect on the expressions of the passengers.

The few seagulls that had glided from the port of Calais alongside the boat had finally decided to abandon their chaperoning duties and return home. Looking out to where the human day-trippers were heading it was now just possible to see a dark shadow on the horizon as if the uneducated hand of an infant had tried to draw a straight line with a thick flat grey marker pen, making characteristic jerky movements. The effort had been improved by a teacher ruling off the bottom section, the English Channel ruling off the coastal features of this most extreme part of South East England. A few white frigates from the United Nations could be seen at a distance, enforcing their blockade at this most intensely guarded gateway to the British mainland. It had been easy enough to block the Channel Tunnel beneath their feet with a ten-metre thick plug of concrete, but preventing access from the sea or air was an altogether more difficult and costlier operation.

Ben's gaze fell on the back of a blonde haired lady in her twenties whose body was also pressed against the white railing. Her short, lacquered bob of a hairstyle seemed to accentuate the shapely bulge of buttocks pushing against the pink material of her mini-skirt. He admired the pale white legs that sprouted from their firm base, eventually tapering to a black pair of felt ankle boots. His eyes remained fixed on those legs, not as smooth and featureless as a model's, but sculptured by the taut definition of muscle into curves that boldly affirmed her sexuality. She could have been an athlete at some stage in her life but was carrying too much weight to be one now. There was no need for him to raise his eyes above waist level, those twin pearly columns had caused enough of a sensation and produced a single-minded intention. On such idiosyncrasies was Ben currently attracted to the female sex: the size of a pair of breasts, the careless positioning of a lock of hair, the unusual curvature of a smile, a moody pair of eyes had all provided the spur for previous conquests. Indeed he had discovered that the absence of feeling these peculiarities engendered had emboldened him to act with far more courage than would have been the case in the past. A mild sea gust blew across the open deck, causing her red blouse to flap in the wind but neither the hair nor mini-skirt was disturbed. When the couple standing next to her moved away and it was clear she was a solitary traveller, a thrill of excitement starting in the stomach surged through her admirer and without a moment's hesitation he moved to fill the recently vacated space.

The thick line on the horizon could now be separated into a white bulk topped by a dark crust. Ben surveyed the familiar scene then let out a sigh.

'Such a shame, such a waste.'

The young woman quickly turned to him. She was less facially attractive than the rear view had led him to believe, with rather thick features and the suggestion of wispy hair about the chin.

'You English?' she asked.

Ben visualised those legs and this rapidly removed the faintly disagreeable impression made by her face, especially as he was able to place the accent almost instantaneously.

'This is getting better and better,' he thought. 'A German.'

Realising that haste was unnecessary and probably even counter-productive, his gaze out to sea did not alter and after a well-judged time interval he replied sadly, 'It is not the happiest nationality to be in these times.' He inwardly admitted however that it was probably one of the best when it came to getting your leg over.

The blonde German woman wanted to talk further but Ben asked to be alone with his thoughts and be allowed to look at the view without interruption. It was not an unreasonable request for one who had suffered so greatly and she was sympathetic to it. The features around the white cliffs gradually became more distinguishable and to the left of three radio masts, above the cranes of the now deserted harbour, Dover castle emerged from what had just been a dark bump.

Ben's mind went back in time to a sunny day spent at Dover castle with his sister, brother-in-law and their two young children. He had walked the full length of the battlements, stopping only to look at the cannons and the impressive views they commanded, in the steps of countless soldiers over the centuries, who had defended this stronghold. From Admiralty Lookout he surveyed the straits of Dover alongside the statue of Vice-Admiral Sir Bertram Ramsey. The secret wartime tunnels, hewn within the heart of the white cliffs, were redolent with World War Two nostalgia. Notices on the walls explained in unashamedly patriotic detail the evacuation of Dunkirk as well as the landings on the beaches of Normandy. Huge telephone exchanges encased in dark wood, antique typewriters and maps filled the otherwise spartanly furnished domed, clammy rooms. The sounds of an air attack, complete with intermittent breaks in the electricity, which plunged the tourists into sudden darkness, were piped through to create the authentic feel of a raid by the Luftwaffe. Above the noise of the falling bombs one could hear the sensible voices of women speaking BBC English, wearing starched white blouses and long grey skirts, trying to remain calm and businesslike. Their brave, bluff male counterparts said things like 'cor blimey' and seemed more preoccupied with the challenge of cadging a 'smoke' off each other.

Moving from the outskirts to the centre of Dover castle is like cutting through an old oak tree: the closer to the middle you are, the further back in time you have travelled. Mentally retracing this journey, Ben remembered the rectangular forms of Henry II's keep, built in the twelfth century. An audio-visual presentation told the story of the siege of 1216, when one hundred and forty knights under Hubert de Burgh resisted the French army of Prince Louis. Emerging, blinking, into the sunlight from the dark and gloomy bowels of this building to be greeted by ice cream sellers on the tranquil lawns, it was almost impossible to imagine the scene of carnage it must once have been. At the core of the complex lay the Saxon church and Roman lighthouse, which was so old as to be devoid of anything of historical interest. A roughly built hollow stone cone is how one could best describe it, the only modern addition being an iron grill set into the circular wall above head height to prevent large pieces of rock and dead birds falling on unsuspecting visitors.

Japanese walked alongside Americans and the information boards were printed in German and Italian. The children climbed on the cannons, peered cautiously over stone parapets and ran headlong down the steep grassy banks. A wedding reception was being prepared at the Officers New Barracks and two smartly dressed gentlemen fussed over fixing a red carpet to the steps leading to the entrance of that imposing Victorian building. A party of elderly people was being ferried along the steep winding roads at a sedate pace on a tourist buggy, overtaking young couples walking hand in hand. It seemed that the worst chapters of history had run their course and were well and truly buried in the past. The durability of Dover castle against the most evil of foes over many centuries was emblematic of the enduring nature of Britain as a whole. This fairest isle had gone on and would go on forever and its future appeared as bright and peaceful as the weather that day.

The boat was allowed to go no nearer than five kilometres from the British coast. Limits set and imposed by the United

Nations in conjunction with the European Union were necessarily in the metric system. A slow turn to the right was the signal that it had reached its permitted boundary and it proceeded to hug the coastline at this respectful distance, travelling Northwards. Ben looked at the German woman and felt his eyes involuntarily homing in on those legs again. Turning his gaze away with an effort, he observed that in fact the white cliffs of Dover were not as white as song and legend would have one believe. Admittedly 'the dirty pale yellow cliffs of Dover, stained here and there with green algae' did not have quite the same ring to it, but it was interesting to consider how that word 'white' could have been used to signify pure, innocent, virtuous and without taint. A beacon of hope to the downtrodden visiting British shores, the virgin bride resolutely defending her honour against the loathsome advances of an unwanted aggressor, a promise for everything good that lay in the land beyond.

To the left of Dover town, and if one knew where to look, it was possible to see the concrete wall enclosing Samphire Hoe, the recently created piece of land made out of the waste produced by the digging of the Channel Tunnel. At the time of construction it was designed as a wild unspoiled nature reserve, planted with grass seed specially brought in from Runnymede. People had come from miles around to see the wavy grassland and observe plant and insect life slowly evolving. A new species was enthusiastically greeted by those who saw a microcosm of Eden taking shape, the random nature of life creation contrasting starkly with the order of their own lives. Most passengers on the boat would have been unaware of the existence of Samphire Hoe, dismissing it as just some vegetation at the foot of the cliffs. Ben picked it out, but observing nothing remarkable, turned away.

He turned to the woman standing beside him and felt it was about time to start a conversation.

'I'm sorry, I forgot to ask you your name.'

'Elisabetta,' came the quick reply to this most predictable of conversation openers.

'You will have to forgive me for not talking so much, I always find this trip difficult,' he continued.

'Did you have any family or friends that were left on the mainland?' Elisabetta asked.

For a while Ben was stunned by the crass stupidity of this question and was at a loss to know quite how to reply.

'All my fucking family, all my fucking friends,' he raged inwardly, gripping tightly onto the white railing.

'Does she really think that everyone I knew, living and working in Britain, by some happy coincidence happened to be out of the country when the attack came?'

With an effort to remain calm and remembering the purpose behind starting this conversation, he pursed his lips then slowly and deliberately said,

'Almost everybody I ever knew never left Britain.'

'Was that very hard for you?' she asked with some sympathy.

'Jesus this woman must have graduated from Toothickfor University with a first class honours degree in asking daft questions,' he thought. 'If everybody you know is suddenly wiped out, is that an easy thing to deal with?'

'Yes,' he continued in a slow monotonic voice trying not to betray any emotion. 'Things have been very difficult.'

'In fact,' he followed up his previous statement almost immediately before she had the chance to drop another ill-considered bombshell of insensitivity on top of him. 'In fact the whole situation is so difficult I'd rather not talk about it.' He noticed her look of disappointment and felt a disappointment of his own. 'At least not now,' he continued. 'This trip brings up so many emotions that I find it difficult to deal with. However you seem like an understanding and sensitive person, perhaps I could give you a phone call after we have returned to France. Do you live close to Paris?'

The boat continued North, past the pier at Deal and on to Sandwich and then Ramsgate. Here and there it was possible to see buildings, towns, beaches, but there was one thing that was not normal about any of these sights. There were no signs of humans, no moving cars, no trains, no smoke coming from a chimney, nothing to indicate a trace of life at all. Neither was there a trace of death as no corpses were visible along the shoreline. At least in Pompeii plaster casts of bodies had been scattered around the ancient ruins in various stages of distress but here there was nothing. It was as if everyone had simultaneously decided to board a large spaceship or been energised into the ether as in Star Trek. At Foreness Point the coastline turned sharply to the west as it started to form what would eventually become the mouth of the River Thames. Here the boat turned around and headed back to Calais by the most direct route.

Ben engaged Elisabetta as best as he could in idle chatter during the remainder of the journey, but upon disembarking had no desire to prolong the conversation. He pleaded urgent business to attend to in Calais, regretting he would not be able to accompany her onward to Paris. He had already gained everything he desired from the strongly attractive German woman: her name, her address and her sympathy.

Chapter 2

The town of Moshi, Tanzania, at the foot of Mount Kilimanjaro

D R ROBERT WILLIAMS detested his new title of Chief of Gynaecology. He had joined the medical profession to save lives and relieve suffering, but now spent too much of his time shuffling paper, attending meetings and making political rather than medical decisions. To cap it all he now faced a serious problem, avoidance of which was made impossible as a result of this increased responsibility. He paced up and down his large office at the Kilimanjaro Christian Medical Centre and pondered what to do. A younger Dr Williams would have poked fun at his moral dilemma, maintaining that there was only one correct way to act. That was a different person in a different time, somehow things had become more complicated as the years progressed.

Robert had seen many changes during his long tenure at KCMC. The idealistic, if thoroughly impractical, policies of Mwalimu Julius Nyerere had been discredited and given way to a greater realism which pervaded all parts of Tanzanian society. Though inevitable and arguably beneficial, it had resulted in money dominating most considerations and a lowering of expectations regarding the innate goodness of the human spirit. The old man who worked at the hospital morgue complained that these days funeral companies wanted to see money in their hands before they would even consider removing anyone for burial. In fact they asked for the money before they asked for the deceased's name. There had also been a reduction in the number of white faces amongst doctors as generously funded aid packages from Europe and North America had dried up. Although Robert was not on anything but friendly terms with his African colleagues, there was inevitably a cultural difference between them. A different way of looking at the world that prevented a deep mutual empathy and the forging of the close personal bonds he had enjoyed in a different era. In the past he could have shared his problem with a trusted confidant. Now he felt that nobody would understand the complexity of his emotions or, perhaps more importantly, could be relied on to keep their mouth shut. His recent promotion had only added to this feeling of isolation.

Dr Olanya was a pleasant man, there was no reason to suppose he was not a good man, a family man who had undoubtedly helped a lot of people since joining the medical staff at KCMC. The problem was that a baby had just died as a result of negligence. The understandably distraught parents had been fobbed off with the excuse that their newly born son had died of 'breathing problems' but an anonymous letter had circulated within the hospital and prompted the launching of an internal inquiry. The cursory report into the incident lay on Dr Williams' desk and contained so many contradictions and medical improbabilities that it was obvious someone was lying and trying to cover up their own incompetence. The subsequent interview with Dr Olanya had confirmed Robert's worst fears: he was evasive and less than candid, making him most likely the culpable party.

What was to be done though? He had once believed that truth was all that mattered and had to be ruthlessly pursued regardless of the cost. Years of working in Tanzania however had taught him that a vigorous exposé of what had taken place would probably benefit no one, least of all himself. Apart from this incident Dr Olanya was a reliable gynaecologist, even if he could be accused of sometimes neglecting his hospital duties in favour of devoting too much time to his private practice in the town of Moshi. Who would replace him and how would the patients at KCMC benefit from having one less doctor to treat them? This was all assuming he was found guilty: a long drawn-out investigation might apportion no blame and most likely result in no action being taken. He would be back to square one, having merely achieved the production of an atmosphere of distrust within the department. His own position could even become so intolerable that he might find himself on a plane out of the country, but to where? That was a question the answer to which he could hardly bear contemplating. On the other hand standards had to be maintained and he was well aware of the eyes of medical technicians, who knew what had happened. They were watching his every move to see what kind of example would be set. Although the possibility of legal action by the victim's parents was remote, what was his duty to them? Medicine is full of moral and ethical quandaries, most of which he would have no problem dealing with. This however was the worst kind of predicament for Dr Williams: it wasn't about the risks of a certain procedure, the cost implications of a new treatment or the right of a patient to choose to die. This brought into question his own honour and defined what kind of man he was.

Dr Williams continued to pace intermittently around his office, hoping that the alternate movement and stopping would jolt his mind into some solution of the problem. A short, slightly built man, with round glasses and a distinguished white closely cropped beard, he gave the appearance of your typical intellectual expatriate in the tropics. All the years of living abroad had taught him one important lesson, however: he would never fully understand this country or radically change it. His actions should be directed by pragmatism instead of idealism and paramount amongst all considerations should be the welfare of the patients.

During one of his periods of immobility he gazed out of the large window in the direction of Mount Kilimanjaro. The hospital owned a large section of land on which various crops were cultivated for consumption by the staff and patients. Beyond that the green and fertile region of Kibosho, watered by mountain rains and densely forested with innumerable banana and coffee trees rose up the gentle slopes that signalled the commencement of the world's highest free-standing mountain. The profile was broad, dramatic in sheer magnitude rather than shape, a gradual swelling on the crust of the earth that demonstrated its consequence by the huge circle of land it commanded. Its complexion was green with random patches of light and dark indicating where the clouds had cast their shadows. Further up, the mountain assumed a smoother demeanour as the jagged features of the forest gave way to a moorland of spindly trees, bushes and grasses. Where the light caught this type of plant life, beautiful green uplands were produced, Elysian fields offering oases of peace. The Masai had not called it the House of God for no reason. The snow-capped peak was not on display today as rather frustratingly an impenetrable barrier of cloud cover prevented one from seeing the uppermost sections of this marvel of nature.

He remembered how he had felt so excited and inspired on coming to this part of the world many years ago. The mountain never ceased to inspire awe and wonder, changing its appearance according to the weather conditions and time of day: a huge animate petrification whose manifold mysteries kept him enthralled with the view. He had cycled for hours along the many small roads and dirt tracks, some no wider than footpaths, that criss-crossed the entire region. Every outing was an adventure as you never knew what to expect and would end up experiencing something novel each time. The Chagga people who inhabited the area were friendly and respectful but maintained a healthy suspicion of strangers. They really lived on the land, not just visiting it from their comfortable homes when necessity or desire demanded. The soil beneath their feet was bound up with everything that constituted their existence, so that the countryside was alive and vibrant with their lives. He believed that his work was important and making a real difference to these people. Then there was the great camaraderie of his colleagues: away from the shackles of their native society they could say and be what they wanted. There was no requirement to pursue material wealth or to conform to what others expected from them. Life was free and they were able to concentrate on the simple pleasures of self-fulfilment. At the end of the day they would sit down at a local bar, drinking cold Tusker and watching the sun go down against a backdrop of mountain and broad banana leaves.

Robert wanted to go home but knew this was impossible as his homeland had been destroyed. Where was his real home anyway? There was no geographical location that could define it. If a home could be described as a situation inducing a state of mind where you truly feel at home, then his home belonged to the time when he had first come to Tanzania. Returning to that period of his life however seemed just as impossible as returning to the country of his birth, unless one believed in time travel. He was isolated from friendship, from his homeland, from his ideals, by his authority and by his memories. What else was he isolated from? Oh yes, his wife.

Robert pulled into the driveway of the large house only one kilometre from KCMC to be saluted by a guard at the gate. The garden enclosed by the wooden stake and barbed wire fence was obscenely large, so much so that it would have been a criminal use of water to try and keep it green all year round. The house was single storey but commodious. In fact the person who first coined the phrase 'sprawling building' could have originated from this part of the world. It seemed to have assumed a life of its own and grown in all directions over the years without any obvious plan. Different building materials, colours and heights contributed to the feeling of a patchwork quilt style of construction. An internal courtyard had even sprung up, more by accident than design.

There was a large group of people sitting in the living room and amongst the gathering was his wife Anna. She smiled as he entered but made no attempt to get up from her position on the sofa. Robert issued a general greeting to everyone, most of whom he did not know. In polite African society it is usually necessary to go around the room shaking hands and greeting each person individually, but he had long ago abandoned this time-consuming and awkward custom. He walked quickly through to his study, the one room in the house that was his sanctuary, where it was possible to sit down and be undisturbed by whatever else happened. This room had become more and more of a retreat in recent years, his habitat shrinking as the rest of the house expanded. Except when eating, sleeping or visiting the bathroom necessitated a change of location, the other rooms hardly existed for him. The guests might leave but there would be others to take their place, a constant stream of banal chatter about nothing in particular. He never felt more lonely than when in a crowded room with others trying to engage him in conversation. When his wife was not entertaining guests there was the television to keep her company. There was virtually nothing they had in common anymore and whatever words were exchanged revolved around the superficial details of daily life. They did not hate each other, they had simply grown apart and realised they had nothing meaningful to share. At times he felt like an ornament; a rare object of great monetary value to be shown off on occasions and admired, only to be put back in its box and forgotten about when everybody else had gone.

Anna had been a pretty nurse and looked particularly fetching in her white nurse's uniform and hat. She performed her duties efficiently and without complaint and had not been one to demonstrate her availability to the doctors too readily. What Robert found most alluring was her kindness and obvious concern for the patients. He noticed the tender look in her eyes as she patiently listened to whatever problems the women had and imagined that same tenderness being extended to himself. It seemed to him almost inconceivable at the time that anything malicious or cruel could ever emanate from this person. In fact nothing hateful had ever come from her, just a wall of neglect and an unwillingness to accommodate him into her lifestyle. Of course he blamed himself for having such unrealistic expectations of her. The warning signs had been there during their courtship but he felt honour-bound to continue the relationship to its conclusion as she provided him with no good reason to break it off. He had foolishly hoped that any differences would be ironed out once they were married but inevitably they only became worse. A few months after the wedding he wondered how it had all happened: he was like a somnambulist walking calmly and blindly to the altar, who had only woken up after his fate had been sealed.

Chapter 3

The Mountains of the Hindu Kush, Afghanistan

THE SPANISH SOLDIER wore the badge of a red cross, the cross of St James, on his light brown combat jacket. Beneath that was another badge depicting St James the Moor-slayer. It was a drawing based on the statue of St James that resided in the cathedral of Santiago de Compostela. He was shown on a white charger, sword held aloft in the air, with the hacked-off heads of his Muslim enemies lying beneath the horse's hooves. His face depicted neither joy nor sadness as he carried out his grisly duty, just an iron-willed determination to get on with it. The Spanish soldier told Tallis that St James had appeared at the battle of Clavijo in 844 on a white cloud, spurring Spanish soldiers on to victory against the Moors. It was thus entirely appropriate that his badge should be worn during the campaign in which they were presently involved. He walked slowly but with purpose towards Tallis, his daysack carried in one hand, whilst a rifle carelessly slung over his opposite shoulder swung as he walked. Tallis had hoped his timekeeping would not be so accurate, giving him the opportunity to finish his game of cards. The Spaniard, however, was just as keen to leave his post as his relief was reluctant to set out and the fact that he had been looking at his watch almost continuously for the last hour made it extremely unlikely he would be late.

Tallis folded his hand of cards and rose slowly out of a camp chair. On the way out of the mess tent he picked up his hat and water bottle and moved to intercept the man just finishing his duty. 'Anything to report?' he asked. The Spanish soldier shook his head wearily as he handed over the binoculars. There had been nothing to report for over a fortnight from any lookout post. Tallis walked up the gentle slope to a rock, which commanded a view of the entire valley beneath them. It would be difficult for anyone to pass unobserved through the valley from this vantage-point. He found the spectacle of this barren landscape uninspiring despite the steep-sided and dramatic mountains. Small paths, goat-trading routes, criss-crossed the valley but there was not much sign of vegetation except for the odd tree or bush. It seemed miraculous how a people could survive amongst such lifeless conditions. Then there was the ubiquitous dust: it got everywhere and invaded every aspect of your being. There was dust in your gun, up your nostrils and in your food, whilst to try and keep clothes clean and free from dust was an exercise in futility.

He had been in Afghanistan for nearly a year now and so far had not fired a shot at the enemy. He desperately longed for some action but only seemed to spend day after day camping, looking for an adversary who never showed up. At times he wondered if it even existed in this remote part of the world, as he had never seen any evidence of its presence. The other men in his unit were a variety of nationalities and backgrounds with different reasons for fighting this war. Some were out-and-out mercenaries who made no attempt to disguise the fact they were in it for the money, whilst others had naïvely joined up seeking an adventure. With Tallis it was personal: he had his own score to settle.

The commander of the unit was a tall Texan named George. His personality was like a large stick of candyfloss: initially attractive and enjoyable but increasingly tiresome as one realised there was no substance behind it. At the start of this tour of duty he had been fairly popular, his tall stories and proud boasts of a former life in the US army providing a welcome diversion from the monotony of daily life and an entertaining way to spend the evenings. As time had progressed however they appeared to be increasingly the product of an overactive imagination and, as with a surfeit of candyfloss, people were becoming sick of them. The lack of esteem in which he was held, particularly by those who had once been soldiers in a national army, was also due to the fact that he knew little about military discipline and certainly could not lead by example. George seemed to sense the growing alienation between himself and the others, produced by their inability to take him seriously. Whilst this clearly bothered him, any speeches he made designed to increase his standing within the unit usually had the opposite effect.

Tallis spent the long hot afternoon sitting on the rock looking down into the valley. It was amazing how quickly the human mind could adjust to doing nothing for long periods of time. He discovered that he could transform the simplest of tasks, like cutting toenails, into an exercise lasting nearly an hour through carefully considering each small action and taking suitable breaks for reflection. He felt as if his mind should be racing with all manner of deep and meaningful ideas given the solitude, but instead was surprised that he hardly thought of anything. What would those who had joined up in search of adventure tell the folks back home? He realised he had just pinpointed a possible reason for George's exaggerated storytelling.

Tallis was relieved of his duty just before nightfall. He dreaded the night lookout duty: there was even less to look at than during the day and if an attacker did burst onto the scene he would be upon you before you realised it. There were the night vision binoculars, of course, but it was difficult to keep them pressed against your eyes all night. Fortunately he rarely had to do the nightshift since, for some perverse reason, others seemed to enjoy it and would willingly volunteer. Following a brief consideration of the hardships of night-time duty, Tallis had come to the worrying conclusion that they all probably slept.

The card game in the mess tent had finished and most men had retired to their tents having eaten their rations for the day. Tallis had reserved one thought for the night, successfully managing to block it out of his mind during the daytime. In one month's time he was due a rest and recreation break. There being no country in the immediate vicinity where one could truly have a good time, he planned to travel down to India. He would be on his own, accountable to no one for his actions, with a bulging wallet, the wages of four months of soldiering. One could visit a great many bars and brothels on that kind of money in the few weeks he had off. Yes, he decided, this was a thought best reserved for the night as he clambered naked into his sleeping bag that was lying on the thin camping mat.

The members of the unit did not really need George to be swinging a handbell outside their tents to be informed that it was morning. With deliberate disdain they ignored his exhortations to move quickly and ready themselves for inspection. They knew they had to assemble at six thirty and would do so without the benefit of his constant harrying. The soldiers stood to attention, though not stiffly, on the makeshift parade ground as he gave the orders for the day. Rotas for everything from guarding to cleaning duties were read out, quite unnecessarily as they were already posted on the notice board in the mess tent. Acknowledging that some might be disappointed at the lack of action so far, he assured them that they were doing a good job and that from intelligence received he was confident they were narrowing in on their enemy. These terrorists were just cowards and would rather attack women and children than fight man to man. He reminded the soldiers that such low life would always run if they could but that they were united on a noble quest to hunt them down to the ends of the earth if necessary and make them pay for what they had done.

The group of about twenty men moved on to a level area of ground where a series of wooden posts had been planted at regular intervals. Attached to each post was a dummy dressed in a white robe and red and white patterned headscarf.

'Show me what you are going to do to those Arabs when you meet them!' George shouted at the top of his voice. 'I want a bullet in the head or a bullet in the heart,' he continued, holding up two plastic bags, one with red dye inside and the other containing black dye.

This was one of his favourite eccentricities: when a bullet hit the head, red dye would spurt out of the plastic bag that had been placed there. He refused however to put red dye in the bag placed in the position of the heart, unequivocally stating that this part of any Arab was black and rotten and so only black liquid should come out.

'Show them no mercy, because you can be sure that they will shoot you in the back.'

One last trick was the rigging up of two large loudspeakers through which the music of The Cure would emerge just before the firing commenced. The familiar sound of George's pet song 'Killing an Arab' began. The shots started and the black and red liquid splattered over the white clothes of the dummies. Above the noise of the gunfire could be heard the repeated refrain, 'I am the stranger, killing an Arab.'

Chapter 4

T HE NEWS ON French television was concerned with the situation in Gibraltar. Spain was pushing hard to be granted sovereignty over the rock at its southern tip but the Gibraltarians were determined to oppose this merger. The case was a diplomat's nightmare and raised unprecedented legal issues. The inhabitants of the rock had already let it be known they would challenge in the European Court any settlement made without their consent. As British citizens they argued that no foreign power had the right to decide on their sovereignty, whilst the Spanish countered by saying that as Britain no longer existed as a force in the world the concept of British nationality was meaningless. The European nations trembled at the prospect of Spanish soldiers marching into Gibraltar and the consequent effect on public opinion if blood started to flow. Northern Ireland had been reunited with the South, through a mixture of generous pay-offs and voluntary repatriation principally sponsored by the Americans. The Falkland Islands had agreed to the status of a United Nations protectorate administered by a Governor General reporting to a committee in New York. Accommodations had been reached in other parts of the world but despite all efforts at cajoling their representatives and no matter what incentives were dreamed up, the Gibraltarians would not budge. It was a particularly bad, if true, joke to say these people were as immovable as the rock of Gibraltar. Tensions were now surfacing within the European Union, created by Spain's urgency to resolve the issue and every other nation's procrastination. It had dawned on the government in Madrid that if Britain was recolonised at some time in the near future they would have lost their best chance in over three hundred years to reclaim their ancient land. Talk of an economic blockade and Spanish troops seen massing near the border had caused a flurry of diplomatic activity in an attempt to defuse the deteriorating situation.

Reporters had been placed either side of the border and their anxious words were transmitted into living rooms worldwide: the mayor of Gibraltar vowed that those he represented would lie down in front of tanks instead of capitulating and living under the heel of the Spanish. A rather innocent-looking eighteen year old soldier, who said he was from the Basque region, claimed he did not know why he had been posted there but that no orders had been given to invade. Ben was only half listening to the analysis back in the studio when there was a ring at the doorbell. He switched off the programme and went downstairs to let in Elisabetta.

During their conversation on the boat he had already established that she was twenty-four years old and Austrian not German. In Paris for six months as part of a course on hotel catering, it was her first time out of her native country. She admitted to being intrigued by all things British, temporarily flummoxing Ben with the statement, 'My parents brought me up on a diet of Beatles.' Further questioning quickly clarified she was talking about the music group and was not in fact insectivorous. The royal family too was an object of admiration, as were 'those guards with red jackets and big black fluffy hats'. Ben told her about an extraordinary auction he had recently read about at the New York branch of Christies, where an original double A-sided single of Strawberry Fields Forever / Penny Lane had fetched a price of $20 000. Both songs had achieved a kind of cult status, one evoking Liverpudlian suburban life of a bygone age and the other how special places become inextricably linked with magical emotions especially during childhood. Yes it was an old single, but $20 000? It had reached number one so imagine how many copies must have been bought. If the manufacturers had had the foresight to print a few hundred extra, they could have earned the eternal gratitude of their children and made them millionaires. Ben had remarked to Elisabetta how he wished his parents had bought him a few more mugs when Charles and Diana were getting married. A few weeks after the social event of the year in St Paul's Cathedral shopowners could hardly give them away.

Elisabetta was wearing pink trousers and a white blouse. She was immediately impressed by the size and décor of the flat, so much grander than the modest dilapidated accommodation arranged by her college, which she had to share with two other female students. The worldwide recession had been going on for two and a half years now and the kind of employment able to support a lifestyle such as this was an enviable rarity. Ben fixed them both drinks and they sat down in the lounge. The photographs on the wall told of another, happier life, which was now just a memory: the one serious girlfriend in his life, his parents' silver wedding anniversary, graduation, summer holidays on the beach with relatives and smiling children. He imagined Elisabetta returning to the bosom of her family back in Austria. There would be the kind and trusting parents, so proud of their little girl, waiting to greet her on her return. She would not allow their image of her to be tainted by revealing everything that had happened in Paris, but would happily live a twin-track life, changing lanes when it suited her to satisfy appearances and her own desires. The comfortable hypocrisy of family life would continue as it had done for generations before. Ben tried to steer the conversation away from families and asked as many questions as he could think of about her course of study. The topic of Gibraltar was held in reserve and would only be called up in an emergency.

Over dinner it was his turn to tell the story of his recent life and how he had ended up in Paris. He had been working for a large drinks company, concentrating on selling beer in former communist bloc countries, his travels taking him to Prague, Moscow, Warsaw and Budapest amongst other places. Sales had started well, as people starved of decent beer for so long drank the company's products with great enthusiasm. Later more competition emerged and local breweries were established but it still proved to be a good export market. When the attack occurred he found himself stranded in Eastern Europe without a job and no home to return to. The company was taken over by the French and the idea of marketing British beer, drawing heavily on the nostalgia for all things British, was hatched. Ben was the ideal person to take on the task of organising this and had already produced Newcastle Brown Ale and London Pride as well as a whole host of other famous names. Nobody was really sure how accurate the recipes were but it was the labels that sold them. Despite the recession they sold well and at the moment he was working on launching a new beer called Stonehenge.

After the meal they retired to the living room, put on some soft music and began to chat. It was at this point that Elisabetta asked about the photographs on the wall and before long her heart was full of pity for this man who had lost everything so near and dear to him. His head nestled in her lap, whilst she ran her fingers through his hair, then, taking both his hands in hers she stood up and led him into the bedroom.

Ben awoke in the morning to find Elisabetta still sleeping beside him. Picking up the small piece of white plastic that had been torn off the corner of the condom wrapping the night before and which now lay on the bedside table, he got out of bed. The plastic was dropped in the rubbish bin as he walked to the wardrobe to put on some boxer shorts. Although a cure for AIDS

24

had recently been discovered, the wearing of a rubber was a habit that had not yet been broken. He switched on the television and followed a programme concerned with the present economic climate. There was still no sign of the much-anticipated upturn in business and though things were not becoming a lot worse, neither were they getting any better. The destruction of British industry had left some companies without the raw materials to manufacture, whilst others had lost a market overnight. In the interdependent international marketplace few had escaped the knock-on effects of this disturbance. The value of stocks, not just a barometer of economic reality but also human emotion, had plummeted as investors grappled to come to terms with the enormous psychological blow dealt to Western society. The price of gold, a refuge in times of uncertainty, had soared whilst that of other commodities had tumbled. The programme cut to a debate between one expert who believed the free market would sort out the whole mess and another who advocated government intervention, quoting the success of Roosevelt's New Deal in 1930's depression-hit America. The discussion was becoming tedious, a rehash of economic arguments that had been going on for decades without resolution. Ben switched channels to view the sport.

Elisabetta was stirring and reached out her arm to stroke his back. He felt a little uncomfortable at this display of intimacy but managed to return a weak smile. This was the time in a relationship he disliked the most as he tried to extricate himself from the situation in which he had been voluntarily placed by the exertions of the previous night. He quickly stood up and announced he was going to make breakfast.

'Nothing for me thanks,' shouted Elisabetta, causing him to change direction en route to the kitchen and head for the bathroom instead to shower.

After a few minutes he heard the glass shower door sliding

and felt the naked body of his lover pressing against his back. The intention of creating some distance between them was abandoned as she rubbed him gently with soap and water. Turning around to face her he made no attempt at self-restraint, not even delaying his actions to find a condom. As she was dropped off at the college Elisabetta asked if she would see him again.

'I'm just not ready for a serious relationship,' replied Ben.

'So this was just a one-night stand then?' she continued, avoiding eye contact and studying her feet.

'Listen, you're a wonderful woman and we had a great time together but I've been through so much that it wouldn't be fair on you to be saddled with someone like me. Surely you understand.'

Elisabetta reached out to open the door. 'I understand,' and with that walked away without looking back.

Ben drove on but was experiencing a feeling of annoyance. It was those last two words she had uttered that were the cause of his dissatisfaction. He simply did not know what meaning to attach to them. If she had said 'I understand' whilst slamming the door and raising the spitefulness level in her voice he would have got the message. Likewise if she had tenderly stroked his cheek, looking with pity into his eyes whilst saying those same words the feeling would have been clear. Running through the scene again in his head to try and ascertain whether they had parted on good or bad terms he could glean no information from the tone of her voice or body language. Trying to decide between these two extremes of emotion, the possibility of a third interpretation gradually began to dawn on him. Perhaps she understood they were going their separate ways but could not care one way or the other if he was a saint or a sinner and was treating her badly or not. 'Yes,' thought Ben, 'that's probably how she felt.'

Chapter 5

'*E*CLAMPSIA (E'KLAMP'SĒƏ.) N. PATHOL. A SUDDEN convulsive seizure without loss of consciousness, especially during pregnancy or childbirth.' The dictionary definition of this condition offered no new insights to Dr Williams. He closed the thick tome carelessly with a slap and reinstated it to its usual position on the shelf in his study. The documented incidence of preeclampsia during pregnancy is five per cent and in his experience was even higher amongst African women. For a qualified gynaecologist not to diagnose and treat this relatively common ailment was unforgivable. Swelling of the hands, weight gain and headaches were all tell-tale indications of preeclampsia and Dr Olanya's patient had them all. She should have been hospitalised, had her progress carefully monitored and been given appropriate medication in an effort to prolong the pregnancy to full term when the baby could be safely delivered. Instead she had been sent home with an instruction to take things easy and had developed eclampsia twenty-six weeks into the pregnancy. Labour had been induced but at such an immature age it was always going to be touch and go whether the foetus would survive. Unfortunately the little boy didn't make it.

How was this possible? Surely the most junior doctor could have spotted such a straightforward problem, which was to be found in any elementary textbook on gynaecology. Robert even started to wonder whether it had in fact been Dr Olanya who made the diagnosis or whether it had been left in the hands of one of his subordinates, perhaps whilst the responsible doctor was away tending to his private practice. He could not permit such reckless dereliction of medical duty to take place without a challenge, yet feared becoming embroiled in a conflict which would sour relations within the department. After much thought he decided that the best course of action would be to attempt to push responsibility for the decision up the management hierarchy. He would arrange a meeting with the Director of KCMC, Dr Fidelis Massawe.

Robert left the secure and familiar surroundings of his study only to be greeted by the harsh, demanding voice of an evangelist on opening the door. The brash, smug North American accent provided some reassurance that the conversion was being done through the medium of television and it would not be necessary to have to evade the attentions of a zealot sermonising in his own living room. He recalled with a shudder of embarrassment how Anna's mother had brought a Walekole, or screaming woman of the Bible, from the village when her daughter had been ill with malaria. Against his better judgement he had tagged along with the accompanying group of singing women as this deranged person placed the Bible all over his wife's body and then to his infinite shame remained passive as she did the same to him. The five women who were presently in the house, still wearing their blue church uniforms, seemed too engrossed in the video to be in the mood for hysterics. Unfortunately the recording was poor quality and had to be played at high volume to overcome the crackling sounds, which only added to the jarring effect it had on Robert's mind. The Good News included a life of sacrifice and servitude for the righteous, whilst the ungodly had to endure an eternity of torment. He had never been able to figure out what was so attractive about that message and sought to make his way to the haven of the garden as quickly as possible.

Anna greeted him in a friendly manner and his heart sank as he realised she wanted to show off her ornament today. A stable marriage, an honourable profession, a comfortable home without ostentatious wealth, no wild or lewd behaviour, he was everything to be admired and gawped at by a group of church women.

'How are you my dear? Do come and join us,' she said, casting her eyes towards the others to see what effect she was having.

'I'm afraid I have to go to the hospital. It's an emergency,' he replied, thinking of the best excuse that would extricate him as quickly as possible from the situation.

'These doctors are always so busy,' she happily complained to the women who were now smiling and had their attention fixed on him.

Robert walked towards the car, the pronouncements of the television evangelist gratifyingly becoming less audible as he made his way along the garden path. The words, however, still resonated in his mind. Why did God require so much from us and punished so severely when he didn't get it? What purpose did it all serve?

He started to drive, without any particular plan in mind as to where he was travelling. The motivation to start this trip had simply been to leave the suffocating atmosphere of the house. He decided to head northwards in the direction of Kilimanjaro and before long was negotiating the dirt roads once cycled in happier times. Inevitably the passage of years had added tarnish to the image created in his mind and the scenery did not seem as special as when it had been viewed through younger and more idealistic eyes. That said, he was surprised at how little had actually changed. The children ran by the car and were the only ones to greet him with unaffected enthusiasm and sincere pleasure. The women were wrapped in chitenge, material that covered their bodies and hair and which could also be used to strap a baby to the back. The majority of men assumed a more western style of clothing of long dark trousers and long-sleeved collared shirts. There was a kind of mutual envy between Robert and these adults: they were jealous of his wealth and possessions, whilst he longed for their uncomplicated existence. The women were working amongst the banana plants that encroached within less than a metre of the road. They were loosening the earth around the roots with a hoe and looked at Robert with an expression of distrust. It was not an easy life but wasn't it better to work hard and sleep soundly without the problems that kept him awake at night? The minibuses passed his car at speed, lurching from side to side as they tried to find the smoothest route through the dust. Apart from these, the main mode of transport were black bicycles, uniform not only in colour, but in manufacturer and simple design. The small concrete bars with flaking paint on the walls and rusting metal rooves, provided a focal point where men sat outside on the low wooden benches to meet and discuss the issues of the day. Not far away from these places millet, which would later be used in the brewing process, was drying on large pieces of brown hessian material. The simple pleasures of comradeship and company depressed Robert as he reflected on the nature of his own life. Was he being too naïve and idealistic? He knew that cases of domestic violence, sexual abuse and illness abounded in this area. But then what is even so upsetting about death if it comes simply and naturally and is accepted by all? The weather was becoming colder as he continued his journey northward and it looked like it might rain. A chicken ran across his path, narrowly missing the car, as chickens invariably manage to do. He turned his car around and spent the remainder of Sunday afternoon on the verandah of Moshi Sports Club enjoying a cold Tusker.

Chapter 6

GEORGE AND HIS laptop were almost inseparable. He would type emails at a furious rate, communicate via video link with the leaders of his organisation and upload maps of the region, which were printed out and pored over endlessly. The tangible consequences of all this activity were barely noticeable as the unit never seemed to achieve anything. Every few weeks they would pack up camp, move on and then pitch their tents again only to repeat the pattern of watching and waiting. In truth the inaction of the unit was not George's fault, he was only following orders and longed for the opportunity to be engaged in combat and prove himself on the field of battle in front of his subordinates. His constant communication with the laptop was scorned as well as being the source of plenty of amusement and speculation. It was alternately known as George's brain or George's mother, since he seemed incapable of making any decision without first consulting it. Just recently his emotional attachment to this machine had reached new levels of intensity. One of the soldiers had visited George's tent late one evening only to find him sweating profusely, shirt unbuttoned, looking at internet images of naked women involved in various erotic acts. Since then the laptop had become George's lover and George's sex toy.

The story he had told his soldiers about being hot on the heels of an Islamic terrorist group was not entirely true; in fact it was a complete falsehood. This inexperienced assortment of combatants had been placed in a remote corner of the country to report on any kind of movement of troops or weapons. Headquarters in Jalalabad had not expected anything in terms of enemy activity to occur and sure enough it hadn't. Now the news that George dreaded had been relayed to him. The unit was being recalled to base, there being no reason to keep them on patrol anymore. They were to retreat to Jalalabad immediately and await further orders. Whilst there may have been those who doubted the veracity of George's promises of imminent conflict, the admission that they contained no truth whatsoever would totally destroy any residual credibility he possessed. He had painted a picture of the slippery Arabs just slipping through their fingers, a frightened and demoralised troupe on the run in fear of the imminent day of reckoning. To admit that this was all a figment of his imagination was too much to bear. He would not and could not issue the order to pack up and return to base. But what was to be done if there was no enemy to fight? The voice at the other end of his earpiece was adamant there was no point in them staying and expressly forbade any kind of action except their immediate retreat. George switched off his laptop – and there was probably an element of truth in what the soldiers said, that his brain was then switched off. After a short period of contemplation he emerged from his tent with a big smile and said, 'Gentlemen, I am pleased to announce that in three days' time we will be undertaking our first military operation.'

The men gathered round as George pointed to a location on one of his maps some hundred kilometres north, where tributaries of the river Amu Darya flowed through wide fertile valleys.

'Is that where the terrorists are hiding?' asked John, a fresh-faced youth who seemed barely old enough to be out of high school, let alone a member of a military outfit.

'This is the terrorists' lifeline and a cause of misery to tens of thousands in our own countries,' replied George. 'Here are the poppy fields, the raw material for heroin, the drug that funds the evil men plotting against our civilisation whilst simultaneously undermining its social fabric.'

'What do you plan?' asked one of the older mercenaries, folding his arms and looking straight at his commander.

'We will hit them at night, burn the poppy fields and await further instructions from headquarters.'

Following the inspection of yet more maps it was decided to pack up and strike camp at a place some ten kilometres from the intended target. As they were moving into a more populated area concealment would be more difficult, but they eventually settled on a spot which suited their requirements and was not too far away from the main road. George seemed to have remarkably good intelligence about the area and knew exactly which farm to attack. The younger members of the unit packed with enthusiasm, the older ones with a more matter-of-fact air, perhaps sensing there was something not quite right about what they had been asked to do. The convoy of vehicles exited the northern slopes of the Hindu Kush and entered a much flatter region, where the vegetation grew in greater abundance.

The day after arriving, Alonzo the Spaniard was sent out to scout with John to try to find out as much information as possible about the poppy farm. They came back some hours later, John eager to report their findings whilst Alonzo remained silent, only moving his head to confirm or deny the intelligence details. There was no doubt that they were growing the opium poppy: the tall plants terminating in a nodding green sphere with reddish purply flowers that were just beginning to blossom were unmistakable even from a distance. There was a long low-roofed farmhouse at the edge of the arable area. It had three access points: doors at the front, rear and one of the sides. There could have been as many as twelve people living there but it was really impossible to tell given the short length of time they had surveyed the building. A map was drawn of the farm and each man assigned a duty for the evening. Some would secure the farmhouse to prevent anyone from leaving, whilst others were to guard key points outside. Twelve men would pour petrol over the fields and set them alight. George had real excitement in his eyes as he repeatedly went over the details of the operation: this was his opportunity to show everybody what he was made of.

The truck carrying the men stopped about one kilometre from the farm. Two teams of three had already been dropped off to start the lighting of the fields from different points. They were to use radios to synchronise their act of pyromania, waiting for the order from George who would be by the farmhouse. The remainder of the unit disembarked and trotted stealthily down the rough track leading to the house. Two positioned themselves by the gate and another four, including Tallis, at strategic points around the farmhouse. Two more teams of three headed off in the direction of the fields with petrol containers, whilst George walked around the whole scene having no specific role except that of self-appointed overseer. John and three others were to take the family in the house hostage whilst the destruction of their livelihood was taking place.

The timing of the attack had been planned to coincide with the whole family having their evening meal. Of course the men and women would be in separate rooms, but at least it would reduce the probability of anybody lurking elsewhere within the house. The four men entered quietly through the unlocked back door: the first the Afghanis knew about their unwelcome visitors was their sudden appearance in combat fatigues and balaclavas in the dining rooms. There was a stunned silence as they were ushered by the barrel of a gun into a corner of the room. The women were brought into the same room as the men and once they were all together one of the soldiers walked through the rooms of the rest of the house to flush out any remaining family members. Some rope was brought and one of the soldiers started tying the hands of the hostages as the other two stood guard with their automatic rifles. The man who had done the room search came back with nothing to report. As they looked out of the windows, flames could be seen rising from the poppy fields. Everything seemed to be going according to plan.

Just then a ten-year-old boy ran into the room and tried to grab a rifle from one of the soldiers. An unequal struggle ensued, which terminated abruptly with the boy being hit on the head with the butt of the rifle. He fell to the ground with blood gushing from his forehead. A woman screamed and one of the men stood up, taking a step towards his captors. John, who was pointing a rifle at the family, suddenly squeezed the trigger, releasing a hail of bullets in the direction of the group huddled into a corner of the room. He seemed unable to release the pressure on the trigger as the bodies convulsed as a result of this relentless onslaught. The rat-a-tat-tat seemed to go on forever but probably lasted no more than half a minute. It was long enough however to ensure that the family who had been enjoying their evening meal an hour earlier were now just a pile of corpses. George rushed in, his face white with shock.

'What the fuck happened here?' he yelled at the top of his voice.

John stood motionless, his gun still pointing to where the family lay, unable to utter a single word.

The men from the fields ran in still holding their petrol containers. Their arrival seemed to calm George down though he was still agitated. He looked at the scene for a short time, breathing heavily, then turned to Tallis.

'See if there's any gasoline left,' he ordered. 'We may as well torch the whole Goddamn place.'

And so the buildings as well as the fields were set alight so that the horror of what had actually transpired would not be too evident. Their temporary camp was hurriedly dismantled that evening and George gave the instruction that the truck was to drive immediately to Jalalabad. Tallis sat in the back of the truck and only now saw the irony of poppies growing where the dead lay just as they had done in Flanders fields so many years before. He looked across at Alonzo, he was a man of few words but the look of despondency on his face told a story. It was probably not the type of military action of which St James would have been particularly proud.

Chapter 7

THE ROOM WAS large and full of people. Everybody had a drink in hand and the mood was convivial with plenty of chatting, joking and laughing. At the centre of the room was Ben's older brother Michael and on his shoulder his small frail mother. Michael did not pay much attention to her as he held court but she never once took her eyes off him, a subdued smile betraying the intense feeling of pride she experienced in watching her first-born child. Only Ben who was standing in one of the corners of the room observed the scene with some disquiet.

'Michael is dead but how can I tell anyone in this room?' he thought desperately.

Turning to his father who was somewhat detached from the general merriment he said, 'Dad this is a dream, nothing here is real.' His father returned a quizzical look, evidently failing to register what he was talking about.

'Dad, what can I do to convince you that this is all an illusion?'

The party continued and it seemed as if his father was not at all interested in what he was saying.

'Dad, please believe me. Talk to mum, tell her this is a dream.' He did not want to be the one to break the awful news and was hoping they would all just wake up in order to face reality.

'Perhaps, Dad, you could slap yourself, pinch yourself, pour a glass of water over your head. Try to open your eyes really wide, screw them tightly shut, now open them again as wide as you can.'

Ben also tried these exercises in the hope that even if nobody else could remove themselves from the dream he would be able to manage it. Nothing worked however and they were all imprisoned in this fantasy together. Finally in exasperation he shouted across the room:

'Mum, Michael is dead!'

She turned to look angrily at him as Michael slowly faded away to nothing, still chatting and laughing as he gradually became transparent.

Ben woke up and fixed his eyes on the bedroom window where the morning light was just beginning to stream through. If he looked at this light long enough then sleep would not return and neither would his nightmare.

'Why was I only concerned with telling the truth about Michael?' he thought. 'Everybody in that room was dead. My denial of that reality was far less forgivable than their wish to believe Michael was alive. Am I awake even now to everything that has happened?'

These and other thoughts preoccupied him as he was getting himself ready and prepared to travel into the centre of Paris.

It was July 14th, Bastille Day, and all businesses were closed except for the bars and restaurants, which expected to do a brisk trade. As a member of the exiled British community living in France, Ben had been invited to the celebrations, which included the opening of a memorial to all the British who had given their lives in the fight against terrorism. The plaque would read that they had promoted the cause of peace and freedom worldwide. This claim had been somewhat controversial: pacifists stated that only those who had given their lives without fighting could claim to be promoting the cause of peace. Others maintained that just being British and dying at the hands of terrorists, a term itself liable to wide interpretation, did not necessarily result in the world becoming a freer place. Ben could see the validity of these points but as had been the case with other well reasoned arguments in recent years, such objections were drowned by the overwhelming tide of sympathy for Britain, which inundated most of Europe.

Ben avoided the large crowds lining the Champs Élysées by walking along the River Seine to Tuileries Gardens where the ceremony was due to take place in the late afternoon. He had plenty of time to look out over the Seine, read a newspaper and walk around the gardens. On the north side of Tuileries Gardens bordering the Rue de Rivoli the President would open a memorial garden with a water feature. There had been general relief that no new sculpture would be added to the extensive collection already residing in the gardens. The artistic, political and diplomatic wrangling would have been interminable as experts from all fields squabbled over the design. When the President came to give his speech the chosen style of memorial also allowed him to draw heavily on gardening metaphors to pay tribute to the dead.

Flowers are like humans: they are both beautiful and delicate. The bloom of a flower is something lovely to behold as is the coming of age of a young person, but it soon withers and dies. Death however is a natural process, allowing room for the new seeds to grow. We see therefore that death creates life and both are part of a cycle with the one depending on the other. Occasionally a pestilence or drought will destroy all the flowers in the garden, but life always returns. Nobody can ever eradicate the seeds of hope. Continuing in this vein, he only neglected to mention which parts of Britain had been in need of a good pruning. Polite applause accompanied the entirely predictable words and he pulled on a silk cord to reveal the inscription on the shining brass plaque. Ben crossed the Rue de Rivoli, retiring to the nearest bar where he ordered a cool draught of Carlsberg.

A small group remained behind at the memorial garden, lost in their own thoughts, remembering their dead. Their mood contrasted sharply with the exuberant spirits of the vast majority of Parisians on Bastille Day. The long narrow road which was the Rue be Rivoli was beginning to fill up with people returning from the Champs Élysées and the day's festivities which had been held there. On seeing the garden through the tall iron railings, which bordered it and the mournful people inside, the mood of the crowd sobered. Voices were hushed, hats removed and the walking pace reduced as a mark of respect to those who had fallen on the other side of the Channel. Some stopped altogether and it wasn't long before the street became congested.

With rather unfortunate timing a group of male Muslims joined the thronging crowd which was slowly making its way down the street. They were easily identified as Muslims, having just come out of evening prayers and still wearing their white robes and skullcaps. It was impossible to be part of that crowd and not come into physical contact with others, though the force and disrespect with which they were jostled suggested feelings of antagonism amongst a large section of those present. The young men looked nervously at each other but decided they just had to grin and bear these indignities.

Suddenly someone shouted from the crowd, 'Hey, why don't those guys take off their hats?'

More pushing ensued then another voice replied, 'Let's teach those bastards some respect.'

Hands reached out to pull off the skullcaps and a couple of punches were thrown. One of the group of Muslims made the mistake of retaliating and he and his comrades were immediately assailed by a hail of blows. Totally encircled, the punches and kicks rained in from all sides and the more they attempted to push their way out of the situation the worse was the retribution of the crush. Whilst some members of the crowd moved away from the violence, others moved towards it and these new arrivals were among the most vicious. Eventually, once the victims seemed resigned to their fate and offered no more resistance the ferocity of the attack seemed to abate. The crowd thinned out, continuing down the Rue de Rivoli to the Place des Pyramides where a golden statue of Joan of Arc stood proudly in the middle of the road, near where she was wounded in an unsuccessful attack against the English in 1429. Nine young men lay on the road, bruised and bloodied with broken bones, though still alive.

Ben had heard the commotion from his table inside the bar on the side of Rue de Rivoli, which boasted some of Paris' most fashionable shops. Although his glass was empty he waited for the noise and crowd to subside before venturing outside to investigate. There was an archway over the sidewalk and he leant against one of the pillars as he looked to see what had happened. It was with some shock that he came upon the scene of men lying on the ground, their faces contorted with pain, making slight groans and small movements. The torn white robes were muddied from being on the ground and underfoot, with streaks of red scored across the material. The remaining stragglers from the celebrations walked straight past them as though nothing had happened and even the gendarmes seemed reluctant to become involved. They formed a loose ring around the victims and waited anxiously for the ambulances to arrive. The sight seemed surreal and only when the ambulances arrived was some semblance of normality returned by the busy action of the paramedics.

Ben was jolted from his observation of the scene by the words of one of the bartenders who had joined him on the sidewalk.

'Terrible mess this, this is not how we want to celebrate Bastille Day, terrible, just terrible.'

Having overcome his shock Ben felt his normal self returning and the angry feelings of hate he had harboured for so long being restored to their usual place within his consciousness. Without turning to the barman standing beside him, he spat out the words with as much venom as he could muster.

'Bloody Mohammedans. Deserve everything that's coming to them.'

Chapter 8

Dr Massawe was more of a politician than a medical practitioner, appointed to mollify and unite the diverse and often stubborn assortment of groups that constituted the stakeholders of KCMC. In a previous life his name had probably been prefixed by the abbreviation Hon. instead of Dr. He was a man whose main preoccupation was to keep everything calm and appearances in order, but who would not shy away from sticking the knife in another's back as a means of saving his own skin. It was thus with some trepidation that Robert walked through the large entrance lobby of KCMC and turned immediately to the left in the direction of Dr Massawe's office. He was ushered into a small waiting room by a secretary and there mentally went over everything he intended to say. He was not going to make any allegations or lay charges but merely seek the advice of his boss. If at least he could shift the blame for any inaction onto the shoulders of a higher authority he would be able to live with himself through believing the lie that his hands had been tied.

Dr Massawe was a short man, wearing a grey pin-stripe suit and small round glasses, which gave him both a businesslike and studious air. His large desk and swivel chair dwarfed him and his office contained enough vacant floor space to play a decent game of golf-putting should anyone so desire. Robert was greeted warmly with a vigorous handshake and a beaming smile. It had been long, far too long since they last met. How was his wife? How were things going in his new job? The exchange of pleasantries lasted some five minutes before Dr Massawe extended his right hand to indicate they should retire to the long sofa that ran the length of one side of the room. After a few more minutes of innocuous chatter they eventually came round to the point of discussing the reason for the visit.

'You see Fidelis,' Dr Williams started, 'I obviously don't want to cause any problem for the hospital or the department. I have always desired and worked for a happy and harmonious relationship between everybody employed in gynaecology.'

Dr Massawe nodded his head in agreement with this opening conciliatory statement.

'What do I do if there is evidence of neglect that could have caused the death of a patient?' He felt himself reddening as he spoke the words that made manifest his own impotence.

'I am aware of the unfortunate case of the little boy,' Dr Massawe said wearily and then fixed him with a look that indicated he was about to ask an important question. 'Are you sure that this baby would have survived had it not been for the mistakes made in your department?'

Robert was a little annoyed at the implication that this was the fault of his department and not an individual, but was even more amazed that a medical practitioner could ask such a question about the survival prospects of a baby.

'How could anyone be sure of such a thing?' he thought. 'The little boy could have died from a thousand other causes. Is it ever possible to guarantee life?' He managed to check his natural response to the question and in those few seconds realised he was being offered a way out of his predicament. He decided to give an answer that was paradoxically both truthful and dishonest, 'No, I cannot be absolutely sure that the baby would have survived.'

'It seems to me then that what is needed is a tightening-up of procedures to make sure that this kind of thing does not happen again. The loss of the baby is of course regrettable, but since it cannot be proved beyond doubt that it died as a result of negligence, I don't think any useful purpose would be served by taking action against the doctor concerned.'

Robert noticed the absence of the word 'reasonable' between 'beyond' and 'doubt' in Dr Massawe's answer. Would it be inserted retrospectively if the Director of KCMC were ever called on to account for his advice? The responsibility had not so much been shifted elsewhere as lost within a haze of semantics.

'It's strange don't you think?' said Dr Massawe

'What is strange?' asked Robert.

'The ironies of life. Here you are, a citizen of a country that has lost millions; millions of dead in the worst terrorist atrocity the world has ever witnessed and yet we spend such a great amount of time worrying over the death of a foetus. Don't get me wrong, I'm not saying it's unimportant, I just find there is something strange about the situation.'

'Something strange?' thought Robert as he was walking away from the office. 'What is strange about trying to prevent death and having a conscience about the fate of our patients? Why do we have a hospital if we don't care about saving human life?' The unpalatable truth, that he was trying desperately hard to ignore, was that he didn't care, at least not enough to put his own livelihood on the line.

The interview with Dr Massawe made him feel guilty about being complicit in a cover-up but also made him feel guilty for another reason. Had he properly mourned all those people he had known from what seemed now to be another life? Britain, the country of his birth, had become increasingly alien to him since starting work in Tanzania. With each visit back he had discovered that the society had moved on without him, leaving him feeling detached and without the new roots that those remaining had grown in order to belong. He perceived the evolution of a much harsher and more uncaring country through its remorseless pursuit of self-interest. In contrast he remembered with great affection the country of his childhood, a land where good manners and considerate behaviour were highly valued qualities and where he had been taught to think of others as well as himself. He recalled a society of great kindness and gentleness because it was well ordered and did not pander to selfishness.

One memory had recurred in recent weeks and now impressed itself on his mind again following his meeting with Dr Massawe. He was a choirboy in a large abbey in the north of England. It was Wednesday evensong and save for a congregation of five pensioners, the boys were singing to themselves. It was a calming evening anthem with a slow melody whose words he had remembered to the present day. The sunlight streamed through the stained glass windows at a shallow angle across the dark wood of the fifteenth century choir stalls and onto the uneven stone floor. He looked up to see the bearded saintly figures with their flowing robes captured in coloured glass within thick lead borders. Jesus was easy to identify from the others since, apart from being the centre of attention, his heart was exposed for all to see. The scene evoked a tremendous reassurance that, no matter what happened, somehow everything would be alright. Robert knew that now there would be no choir singing in the abbey and no congregation to hear them. Perhaps, however, the evening sun still streamed through the heart of Jesus casting a mellow light on the ancient stone.

Chapter 9

ALLIS WAS USHERED into a plain windowless concrete room with whitewashed walls. In the middle of the room was a simple table with a vacant wooden chair on one side of it. Facing this on the other side of the table three men were seated, two dressed in military fatigues and the other in civilian clothes. Tallis immediately recognised one of the military men as Major Kaufman, head of the Afghan Volunteer Force, the organisation to which he was attached. He did not know who the other two were and they made no attempt to introduce themselves, though Tallis could tell from the stripes on the other soldier's shoulders that he was a colonel.

'Please sit down,' said the Major curtly without standing up or shaking his hand as he entered the room.

'Tallis Halliday, former British citizen and landscape gardener. Joined the volunteer force two years ago, trained at our base in Turkey after an initial posting to Georgia, USA, and has been in Afghanistan for one year now. Two assignments: a four month posting on the Pakistan border south of Jalalabad and latterly in the mountains of the Hindu Kush, nearest settlement Pol-e Khamri, under the command of Lieutenant George Bell.'

The other two men nodded as this potted history of Tallis' last two years was read out at speed by his boss.

'Any disciplinary cases on his file?' asked the man in plain clothes.

'None,' came the reply 'Private Halliday's file is remarkably thin.'

This was said in such a way that it seemed more like an insult than a compliment. Tallis felt uncomfortable and knew he was in for a rough ride.

'I don't want to waste any more time than is necessary, Private Halliday,' said the man in plain clothes. 'I suppose you know why you're here anyway. We are enquiring about the unauthorised military activity in which your unit participated two days ago.'

Tallis felt the hairs on the back of his head stand up at the mention of the word 'unauthorised'. So George had lied to them all about the instructions from headquarters, meaning that all the men could be accused of colluding in a criminal act, an act of murder no less. Few of the unit felt any loyalty to George and this reckless attempt to prove himself a man at others' expense must have incensed every single one of them. There was no point, Tallis reasoned, in telling anything but the truth since this would be what everybody would do. So what if George got into trouble, he deserved it and there was no way Tallis would risk having any blame pinned on him and being slammed into prison. At the prompt 'Tell me in your own words exactly what happened,' Tallis did precisely that.

The trio of interrogators listened patiently to his side of the story, but there was no noticeable softening of their attitude as he recounted how he had been duped by a superior officer and was simply following orders. At the end of his statement the colonel started his questioning.

'What was your reaction when you were told of your mission?'

'My reaction was that I should do exactly what headquarters had instructed,' answered Tallis.

'Did you not think it a strange order to be told to attack a group of Afghan civilians?'

'To be honest, sir, I didn't think much about it all, I just felt I had to get on and do it.'

His questioner was determined to pursue this point.

'Tell me, why should a surveillance unit such as yourselves think that headquarters would require you to participate in a military action?'

'I wasn't aware that we were there simply on a surveillance mission.'

'What on earth did you think you were there to do? Pick the mountain flowers and admire the goat herders' daughters?'

Tallis felt himself reddening and knew by now that his next statement would bring general derision. Still he had gone too far to turn back now.

'I was under the impression that we were tracking down a group of Islamic terrorists.'

The colonel stared at him in disbelief and was unable to speak for a few seconds.

'Do you really think we would send a bunch of half-wits like yourselves after a group of terrorists? Your ashes would end up as powder for their hashish pipes. Who the fuck do you think you are anyway, the magnificent fucking seven?'

The man in civilian clothes saw the increasing volume and vitriol of his colleague's speech as his cue to start a line of questioning and return the dialogue to a calmer and more productive establishment of the facts.

'What were your rules of engagement?'

'I'm sorry, can you explain that?' asked Tallis, a little perplexed.

'What level of force were you authorised to use and under what circumstances?'

'I was simply told to guard the farmhouse and make sure nobody entered or left.'

'I am fully aware you were guarding the farmhouse,' his interrogator responded testily. 'But wouldn't you agree it is rather foolish to put a gun in somebody's hands if he does not know under what conditions he is supposed to use it?'

'That was not made clear to me, sir, I suppose I was expected to use my own initiative.'

'Let me get this right, you were not told under what circumstances to fire your gun?'

'Yes, that is correct, sir.'

The man let out a sigh of disbelief, shaking his head in the process, then in a quieter tone of voice, which suggested a more serious concern on his part, asked, 'Why did you hand your commanding officer the can of petrol?'

'Because he asked for it.'

He now looked Tallis directly in the eye. 'Are you sure that is the only reason? I put it to you that you wanted to destroy the evidence of your action.'

'No, sir, it was not my idea to start the fire in the farmhouse.'

'But you didn't try to stop it. Are you aware that you could be charged with being an accessory to murder as well as assisting in destroying the evidence afterwards? Are you aware that you could be facing a long prison term?'

'I thought I was just doing my job, sir.'

The man fixed him with an intense look and said quietly, 'You did not think at all, Private Halliday.'

Major Kaufman, who had been looking increasingly uncomfortable during the interview, at last broke the silence that followed that last statement.

'If there are no further questions then this interview is over,' he said whilst looking uneasily at the other two men. 'You will be confined to barracks whilst this investigation is being conducted. You are not to talk to anybody about what has been said in this room or indeed say anything about the events of two days ago. You may now leave the room, Private Halliday.'

Tallis lay on his back on the single metal-framed bed in his room and looked at the naked light bulb hanging on a long piece of wire from the high ceiling. One of his ways of occupying his time was to see if he could perceive any movement at all of this glass globe in the faint breeze that his body was only just capable of detecting. Had they left that length so long so that he could hang himself in his cell, or perhaps the light bulb was deliberately uncovered so that he would get the idea to electrocute himself. Not that he would need to climb up on to his bed to achieve that particular task, he could probably connect some wires from the plug in the wall to the frame of his bed so that he could be fried in his sleep. No this room would not have passed a safety check from Her Majesty's Inspector of Prisons. It was an amateurish holding pen, just as those three men in the room had been amateurs, just as his unit had been a bunch of bungling amateurs. Incompetence had followed him everywhere since joining the volunteer force and he was ashamed to admit that he was part of it.

The biggest buffoon of course was George. No, buffoon was the wrong word since it suggested something comic about his inadequacies. No matter how big a fool you thought him, it was not possible to laugh at what George had achieved. His shortcomings were truly evil and without a second's thought he had landed a whole lot of men in a whole lot of trouble. Tallis was somehow not bothered too much about the prospect of prison. He had accustomed himself so much to the idea of dying since the attack on his homeland that death or hardship no longer held any fear for him. There were no rosy dreams of a bright future filled with a loving family and a fulfilling job and he had long thought that his preferred fate would be to die fighting the enemy. If he was taken prisoner by Islamic terrorists he had resolved not to plead for his life and have videotapes of pathetic supplication played out by the international news media against a backdrop of hooded figures with Kalashnikovs and verses from the Koran. He would spit in the eye of his captor and dare the coward to take out his knife and do his worst. He would tear up any messages they gave him to read out and tell any camera pointing in his direction not to bother about his life but simply come and bomb the bastards to smithereens. No, he was not afraid of suffering, but what would be almost unendurable would be suffering as a result of George. Send him out as cannon fodder or with a suicide bomb strapped to his waist but don't let him spend his days pacing a small cell thinking about the man whose stupidity and posturing had sent him there.

At least the simple surroundings were clean and comfortable and he didn't have to cope with the sun beating on his back or the dust encompassing him. Tallis didn't mind the few days he had on his own, it was no less boring than being on a tour of duty and certainly less uncomfortable and stressful. The meals were brought at regular intervals and save for the guard patrolling the corridor he had no contact with anyone. Not that he was desirous of any conversation or even thought about tapping on walls to make contact; the state of incommunicado suited him just fine. It was a reasonable guess that there were other prisoners held further along the corridor from the way the guard paced up and down looking through the metal slat on the door, which was usually kept open. A pen and paper had been left in case Tallis wished to add anything to his verbal statement. He saw little point however in making use of this opportunity, reasoning that the decision had almost certainly been made and all that was left for him to do was to wait and see what would happen.

He must have spent four days being held in that cell before being informed by the guard one morning that his presence was required in one hour. Tallis made his way to the same windowless room that had been the setting for the initial interrogation. Inside was Major Kaufman who gestured to him to take a chair. His expression seemed softer than when they had previously met but there was still an air of anxiety about him.

'Private Halliday, we have concluded our investigation

and whilst finding that you were guilty of incredible naïveté and foolishness, we do not have sufficient evidence to bring disciplinary charges against you. In short you will be free to go.'

Tallis felt a rush of relief pass through his body. He resisted the urge to thank his boss and felt he should behave more like a soldier on this occasion by asking what his next orders were.

'I don't mind telling you this is one big fuck-up,' sighed Major Kaufman, looking disconsolate. 'God knows how we're going to keep it quiet or explain it to the Afghan government. The best thing is to get you out of this country as soon as possible.' He paused as he looked through Tallis' file. 'I see you're due for leave in a few weeks anyway. Go back to your room, pack your things then report to the personnel department. They'll arrange for your payment and travel out of Afghanistan.'

Tallis hesitated before leaving the room then turned to Major Kaufman.

'Do I still work for the Afghan Volunteer Force or am I being discharged?'

'To be honest Private Halliday I just don't know. Everything is in such a mess at the moment. You leave your email with personnel and if we need you for anything we'll be in touch.'

Chapter 10

THE OBSTACLES TO a recolonisation of Britain were twofold: first was the task of ensuring the land was safe for human habitation; second was devising a framework for the resettlement process, deciding who was entitled to return, how much land they should be apportioned and how they should be governed. The second problem was at least as big as the first: millions of claims had been submitted worldwide from people professing British ancestry, usually with an accompanying request for a small part of their motherland. All this data had to be checked and cross-referenced and not surprisingly a large number of frauds had been attempted, driven by the prospect of large parcels of land being handed over for free. Luckily the British government had compiled a comprehensive genetic database of the entire population prior to the attack. Originally designed for use in the fight against crime and bogus asylum seekers, it was immediately able to associate DNA found by the police with that of a specific individual. Now instead of being used to exclude a person from society behind prison walls or beyond national borders, its purpose was to help decide whom to include in a future British society. It had been more successful than anyone had imagined in weeding out numerous imposters. Indeed rather too successful, resulting in the system being under constant attack twenty-four hours a day from hackers around the world. The stage was being reached where concerns over the security of the database were outweighing its usefulness in processing applications and there were rumours that unless it could be made less vulnerable its operation would be discontinued.

Ben walked along the corridor in the building housing the United Nations Department for British Affairs. He was here in response to an advertising campaign that had been running for weeks urging those who suspected they had even the smallest amount of British blood coursing through their veins to register with the authorities. Although Ben had his papers in order and the case seemed clear-cut, his interview, lasting well over an hour, had been both exhaustive and exhausting. He was now on the way to the clinic to give blood for use in genetic fingerprinting. It was almost impossible to conceive how each claimant could be effectively processed at this rate, especially those who did not have the correct documentation. The data collection had started whilst politicians still vacillated over a number of thorny issues. One pressure group had been campaigning for Muslims to be excluded from the possibility of resettling in Britain. Whilst this wish was unlikely to be granted, it raised the question of who should control the recolonisation process when it eventually got underway. Although the United Nations was officially in charge, British expatriates had staked a claim to have some say in how the future of their island should be shaped and had received qualified support from most western governments for this stance.

A collective sigh of relief had been breathed throughout Europe after an agreement had been reached with Spain defusing the tension along its border with Gibraltar. The European Union with the blessing of the United Nations had agreed with Spain that no recolonisation of Britain would occur until the future of Gibraltar had been settled once and for all. This agreement satisfied everybody except those it affected: the citizens of Spain argued that there were no assurances that the territory would be eventually returned to them, whilst the Gibraltarians suspected a behind-the-scenes deal had been struck to hand over the island. The British Diaspora saw it as just another impediment that would delay the longed-for time when they could return to their island. It had been a typical politician's ploy: discovering a clever way to avoid making a decision then dressing up their procrastination in such a way that all parties saved face. At least the troops had been removed and there was no danger of imminent conflict.

Ben walked into the clinic and took a seat. Suddenly he felt a hand roughly clap his shoulder and a loud voice say, 'Ben you old devil, where have you been?'

Ben instantly recognised the voice of Frank Oates and turned around to see a tall, portly, sandy-haired figure smiling down at him.

'What have you been up to anyway?' asked Frank. 'It must have been over a year now.'

'Oh working hard, trying to make a living.'

'Aren't we all my friend? This recession's a real bugger. Those bloody ragheads, not only do they destroy our homeland, they make it difficult for decent folk like you and me to make ends meet.'

Frank never reduced his volume during any of his tirades and did not care who he offended with his forthright opinions and prejudices. If there had been any Muslims sitting nearby he would not have thought twice about saying, 'Yes I'm talking about you buggers.'

'How are things at the club?' asked Ben, smiling at his friend's lack of diplomacy.

'Oh can't complain you know. Of course these days we have a lot of shysters pretending they're Brits coming along, trying to pass themselves off as the genuine article. They don't know the Thames from the Tyne and think that a Yorkshire pudding is something you eat with ice cream. Pisses me off something rotten when you have folk wanting to stay in Britain who can't even speak the Queen's English.'

'It's just the money,' replied Ben, 'They think they can get something for nothing and so they try.'

'And do you know what they're doing now?' continued Frank, not pausing to reflect on Ben's words. 'They're saying my brother, sister, half cousin twice removed or whoever was on holiday in Britain when the attack came therefore I have a right to settle there.'

'Do you think the resettlement will come soon?' asked Ben.

Frank shook his head despondently. 'You know the problem?' He paused for a few seconds. 'It's not the land, it's the bloody bureaucrats. Don't know what to do, can't agree on anything and now they've sold us down the river to the bloody dagoes. They've got their heads up their arses and don't know what they want. I say stuff the lot of them and let us Brits sort out the problem. We know how to take care of our own.'

'Is the land safe to return to then?' asked Ben with some surprise.

'Of course it is,' bellowed Frank. 'The UN doesn't want Britain recolonised, it would cause too many problems for them, so they tell their scientists to forge the soil test results and claim it's too dangerous for the likes of you and me.'

'You can prove this, can you?' asked Ben.

'Listen,' Frank continued, lowering his voice for once. 'Why don't you come to our meeting next Friday? Should be interesting: we have film shot from a drone that was sent over Britain. Had to blow the thing up before it returned to Europe and got us all into trouble, but not before it sent back a whole load of interesting images.'

'Mr Benedict Collins,' the shrill voice of a nurse pierced the air.

'I'll think about it Frank, got to go now.'

'I'm counting on you old man. Keep your pecker up and one day I'll buy you a pint in my local back in Old Blighty.'

Ben smiled at this unrealistic prospect but nevertheless said,

'It's a date Frank.'

Upon returning to his apartment that evening, Ben switched on his computer. Stored on the hard disk were a large number of iconic British symbols, which had been collected over time. Whenever a suitable image came to mind, perhaps through a conversation or something he saw whilst walking down the street, a note was made of it. It could be something as simple as a milk bottle or as complex as the intricate stonework at St Pancras Station. Following his discussion with Frank he added a drawing of a Yorkshire pudding and a bird's eye view of the River Thames. No one would recognise the corresponding perspective of the River Tyne and besides he already had a sketch of the Tyne Bridge that spanned the river at Newcastle. He had been trying to devise some system where each image was given a score corresponding to its emotional value, recognisability and aesthetic appeal. Needless to say this was no easy task and if done properly would involve surveying large numbers of people for their opinions. Once the database was created, however, he would be able to mix and match the images to produce the necessary reaction in customers and sell his products. He tried to rate the images himself, which explains why he had been staring at a drawing of a chip butty on his computer screen for the last five minutes. On a scale of one to five the emotional value might be two, recognisability three and aesthetic appeal three. No, this was incorrect, how could a chip butty score three for aesthetic appeal? Better reduce it to one, or was he being too harsh? Remembering the artistic acclaim that greeted Andy Warhol's painting of a tin of Campbell's soup, perhaps a two might be more appropriate. It was one of those tasks that became more difficult the longer one spent on it, since more questions and doubts arose over each decision with the passage of time. Eventually you wondered if you were making any sense at all out of the exercise. When the general public was being questioned, there had to be a time limit, in fact they should give an almost instantaneous response and not be allowed to change their minds. He fixed himself a drink and watched an old film on TV. If he was able to perfect this system it could be patented and sold to all manner of companies wishing to advertise their goods. It could be adapted to suit different customer bases, using different sets of images. An extension to look at the emotional content of words might even be possible, which would then be used to construct a sentence. The possibilities seemed endless but one question kept nagging away at the back of his mind: would it ever work?

Ben was in a room with his brother Michael. They were sitting together, then Michael got up to make a speech, accompanied by polite applause from a small audience. The pleasant, if modest, expectations of the onlookers were soon disappointed however as his first few words indicated that he was going to use the occasion to make fun of Ben. His first joke fell flat then he started to have difficulty getting the words out. There was a stony silence as Michael became more flustered with his fruitless efforts to make everybody laugh. Each attempt at humour missed its intended target and rebounded back on him with greater force so that he appeared more and more ridiculous. The harder he tried to embarrass his younger brother the more frustrated he became and now people were starting to whisper amongst themselves and snigger silently. Finally he sat down, only his anger preventing tears, red faced and totally humiliated. Ben woke from his spot on the sofa wondering why he had had such a strange dream before he picked himself up to go to sleep in his bed.

Chapter 11

THERE WAS A kind of hierarchy amongst the cleaners at the Kilimanjaro Christian Medical Centre. The toilet cleaners occupied the most lowly position, the window cleaner's standing was enhanced since he worked independently and his duties involved an element of danger, whilst those swabbing the floors after an operation pretended to have some special medical knowledge. The man with the automatic floor polisher, however, commanded an unassailable position at the pinnacle of this scale of respect. All other cleaners had to give way when he came down the corridor slowly gliding his purring machine from side to side. He had been known to push nurses out of the way and even delay a patient's journey to the operating theatre in the paramount interest of having shiny floors.

The corridor of the gynaecology department had just been the beneficiary of a visit by this man and machine and the white floor gleamed in the morning sunlight. The glow even reached an alcove built into the wall where blue plastic seats were attached to a tubular steel frame, forming a small waiting area. Two of these seats were occupied by a couple who sat quietly waiting to see Dr Olanya. The man must have been about ten years older than his young wife, dressed in a dark suit and tie with a proud but not haughty bearing. He was obviously gainfully employed in a profession that provided enough money to be able to support a family in relative comfort. The woman seemed in awe of her husband, the distinction in their standings being reflected in their contrasting modes of attire. She was dressed in traditional chitenge wraparounds that would not have been out of place in the villages. The two of them had been sitting there for over half an hour and had so far not talked to anyone. The nurses seemed far too busy with their assigned tasks to pay them much attention and Dr Olanya had yet to emerge from his office. When he did eventually come out he walked straight past his visitors without any form of acknowledgement.

It was not long after that occurrence that the rapid and loud footsteps of the senior nurse could be heard, disturbing the peace of the early morning routines, as she sought out this couple.

'Is there anything I can do for you?' she asked in a superior tone of voice.

'We have come to see Dr Olanya,' replied the man politely, ignoring the manner in which he had been addressed.

'I am afraid Dr Olanya is busy and can't be disturbed,' she said peremptorily, indicating that she was clearly annoyed with the request from these time wasters.

'We lost our baby and wanted to talk to him about it.'

'I am well aware of that but Dr Olanya simply does not have the time to talk to you. He is a very busy man.'

'We just want a few minutes,' said the man, obviously upset but still managing to retain his dignity.

'No amount of words will bring back your baby. These things happen all the time, I am afraid we can't help you.'

The voice of the senior nurse did not soften once during the conversation. It was as if she was trying to get rid of an irritating bore from a party in an effort to make it run more smoothly and harmoniously. The man stood up and his wife followed suit. They walked slowly out of the hospital building, only altering their steps so as not to collide with the automatic floor polisher, the tempo of whose movement would not be altered for the likes of them.

Dr Williams was not in the hospital that morning but in a

nearby building where the teaching of medical students was conducted. Watching from a classroom on the second floor, he recognised the couple leaving from a side entrance and felt a pang of sadness as they walked slowly to an old Peugeot in the car park. The vehicle made its way sluggishly along the long KCMC driveway, stopping briefly at the exit before turning right towards the town of Moshi and disappearing from view. He wondered why they had come, and experienced a peculiar mixture of disappointment tinged with relief at not having talked to them.

Robert was killing two birds with one stone with his short series of lectures. He had been researching quality control and patient care systems with the objective of writing the departmental manual. The same material was being used to instruct students as to the best procedures to follow. He had hoped to use them as a sounding board for some of his more contentious proposals, but there had been disappointingly little in the way of lively debate. They obediently took notes and did not see it as their job to question him too much. Would his words have much of an impact anyway? They would be faithfully regurgitated in an examination and most of the students would end up passing, but what effect would they have when these young people became doctors? A doctor in Africa received so much respect it was almost unhealthy, leading many of them to think and behave as if they were gods. Somehow words did not seem to have much power to change people's beliefs and attitudes on this continent. He remembered when AIDS had been a problem of huge magnitude for health workers in Tanzania. The endless meetings, poster campaigns and training programmes generously funded from overseas had had little effect. His mind went back to a theatrical production concerned with the illness when half the audience consisted of WHO officials and foreigners from other organisations. Now the disease was treatable the instances of unplanned pregnancies and sexually transmitted diseases was just the same as in the days of propaganda. He sighed as he looked at his class; thirty faces from different nationalities were looking his way as he paused in his delivery. With a certain degree of indifference he then turned to the whiteboard and wrote down the main principles of patient care.

The afternoon was spent in the gynaecology department attending to patients and visiting the wards. He intended to ask Dr Olanya about the visit of the parents of the dead baby but somehow the opportunity did not present itself. Upon reflection he decided it was probably better to ask the senior nurse, who replied that there was no record of them coming for an appointment. Although he didn't believe her it would now be pointless to ask Dr Olanya about the matter. Robert began to think of some infallible system of recording all those who came to the department so that nobody could get away with such lies in the future. When it had been perfected it would be added to the departmental manual.

It had been a long day and Dr Williams walked wearily to the foyer of KCMC. On the way there he passed the chapel where the late afternoon service had just ended. Now that everybody had left it was a good opportunity to sit down for a few moments of quiet reflection. He looked around and wondered if the solutions to his life's problems would ever be found in a place like this. He had made numerous starts at trying to be a Christian but had never been able to discover the joy and peace about which others raved. Each time there was a part of him that had doubts and could not be swayed no matter how hard he attempted and desperately wanted to believe. Accordingly it was a relief to have missed the service and he expected to have the chapel to himself. The sun was streaming in through the windows, reminding him of his recurrent dream of being a choirboy in Britain. It seemed strange that the rays and shadows cast by the sun in Africa could remind him of a place thousands of miles away and even induce nostalgia of a happier and simpler time.

He was surprised to discover that he was not in fact alone in the chapel. At one end of the first row of chairs sat a woman with her head bowed, alone with her thoughts. When she stood up and turned around to leave Robert saw that she was one of his students, a Zambian in her twenties named Mwamba. He had noticed her before in the lecture room and had considered her attractive without being stunningly beautiful. What struck him particularly as she came closer to where he was seated was the look of perfect peace spread across her whole face. It was the outward manifestation of an inner calm and contented understanding of the world, which he craved. She smiled politely, said 'hello' and was on the way to the door when Robert felt the need to say something to her.

'It's a shame you missed the service,' he said.

'I always miss the service,' she replied, smiling.

'Don't you like the company of others?' Robert continued, intrigued.

'I come here to talk to my best friend, why should I want other people around?'

'I thought Christians were supposed to worship in groups.'

'Who says I'm a Christian? And the God I believe in wants friendship not worship.'

Robert was becoming more and more confused at the direction this conversation was taking.

'What do you believe in Mwamba?' The use of her first name established a degree of intimacy between them and she became more serious.

'Dr Williams, why do you want to know what I believe?'

'I am always interested in what others believe and have yet to find a faith with all the answers and with which I feel comfortable.'

'What is it you don't like about other religions?'

'The harshness, the self sacrifice, the duties, the guilt, the punishments, the fear of not doing the right thing, the intolerance towards those with different beliefs.'

Dr Williams had clearly said something that had got through to Mwamba as she smiled at him and said: 'I will bring you some books tomorrow.'

Chapter 12

THE PLANE FROM Kabul to Mumbai touched down about 14.00 hours. Amongst the fairly eclectic assortment of passengers making this uncustomary journey was a man in his early twenties, happy and relieved to be making his first trip to India. Tallis was travelling on his own, had no commitments, a sackful of money in the bank and was armed with a determination to enjoy himself to the full. For some reason the first breaths of Indian air had an uplifting effect and the sun beating down on his back seemed only to confirm the sensation of having arrived in a place close to paradise. The faces of customs and airport officials were relaxed and friendly despite the crowds, and this new visitor to the country was delighted to be there.

After checking through, he noticed a sign to one of the airport bars. Despite the temptation to experience a few of life's pleasures straight away, Tallis decided that a better course of action would be to find a hotel and deposit his luggage. A taxi was summoned and instructed to head for the Kolhapur Hotel, which destination it eventually reached after a few near misses with other cars, bicycles and pedestrians. The Kolhapur Hotel was a modest enterprise recommended by the travel book, no flea-pit but certainly not the most expensive in town. The intention was to stay in Mumbai for some time, perhaps eventually even finding rented accommodation to prolong the visit so there was no need for extravagance.

The feeling of excitement which had started at the airport

had not yet deserted him and it was a surprise to find that he was almost running with his suitcase to the room. It was only with an effort that he managed to slow down: it was like being a child in a sweetshop, there were so many attractions it was difficult to know what to do first. The option of a good meal in the Hotel restaurant, accompanied by expensive drinks, was selected before venturing out onto the streets to explore the immediate neighbourhood. This was not as leisurely and carefree an experience as he had hoped and he was glad of the opportunity to find refuge in a nearby bar, which was not too crowded at that time of the afternoon. Pondering the nature of the mêlée on the other side of the glass windows he sat alone at a table and ordered a cool lager to offset the heat of the day. He didn't know where to go to find what he wanted and slowly became more inebriated as the afternoon progressed until he realised that this course of action was getting him nowhere. He returned to the Kolhapur Hotel in the hope of gaining a little local intelligence. In the foyer of the hotel was a notice advertising a troupe of female dancers who seemed to perform there on a regular basis. There being no better alternative way of passing the evening Tallis decided to attend this event.

He returned to his room, showered and changed and reasoned that he had at least some chance of meeting female company that day. He remembered the words of some of the soldiers back in Afghanistan, that all you needed to do was to flash your wallet to have your own personal harem, but tried hard not to get too excited beforehand. Despite this he could not help but feel disappointed as he walked into the darkly lit room with its poorly illuminated stage. The event was not well attended and apart from a few couples who kept themselves to themselves at tables on the periphery of the room, the audience was entirely male. A party of Korean businessmen occupied a table near the stage and applauded the dancing with great enthusiasm. The girls smiled most at those customers who were noisy and demonstrative so this group received a lot of attention, which made them applaud even more.

The dancers were in their twenties, wearing long robes of purple, orange, green or some equally garish colour. The only part of them that was exposed was the midriff complete with a bejeweled navel. Their dancing was typically Indian, accompanied by Indian music with plenty of jumping from one foot to the other, twirling around and raising of the arms. Tallis found it strangely seductive notwithstanding the lack of bare flesh on show. There was one lady in particular dressed in yellow, who caught his attention. She was tall and statuesque with long black hair flowing down her back. Despite her imposing bearing she moved freely and naturally and her flashing eyes and smile portrayed a vitality which was captivating. She was attractive but without her radiant energy would probably be considered unremarkable. Tallis tried to attract her attention in a subtle manner but she was oblivious to these cautious advances and seemed more interested in smiling at the Korean table or laughing with her fellow dancers.

The waiters who brought drinks to the tables doubled as flower sellers. For ten rupees one could buy a rose which would be passed on to the dancer of your choice via the waiter. Although a rather artless system, Tallis felt this would be a good way to attract the attention of the woman in yellow. She took the rose in her hand and looked in his direction, smelling the flower and dancing with it as she smiled at him for a short time. The show continued as Tallis became more intoxicated with the alcohol and the dancing girl. Half an hour before the show was due to end he bought another flower, this time writing his room number on a piece of paper and folding a five hundred rupee note inside it so that the money could not be seen. He handed the note and flower to a waiter to pass on then abruptly got up to leave before he could see the dancer reading his note.

Tallis lay on the bed in his room and looked at the time. He was expecting a knock on the door anytime and imagined what he would do when the dancer in yellow walked in. Perhaps she would be too shy to knock. He got up and opened the door slightly, looking down the corridor as he did so only to see that nobody was yet on their way. This wasn't too surprising: maybe the show continued for longer than anticipated and of course she would have to change afterwards, perhaps have a shower. He lay in bed for some time longer and wished she would come in her yellow dress still sweating from the performance, but nothing happened. He glanced at his watch again, it was midnight and the show had been scheduled to finish at eleven. Another look down the corridor was accompanied by another feeling of disappointment. The idea then occurred to him to call room service; he could ask if the show was finished and who knows, a pretty waitress may even bring his order. This latter hope was immediately dashed by the appearance of a waiter at the door carrying a tray with a cheeseburger and whisky and soda on it. The man confirmed that the show always ended on time and in truth Tallis could not imagine it continuing for many encores. He lay on the bed and knew that he would have to do his best to imagine the woman with the flashing eyes and yellow dress in order to satisfy the aching in his groin.

After a restless night's sleep induced by the amount of alcohol in his body and a badly adjusted air conditioner, Tallis sat on his own in the restaurant of the Kolhapur Hotel. The morning light streamed brightly through the large windows, glinting off the cutlery, glassware and white starched tablecloths. A buffet of bread, jams, fruit and cereal was laid on whilst waiters in purple jackets and black trousers took orders for any hot items. He was not hungry and nibbled unenthusiastically at a piece of toast, which was accompanied by copious amounts of fruit juice and coffee in an attempt to quench the raging thirst and ease the splitting headache he was experiencing. The previous evening had been something of a disaster: all he had to show for his efforts was a tired body, the loss of a few hundred rupees and a stained bed-sheet, an act of defilement he had accomplished unfortunately entirely on his own. Things were not going to be as easy as expected. He was able to glance through the open double door of the restaurant and watch the lady at the reception desk. She was attractive but most likely unavailable, the management would probably take a dim view if she widened her job description to include catering for the needs of patrons in their rooms after hours. Maybe she had some friends who could be interested in a man like him, but on second thoughts this might lead to unwanted long-term relationships. He wanted to keep his liaisons short, uncomplicated and varied and realised he would probably have to part with a few rupees to achieve this.

Tallis returned to his room and switched on his laptop computer. He received few emails, apart from those from the plethora of organisations which wanted to keep in contact with British citizens. There was however one note of interest, which had been circulated to all the former members of the now disbanded Afghan Volunteer Force. It urged each one to stay in contact as there was the possibility of further operations in the future, though probably not in Afghanistan. It was also reported that George and John had been returned to the United States where they would face a court martial for their part in the massacre, and as far as anyone else was concerned the matter was now closed. Tallis felt more sorry for John than George, despite the fact that he had been the one to fire the fatal shots. George had cynically lied to everyone out of personal vanity, whilst John had merely panicked when faced with an unfamiliar situation. Tallis returned the email stating he was receptive to offers and pleased he would not be returning to Afghanistan.

He spent the afternoon walking around the Mumbai docks area. There was something soothing about the palm trees blowing in the wind and the vast expanse of water stretching out towards the horizon, though it was still extremely busy, reputedly handling half of all of India's foreign trade. Old graceful buildings built by the British jostled for space with tall skyscrapers, whilst thousands tried to make a living on the ground from the knock-on opportunities associated with this centre of economic activity and commerce. It would have been a very different scene to the one that would have first greeted the pioneers from the British East India Company when they made this their original base of operations more than three hundred years ago.

Down one of the side roads leading away from the harbour area Tallis discovered a fish restaurant called the Kingfisher. He was attracted to it by the smart frontage and elegantly dressed tables inside, which suggested a degree of cleanliness in the kitchen. It was also a relief to see that it was not particularly full so that it should be possible to find a quiet corner where he could enjoy his meal in peace. Unfortunately because it was not too crowded the waiters had time on their hands and contrived to annoy him by constantly asking whether everything was OK. The owner who stood beside the cashier's table was a distinguished-looking gentleman in his sixties with silvery grey hair who took a great interest in Tallis once he discovered his nationality.

'When we heard the news of the attack it was to us Indians as if we had lost an older brother,' he said sadly. 'Particularly my generation, we always respected the British. Yes, India was a colony but the British always treated us fairly.' His eyes began to darken. 'Those damn Muslims cause problems everywhere, even here in India with us Hindus. They bring nothing but trouble and are so cruel. I wish they all go to Hell.'

Tallis felt his animosity turning his mind giddy. 'You know, it's good to find someone who understands the situation. I wish the lot of them could be swallowed up by a big hole in the earth so that we could be rid of this menace forever. I'll always hate them for what they did to my family and friends.'

The old man looked at him with great pity. 'You have suffered so much it really pains me to see. Here is my card, call me sometime. I want to invite you round to see my family.'

Through a mixture of studying the guidebook, reading the newspapers and interviewing the hotel receptionist, Tallis had decided that the Red Dragon night club might be the best place to find some female company. It was expensive enough to attract a high class of customer but neither was its reputation squeaky clean. If he did not achieve success there he might have to resort to trawling the red light areas of town, which was not a particularly appealing prospect. He had read about Kamathipura, Mumbai's oldest and Asia's largest red light area, where the sex workers were said to be so numerous they plied their trade on the street and once they found a client would rent a bed by the hour from the inhabitants. He considered whether or not to invite the hotel receptionist with him but quickly dismissed the idea as it might cramp his freedom and he definitely wanted to move around unfettered that evening.

The Red Dragon night club had a lighted dance floor whose squares went off and on in time to the beat of the music. There was a long bar which nevertheless seemed crowded when it came to trying to buy a drink. A number of private seating areas were positioned around the place and after buying a drink Tallis headed for the one furthest away from the dance floor. He watched the dancing for a while, trying to gauge the mood and atmosphere of the establishment and its customers. A number of women had passed and been the recipients of his smile before one stopped and looked at him closely. He smiled again and this woman returned the gesture.

'What is your name?' asked Tallis.

'Perisha,' replied the woman, still looking him up and down.

'Well Perisha, can I buy you a drink?'

'I would like a gin and tonic,' she answered.

The music was too loud to have any real conversation, apart from the odd question or comment. What was perhaps of more significance was their body language, which communicated a mutual desire to end up in each other's arms albeit for totally different reasons. After an hour or so they were tightly squeezed together and Tallis had his arm around her shoulders. He suggested they go somewhere else, partly to investigate the other 'happening' bars and partly for the opportunity to kiss Perisha once they made themselves comfortable on the dark back seat of a taxi.

A succession of these vehicles whisked them from one place to another, each fairly similar with loud music and a darkness occupied by brightly coloured flashing lights. Tallis made a mental note to visit some of these establishments during daylight hours and build up contacts with the owners, bartenders and patrons. He would finally be moving in the intended social circles and who knows what that would bring. At the end of the evening the problem arose as to whose place to go to, the comfort and security of the Kolhapur Hotel was preferable to the unknown quantity, which was Perisha's abode. The only problem was that attractive hotel receptionist with whom his bridges would definitely be burned. What the hell: she might not be on duty and was not the only pretty hotel receptionist in Mumbai.

The morning dawned bright and sunny but Tallis didn't feel like drawing back the curtains to appreciate it just yet. He stretched out his hand and touched the naked body of Perisha lying on the bed still asleep. He snuggled up to her and heard an incoherent murmur as their legs rubbed together. Lying in that position he began to study her in a detail, which had not been possible the previous evening. In common with the majority of Indian women he had seen she possessed long straight black hair.

Her nose was longish and the eyes slightly slanted, suggesting the presence of someone from further east on some part of her family tree. She was of medium height and slim build and had been a pleasant enough woman with whom to spend the night. After she awoke there didn't appear to be any desire on her part to hang around, and she talked in a matter-of-fact manner about her plans for the day as if nothing had happened the night before. The inevitable stage came when the money had to be handed over. Tallis had no idea what was the going rate so decided it would be best for her to start off the bartering process.

'Tallis my darling, I need some help with the bus fare home. I wonder if you could help, also I need to buy food for my family and then there is my sick grandmother.'

'How much would you like?' asked Tallis.

Perisha winced at the bluntness of the question. 'You give me what your heart tells you to give a woman in such a difficult situation.'

Tallis decided to play along with the game. 'A bus fare is twenty rupees, food for your family maybe one hundred and medicine for your grandmother, let me give you two hundred and fifty rupees.'

'I would also like to go and get my hair done.'

'Here is three hundred rupees,' replied Tallis, placing it in her hand to indicate that he wished to conclude negotiations.

The amount was clearly sufficient as no more pleas were made for a further increase, and she even asked if they would be able to meet again.

'I will find you at the Red Dragon,' said Tallis, mulling on the fact that the dancing woman in yellow had done pretty well out of him the other night and it couldn't have been lack of funds that prevented her coming to his room.

Chapter 13

I T BEING A Saturday, Ben lay in bed for an hour longer than usual. The stained sheets bore testament to the fact that he had spent his time thinking about the women he had made love to over the past months. Despite the tension that had been removed from his system he still felt unhappy at the emotional void in his life that could not be filled by sex. He craved a partner who would love him and with whom trusting moments of tenderness could be shared. The kind of life he was living mitigated against the formation of long-term relationships but he felt powerless to change it. He looked at the photographs of his family on the wall and felt they would be ashamed if they could see him now. That shame grew more intense when he remembered how he had used their memory to plead an emotional need, which invariably led to sex.

For some reason his mind drifted back to Elisabetta. She may have been good at sex and as dim as a twenty-watt light bulb, but there was something different about her than all the other women he had been with. They had a hardness, a veneer of emotional invulnerability which never cracked. With Elisabetta he seemed to have got through to a sensitive heart, which had demonstrated genuine affection for him. She was still a girl in many respects and he felt remorse on remembering her look of disappointment when he had let her down the last time they were together. He was also curious as to whether she had closed the door not only physically but metaphorically when she stepped out of his car on the morning after the night before. Could that nascent relationship be brought back to life or was it beyond all hope of resuscitation? Did he even want to repair the relationship or was he guilty of a kind of curious selfishness? A quest to discover what his effect had been on her only to dump her and cause more pain again. Did he want or was he indeed capable of a long-term relationship?

As he drove to the spot where he had last seen Elisabetta, he had still not fully resolved what his intentions were. He parked the car and started to walk to where he thought she stayed. The piece of paper with her address on had foolishly been thrown away at a time when the intention was that they should never meet again. He spoke through a few intercoms.

'Do you know Elisabetta, Austrian student, lives near here?'

For some reason he found this experience intensely humiliating, giving total strangers the impression that the lady he sought hadn't cared enough to tell him where she lived and he was just some lovesick fool clutching at the straws of an unrequited love. A few enquiries soon established her place of abode but as he pressed the buzzer on the door a sudden pang of anxiety ran through his chest. So strange that he was so much calmer when his intentions had been more dishonourable. Then he thought, 'What if she's not at home? What if her boyfriend answers the door? What if she's still in bed with her boyfriend?' A whole host of embarrassing scenarios started to form in his mind and he regretted not having phoned first. How he hated intercoms: there could be a group of giggling students on the other side laughing at his amorous awkwardness, or she could tell him just to go away, increasing his sense of frustration. Far better the good old days of the doorbell or knocker, which necessitated a face-to-face meeting.

'Ben Collins, come to see Elisabetta,' he said into the holes of the plastic case stuck to the door frame.

'Just a minute,' came the reply and Elisabetta opened the

door, looking at him. Her slightly unkempt morning appearance suited her. She was wearing a baggy yellow sports pullover and faded blue jeans, whilst she hadn't yet got around to putting anything on her feet. The awkwardness in the atmosphere was palpable, compelling Ben to say a few words, no matter what, to break the silence.

'How are you doing?' he asked.

'Oh fine, just fine,' she nodded, as if trying to convince herself that everything was just fine.

'I wanted to see you to talk, can I come in?'

'Sure,' she said, flinging the door open.

Ben felt relieved that there was no man in the house with her. He was shown into a small kitchen with a table at one end, where he sat to drink the coffee that was given to him.

'How's your course going?'

'Oh fine, can't complain. I should be the best qualified waitress in Salzburg when I return next month.'

Next month! The words shocked Ben and dealt a serious blow to his as yet unformed ambitions.

'Listen, I'm sorry about last time, I was just in a confused state of mind.' Ben felt he had to terminate the small talk but was instantly annoyed with himself for using his nationality as an excuse for any emotional shortcomings. 'No, I behaved badly, there's no excuse. I've come to apologise.'

'Apology accepted,' said Elisabetta, still not deigning to look him in the eye and assuming an air of indifference.

'Is there anything I can do to repair the damage I've caused?'

Elisabetta stopped what she was doing and now looked him squarely in the face.

'Ben, what is it you want? Why did you come here?'

'I want to talk to you, I've been thinking about you since that last time we parted.'

Any attempt to profess his undying love for a woman he

had been with for less than twenty-four hours would scarcely be credible, so Ben opted for a more modest proposition.

'I just want to talk, no strings attached, no promises. Let's just see each other and find out where it takes us.'

From her expression it was evident that Elisabetta was softening her attitude toward him.

'You know you really upset me last time. I don't go to bed with just anybody, especially on a first date.'

'I understand that,' said Ben.

The silence following those last words was broken by the arrival of a slightly older woman who was obviously sharing the house with Elisabetta. She had shoulder length straight hair of a mousy grey colour. If she were to seek the services of a hair stylist armed with colouring agents there was considerable room for improvement. She was thinner than Elisabetta with aquiline facial features and only seemed to smile with an effort. Introduced to Ben as Angela from Amsterdam, she had originally some association with Elisabetta's college but had long since abandoned her studies. During the introductory pleasantries it was mentioned that Ben was from Britain.

'I suppose you expect me to feel sorry for you,' said Angela.

'No I don't,' replied Ben, taken aback. 'Why do you say that?'

'Because that's what all the Brits I meet seem to think,' she continued. 'We're the victims, the world deserves us a living, the world has to look after us and must attack the Muslims to do so.'

'I think that's a very sweeping generalisation,' said Ben, trying to remain cool and appear reasonable at the same time.

'Is it?' she said, raising her voice slightly. 'Do you know that I have been working with ten Muslim families who have been driven from their homes by thugs threatening violence? Only last week three Muslim men were killed in suspicious circumstances and I personally know of two women who have been raped. What does the government and media do though? They simply ignore it. Can't upset the Brits, look how they've suffered.'

'Do you know, fifty-eight million people, British citizens, died in the attack?' replied Ben with some hostility.

'There you go, proving my point. Violence justifies violence even if directed against those who did not perpetrate the violence. Israel did whatever it wanted for years because the west had the guilt of six million dead Jews in World War Two concentration camps on its conscience. Now history is repeating itself, only it's much more worse.'

Ben hadn't been prepared for this onslaught and had no desire to prolong the argument, especially with Elisabetta present.

'I haven't come here to argue,' he said, turning to Elisabetta. 'Can I see you again soon? Maybe pick you up tomorrow morning and we can go somewhere for lunch.'

'Let me walk you to the door,' said Elisabetta.

In fact she accompanied Ben through the door and some hundred metres down the street outside.

'Don't mind Angela,' said Elisabetta. 'She's just been spending so much time with these charities that she gets worked up about the injustices she sees and can't stop herself from lashing out sometimes.'

'Don't worry about it,' replied Ben. 'I didn't come here to see her anyway, I came to see you. So what about my invitation?'

'Oh yes, tomorrow will be fine, but perhaps it's best if I come to your place rather than you come here. We don't want another argument.'

'Whatever you say,' replied Ben cheerfully on seeing that some progress was being made in rebuilding this relationship.

They came to a busy street which formed a natural place for Elisabetta to turn round and go home.

'Can I kiss you goodbye?'

Ben had kissed many women in his life but had never once asked their permission first. He was surprised at himself for doing so now, but somehow it seemed the right thing to do.

'Of course,' replied Elisabetta, smiling.

It was a strange situation, Ben thought, to find it difficult to express love or appreciation for someone he had been having sex with not so long ago. Here however the two of them were, sitting in a French café having just finished their lunch, and that was precisely how he felt. The ice had been broken and they could talk freely about everyday things, but how was he to establish the emotional intimacy he craved? Proclamations of undying love were premature and therefore insincere, yet any attempt at rekindling the physical aspect of their relationship by putting an arm around her or touching a knee seemed cheap and tawdry. It would have appeared as if he just wanted to repeat the experience of their first night together. The physical expression of feelings was however an integral part of a loving relationship and he felt that this was what he wanted. How to demonstrate his honourable intentions yet move the relationship on was the dilemma now being faced. The rain was pelting down outside and condensation had formed on the glass windows which afforded a view of the normally crowded street outside. Would he be sitting in this same café on a Sunday afternoon next month, with Elisabetta gone, wondering what might have been if he had only known the right way to act? Suddenly he had a brainwave.

'I want to come to Austria with you.'

'You want to do what?' asked Elisabetta, taken aback by the statement.

'You heard me, I want to meet your family, your friends, I want to see where you went to school. It would help me to understand you so much better.'

'I really don't understand you,' she said, smiling and shaking her head. 'One time you give me the cold shoulder after a one-night stand, the next time we meet you want to be introduced to my family.'

'I mean it,' said Ben. 'Don't worry, I won't let you down a second time.'

'You let me down over there and you'll have my two brothers to contend with. Let me think about it. In the meantime lets just get to know each other a little better.'

She reached her hand out and stroked Ben on the cheek, like an older woman offering comfort to the earnest and sincere, yet awkward, attempts of a young boy making his first proposal of love.

They spent the rest of the afternoon at Ben's place, just lounging on the sofa, their arms intermittently entwined around each other between breaks for conversation, TV watching or getting another drink. Neither rejected the advances of the other, but these overtures did not communicate any sexual intent. It was a comforting experience for Ben and he wondered if that emotional void in his life was starting to be filled.

Chapter 14

ANNA WILLIAMS WAS a worried woman. There was something disconcerting in the behaviour of her husband the doctor. He was outwardly polite and respectful and she felt secure in the knowledge that he would never have an affair, but something nevertheless had definitely changed. He no longer seemed affected by what she said and walked with a more self-assured demeanour about the house. No attempt was made to hide away in his office when visitors came, despite the fact that he wanted little to do with them, and nothing seemed to faze him. It was as if an extra layer of invisible skin had been grown, which could not be penetrated by any surrounding circumstance to alter his mood. To make matters worse he actually seemed to be enjoying himself. Anna had felt so embarrassed one afternoon when a friend from the church had come round. To the question posed by her husband, 'Why did Jesus die?' this lady had answered that it was really none of her business and she didn't want to start an argument. Robert just laughed and laughed on hearing this response. It was a real dilemma to know what to do about this problem, made even worse by the fact that Robert had not actually done anything wrong and so there were no allegations that could be made. In fact if anything he was more amiable and considerate than had been the case in the past.

Robert did not feel so much as if he had grown a new skin, rather as if he had cast off an old one. It was a heavy skin of worries and fears, which blunted perception and made him feel impotent.

A snake becomes blind when it sheds its skin and must feel it is seeing things anew once the process is complete. So it was with Robert and he felt reinvigorated without the old encumbrance. An interview with Dr Olanya had finally been arranged. This had been postponed many times in the past but Robert now felt ready to meet with his colleague and go through the incident of the death of the little boy. He hoped the two of them would be able to look to the future to see how such incidents could be avoided. Dr Olanya walked into his boss's office, was received courteously and offered a chair.

'Dr Olanya,' said Robert in a calm and gentle voice, 'I have been wanting to talk to you for some time concerning the case of the little boy who died.'

'Foetus,' interjected Dr Olanya. 'And I was not to blame, the case was looked into by the hospital and there was no evidence of negligence or malpractice.'

'I am aware of what the hospital report said,' continued Robert slowly, looking straight into the eyes of his fellow doctor, a look so intent its recipient had to turn away. 'I did not ask you to come here to apportion blame.'

'Why have you brought me here?'

'To clear the air, to make sure you and I can work well together in the future. I also want to help you take a long hard look at your medical procedures and working practices to make sure a case like this does not happen again.'

'I have no problem with you Dr Williams, but I don't see why you should try to help me. Do you realise I have been a qualified doctor for over fifteen years? What kind of help can you give me?'

Robert had been dreading the occurrence of this interview, fearing that his colleague would become defensive and verbally aggressive. He did not like confrontation and hated having to deal with loud and argumentative people. Now as he looked at

Dr Olanya he did not see anything to be scared about. Here was no omnipotent adversary sitting in his office but somebody who was weak and frightened. He was frightened to take responsibility for his actions, was frightened to see the parents, was frightened of talking about the issue and was frightened to take any advice. Dr Olanya was indeed a weak man.

'I can't help you,' said Robert, 'so long as you refuse to look at yourself and examine your behaviour. I am not here to discipline you, only to urge you to have the courage to look in the mirror.'

'I don't need yours or anybody else's help or advice,' said Dr Olanya and stood up abruptly to leave the office.

Dr Williams sighed and reached for the in tray on his desk where the morning mail was waiting. Amongst the usual items was an envelope from an international firm of real estate agents with the writing 'Release Your Locked Up Capital Now'. The substance of the letter was that they were offering six-figure sums to British expatriates to sign over their rights to land or property that might come their way once Britain was recolonised. There were apparently thousands of people queuing up to purchase a part of Britain. The letter neither pleased nor angered Robert but was placed in the bin without a lot of thought. He reflected on how indifference could prove to be a powerful defence against overtures designed to push you one way or the other. Neither land in the UK nor a large sum of money produced particular excitement in him so it was easy to dismiss both. In any case it was certain that more and improved offers would come along as the time for a recolonisation drew nearer.

What would he do if the possibility of a move back to Britain ever arose? Now there was a question. For so long he had feared losing his job at KCMC and the disastrous effect this would have on his marriage. Now neither of these seemed so important and he dared to think of another life outside Tanzania: a new life in Britain, a new start, possibly as a doctor, possibly not. Was there anything to be afraid of in that and would he really be that bothered if his wife didn't join him? Why not return to the land of his birth, not to pick up the pieces of an old life but to start an entirely new one? The more he thought about it the more the idea appealed to him.

Robert found his friendship with Mwamba difficult to handle, not so much between the two of them but in the signals it gave to others. Her company was engaging and he wanted to spend as much time as possible with her, whilst at the same time being acutely aware of the awkward position in which such companionship could place both of them. If he were honest, it would be untruthful to deny that he had feelings for her: in their talks together he had exposed a part of his soul, resulting in the formation of a mutual emotional bond. He shuddered however at the thought of an affair: he had always despised teachers, lecturers or indeed anyone in a position of authority who abused their power to gain sexual gratification from subordinates. That anybody should think of him as such an unprincipled rake or Mwamba so free with her favours was an unbearable idea. Robert felt that she had helped open his eyes to a whole new way of thinking about life and God, and any physical contact would undermine the significance of the revelations he had received.

'How do you deal with guilt?' he asked her once whilst thinking of some of the problems plaguing his life.

'I don't deal with guilt, because I never allow myself to feel guilty about anything,' she replied.

'That's easy to say but you must have done some things which you feel ashamed about.'

'Guilt and shame are entirely negative emotions with no positive side effects. I try not to view experiences as bad either, since every experience in life whether painful or pleasurable is a learning experience and can help you become a better person. To say something is shameful is to lock it away and only bring it out when you feel like punishing yourself. It is not difficult to ignore guilt if you view your life as a journey where you gain enlightenment from everything that happens.' She accompanied these words with a smile as if to reinforce that it really was not a problem.

'I wonder what I have learnt from the death of the little boy,' thought Robert.

Chapter 15

Tallis sat at the bar of "The Shangri La" and sipped his glass of lager without enthusiasm. The cold liquid effervesced unpleasantly with the coating of his mouth and continued its journey with difficulty on to the stomach. Three other men, average age fifty-five, were also propping up the bar and demolishing the contents of their tall glasses at an equally slow rate. It was lunchtime and the dark interior of the bar contrasted sharply with the bright sunshine, which could be glimpsed through a chink in the door. The boredom of the elderly trio's gatherings had been lessened with the arrival of their young drinking partner, though Tallis was not at all sure he enjoyed being the centre of attention and all their efforts to impress him.

Ian was sitting to his left recounting some long convoluted tale of life in the early days after independence. It was possible he had a smattering of Indian blood, though he assumed the air of an English gentleman in the colonies. Tallis was totally uninterested in what was being said, though he attempted to show a degree of curiosity out of politeness. In fact he was not listening to a word that was being said but focusing more on the appearance of this wearisome raconteur. The pink skin fell loosely about his face and his teeth were stained yellow from years of smoking. His grey blonde hair was thinning though someone had taken the trouble to comb it neatly that morning. Despite the fact that he talked constantly, his eyes were dull, indicating a tedious existence and a jaded view of life. Tallis speculated on what contribution this individual made to society. An empty-headed, unattractive, prejudiced, unemployed talking machine fuelled by lager. There was more vitality in the faces of the young men outside the bar who scratched a living selling whatever goods they could lay their hands on. Their stay on earth was also probably more meaningful and happier.

Tallis had been in Mumbai for just over a month now and the initial excitement of being there had definitely started to wane. There was nothing to admire about the daily routines of his companions at the bar and it was obvious that if he didn't change his present lifestyle he would eventually end up just like them. Leaving The Shangri La by three o'clock, possibly after a game of pool, he would wander back by a fairly circuitous route, taking in as many shops as possible, to the Kolhapur Hotel where he would get ready for the evening's entertainment. Later he would be joined by a different, though certainly no more admirable set of cronies. There was still a thrill of excitement, wondering what kind of woman he would pick up at night, though the pointlessness of this existence was beginning to bother him.

On returning to the hotel room Tallis switched on his laptop only to find another communication from the now renamed Afghan Volunteer Force. They had aligned themselves with another organisation and were now called The Crusading Knights for Justice. There were opportunities to serve worldwide as a soldier, though there was no way he was returning to Afghanistan or indeed any part of the Middle East. A special news item reporting on the tactics of starvation and torture being used by Muslim militias to control Christian tribes in southern Sudan was accompanied by some harrowing photographs. The Kenyan government was concerned the militias would attack settlements in northern Kenya and attempt to destabilise that part of their country. For obvious reasons they were uncomfortable about seeking military assistance from other countries and did not want a long drawn-out campaign that would sap the resources of its own army. The Crusading Knights for Justice had offered their services free of charge and high ranking officials were more than happy to turn a blind eye to their operations. Muslim militias could fight with Christian mercenaries but the Kenyan and Sudanese governments could pretend nothing was going on and still remain on friendly terms. Reading through the conditions of service for soldiers Tallis noticed that the pay was better than in Afghanistan and there would be bars, women and night life, unlike the barren joyless towns he'd had to endure a few months earlier. He would be able to holiday in game parks with spectacular scenery, but most of all some meaning would return to his life. He would feel he was doing something worthwhile by staunching the flow of Muslim influence in Africa. He submitted his details and began to feel excited again about the prospect of being involved in military action.

In a side pocket within the leather covering of his laptop Tallis saw the business card that had been given to him by the proprietor of the Kingfisher restaurant. *Abraham Venu*, read the first line in gold coloured italics, *seafood restaurateur*. He responded to the email address at the bottom: there was nothing better to do with his days than visit this gentleman and who knows, he could even receive a free meal out of it.

Tallis started to prepare for the evening with a bath then picked up the freshly laundered clothes that had been left on the bed. Looking in the mirror he appeared much the same as he had done every evening since arriving in Mumbai, but today he did not particularly look forward to going out: the same drunken lecherous faces, the same conversations, the noise of the bar, the flashing lights. Two desperate souls pretending to be desperately in love with each other, despite never having previously met, and each encouraging the other's lies. A feeling of depression at going through the same routine filled his being and, having once acknowledged this sensation, the realisation dawned that he did not have to go out. If he so desired he could stay in for the evening and watch television. The idea evoked memories of unremarkable evenings spent sitting on a sofa in Britain watching a film or football match. He could be on his own or maybe friends had visited with a collection of six-packs, they could even send out for fish and chips. Remembering those simple pleasures of a life that was now over depressed him still further. No, he didn't want to go out to the night clubs but couldn't stay in the hotel room all evening even with the company of the television. He delved into the leather covering of his laptop and pulled out Abraham's card once more. This time he telephoned the number printed on it.

A child answered and there was a pause occupied by sounds in the background calling for Abraham to come and answer the phone. Tallis imagined a scene of comfortable domesticity, the children running around the house in pyjamas, diving into armchairs too big for them and feeling secure in the warmth of the family home. It made him think of a time when he had parents and a kind of happiness he doubted he would ever again possess.

'Hello Tallis, how are you? Glad you phoned.' Abraham answered the phone and seemed genuinely pleased he had rung. 'Listen I'm a bit busy tonight but why don't you come to the restaurant early tomorrow morning? We can go on a boat trip, I'm sure you will enjoy it.'

Tallis thanked him very much for the invitation. That was tomorrow sorted out but the problem of what to do this evening still remained, so he decided to go out for a walk.

A couple of women were sitting in the reception area dressed in jeans and T-shirts. Tallis immediately recognised one of them as the dancer in yellow he had so presumptuously and unsuccessfully propositioned on his first evening in Mumbai. How would she react when she saw him again? More to the point how would he react? He could hardly ask for his money back, though any form of acknowledgement would bring back the memory of the five hundred rupee note folded in the paper bearing his room number. There would probably be an embarrassed atmosphere with both of them studiously observing the floor as they passed. As it was she didn't even notice his presence and went on talking to her friend as if nothing had happened. He reached the door to the street rather put out that she didn't at least have the good grace to feel uncomfortable in his proximity, and was about to turn around to say something but realised there would be no point.

He walked round the busy shopping centres gazing through the large glass panes of the expensive establishments as well as the innumerable informal traders operating on the streets. He realised with some sadness that he was no more a part of this city than he had been on the first day of arrival and was merely a spectator of all the life and vitality surrounding him. He returned to the Kolhapur Hotel and positioned himself on a corner of the sofa that ran around the edge of the bar and afforded uninterrupted views of the television. The bar was its usual deserted self but he was content just to sit there drinking his lager, watching the television and observing the indolent bar staff. He could hear from a distance the music accompanying the Indian dancers, but had no desire to go there.

Chapter 16

ON WEDNESDAY MORNING an invitation appeared on
Ben's computer screen. It was from the British Refugee
Society of France inviting him to a talk entitled
'Reclamation of our island – when will it happen?' He knew that
this invitation was a result of his brief meeting with Frank Oates
who was chairman of the society. The talk was to be given by Ken
Louis, a controversial politician during his time at the Palace of
Westminster, who these days made much political capital over
the treatment of British expatriates and the sluggishness with
which the United Nations was dealing with the recolonisation
of the island. He was to be assisted by scientific testimony from
Dr Alan Parker, a specialist in the field of chemical and biological
weapons. This eminent academic had recently returned from
North Korea where he had been involved in decommissioning
their enormous stockpiles of weapons of mass destruction. A
surprise video was also promised and the phrase at the bottom
of the invitation read, 'Entry strictly limited to British citizens
with no exceptions.' Ben reflected on the fact that they would
never have got away with such a statement in a different, more
tolerant time.

Friday evening was an inconvenient time for him but as the
talk began at six p.m., he reckoned he had enough time afterwards
to take Elisabetta out. Since Sunday they had seen each other
every day as if both of them had been staking a claim through the
ties of long periods of time. It was much the same way as a lion
marks its territory through the sacrifice of copious amounts of

urine until it becomes the recognised owner. Ben found her easy to talk to and the conversation was a good bit more interesting than originally anticipated. Elisabetta was fascinated by his former life in Britain, and he didn't mind talking about himself. What was amazing was that none of Angela's negativity and anti-British sentiment had rubbed off on her. She maintained a child-like appreciation for her lover's lost homeland, whilst still managing not to fall out or argue with her housemate.

Angela fascinated, scared and angered Ben. Who employed her and what exactly she did all day, were questions that never seemed to get answered. Elisabetta discouraged any discussion of her and made light of her more extreme views, dismissing them as over-enthusiasm for her cause. Ben on the other hand wanted to know why she thought the way she did, what drove her to take up a position so contrary to the prevailing wisdom. Were his countrymen really like the Israelites? Maybe they were now spending their time in the wilderness searching for the promised land. Maybe they were being tested by a divine authority to see if they were worthy to return. But he didn't want to harm anybody, just live in peace in the country of his birth. How we would love to part the waters of the English Channel and lead hordes of Britons, walking along the sea bed back to their island. A drawing of such a scene might prove a powerful propaganda image for the British Refugee Society, the only problem being that Ken Louis would probably want to supplant Ben at the head of the queue leading everybody home.

'It gives me great pleasure to introduce Ken Louis as our guest speaker tonight. The former Labour MP for Walthamstow South, he has consistently championed our cause and exposed the criminal bureaucracy of the United Nations in dealing with the British issue. I am sure he has some golden words of wisdom for us tonight so please give him a warm British welcome.'

Frank Oates beamed with pleasure as he uttered these words

and the guest speaker was greeted by rapturous applause. Ken Louis walked slowly to the small podium that had been set up centre-stage and confidently looked at his audience.

'Ladies and gentlemen,' another slight pause, at the end of which he stretched out his arms and smiled. 'Fellow citizens of our great and noble country. It gives me great pleasure to be able to speak to you today here in Paris, but also great sadness. I wish there was no need for this meeting and I wish I could be greeting my brothers and sisters on British soil. There is a song I remember from my youth with the following words: "Don't it always seem to go that you don't know what you've got till it's gone." I'm sure all of us will echo those sentiments when we think of what we once had. Not only our families and friends who will live in our hearts forever, but also our way of life: cricket on the village green, the gentle countryside, our ancient customs, one of the richest historical legacies in the world, a wonderful literary, scientific and artistic tradition. To think of Shakespeare, Dickens, Newton, Churchill and Lennon to name but a few is to marvel at the fantastic achievements of our small island. An individual simply cannot sum up what it means to be British, but perhaps Leander Starr Jameson came close when he described us as the finest flower of civilisation. We will never be able to bring back the dead but we can reclaim our country and maintain our traditions. We can remake a society of which our ancestors would be proud.

'I am pleased that we only have Britons in the audience tonight, because you all have an understanding of what it means to be British: not like those faceless bureaucrats who sit on committee after committee at UN headquarters in New York. Continuing the words of the song I quoted at the beginning of my speech, "They'd pave paradise to put up a parking lot." Let me quote from Dr Hans Schneider, an influential member of the European Parliament: "The recolonisation of Britain presents significant economic and social challenges for Europe and the world beyond. The wishes of British expatriates should not be paramount as we must consider the wider implications for the whole continent." A professor of Politics at Harvard University has warned of the dangers of an undemocratic and militaristic government being set up one day in the United Kingdom. The United Nations does not want to offend anybody so ends up doing nothing. Ladies and gentlemen, forces and arguments are emerging opposed to a recolonisation of our island and the United Nations does not have the strength of character to adopt the morally correct course of action. To cap it all we now have this agreement with Spain over Gibraltar, which is just another obstacle put in our path. Slowly there is a coming together of powers which is strangling our aspiration to return to our homeland. The longer the present situation continues the more difficult it will be for us ever to go home.'

Continuing in this vein he painted a picture of a world that would find the existence of the British nation a prospect too inconvenient to support. A dark, faceless, amorphous aggregate of vested interests blocking the birthright of a few brave patriotic individuals. Exhorting the crowd never to forget who they were and where they had come from he sat down to thunderous applause.

Frank Oates rose to his feet and shook the hand of the guest speaker. Turning to address everyone else he publicly thanked Ken Louis effusively for his wise words, stating that they were a challenge for all present to continue the fight for their land. Moving on to the next item on the agenda, which was the video shot from the unmanned aircraft, the smile disappeared from his face and he glanced apprehensively at a colleague operating the media equipment.

'Fellow citizens, since the ridiculous decision by the UN to ban all satellite photography of the United Kingdom, we have been investigating ways in which we can view our beloved homeland. This being our first attempt to use an unmanned aircraft, we did experience a few technical hitches during the process. The main difficulties were with the guidance system and the camera position so the images you are about to see are not the most interesting ones.' He hesitated to clear his throat then continued: 'Also you may have trouble seeing –'

'Just shut up Frank and let's get on with the show,' shouted one loud voice from the audience, accompanied by murmurs of approval from the others.

This admonishment seemed to restore some humour to Frank as he said, 'Right you are gentlemen, let's get started.'

The lights dimmed and the first pictures appeared, showing the water of the North Sea passing underneath the drone at speed. Suddenly the grey water gave way to sand, almost immediately followed by green grass. As the camera was pointing down there was no opportunity to see the land set against the skyline. The plane was too close to the ground to see it in the context of a panorama, just snippets of different coloured pieces of land. Those controlling the drone from Europe must have realised this problem when the pictures were relayed to them as the elevation of the craft was increased to give a better view. Inevitably some detail was lost in doing this but at least the images started to make more sense.

'We sent it over southern Scotland to avoid it being shot down by a ship's gun on a better protected stretch of coastline,' explained Frank.

Whilst this was arguably a wise decision it resulted in a complete absence of interesting landmarks. What people had come for was Buckingham Palace, Westminster Cathedral or Old Trafford football pitch. Even a view of a deserted town at close quarters would have been of interest but all that was shown were green fields, criss-crossed with grey roads and here and there a clump of buildings where a settlement had been. It was impossible to see any evidence of life, either human or animal. The drone circled around showing much the same kind of thing then abruptly the film stopped.

'That was when we blew the plane up,' explained Frank.

Mutterings of discontent arose from the audience.

'I know, I know,' said Frank. 'I had frankly expected more too, but you must realise this was a first for our organisation. I can assure you that things will be better next time.'

He then stopped and scanned the front row for a man who had been sitting pensively throughout the evening's drama.

'We are fortunate however to have with us here tonight Dr Alan Parker, an expert in biological and chemical weapons who can perhaps shed some light and answer your questions on the prospect of life returning to Britain.'

Polite applause accompanied Dr Alan Parker's nervous walk to the podium. Frank Oates' hopes that perhaps he could turn around a difficult situation were not fulfilled. If the video had been disappointing the doctor's question and answer session was even worse. He was too much of an academic to be addressing a crowd of this nature and temperament. What they needed was a rabble rouser and he was singularly inadequate to give them the certainties they craved. Opinions were couched in such a cautious manner with so many caveats they became virtually meaningless to those who were there. When would the land be safe for human habitation? It was just not possible to give a time frame from the available evidence but it could be anything from one to ten years. Did he think the scientific evidence was being falsified? He could see no justification for saying so based on what had come out and was not qualified to make a political judgement on the situation as he was not a politician. When asked as to how the attack had affected the bodies of those on the island he started to give a dry, comprehensive scientific monologue which could have lasted over fifteen minutes had not Frank Oates intervened to cut him short. Dr Parker stoically resisted all invitations and prompting to give more clear-cut answers and after forty-five minutes was thanked politely for his time and sat down to almost noiseless applause.

The meeting came to an end with the singing of 'God Save The Queen'. It was customary for the British Refugee Society to continue with verses two and three with their references to the 'knavish tricks' of other nations, a sentiment that most present were able to relate to. Despite the passion of the singing most left the meeting feeling rather deflated.

Ben went out into the street feeling more annoyed than angry. The source of his frustration was how much of his Friday evening had been eaten into. He could have punched Frank Oates in the face. The old fool had felt the need to make a long farewell speech in an effort to smooth over the earlier debacles and try to placate his disgruntled compatriots. Although Elisabetta would not complain of his tardiness and had no difficulty in occupying herself when he was not there, he felt cheated of her company and more disappointed for himself than for her on missing out on the time they could have spent together. They had a quiet and late dinner before Ben drove her home.

'You had better find a safer place to park your car than here,' said Elisabetta as they pulled up on the street outside her front door.

'Why's that?' asked Ben, taken aback.

'Because you're staying the night with me.' Ben felt pleased at receiving such a direct order and gladly complied with his instructions.

Angela was in the living room with some guests, and Elisabetta continued with her pleasantly authoritarian manner, directing him to go straight to the bedroom without stopping to see who was being entertained. This was the first time they had made love in this new phase of their relationship and the tenderness caused by shyness made it so much more satisfying than the previous occasion. Later on Ben got out of bed to go to the toilet, pulling on a pair of boxer shorts before leaving the room. On the way back from relieving himself he took a detour to the kitchen to make a cool drink. Passing by the living room door and hearing slow foreign-sounding voices on the other side of it, it was evident the meeting was still in full swing. The kitchen light was on and there was a woman with her back towards him standing at the kitchen sink. She was wearing a light blue headscarf and a shapeless white dress that covered her body completely to the ankles.

'Excuse me, do you know where the glasses are?' asked Ben with as much politeness as he could muster.

At the first sound of his voice the woman swung round violently, revealing a dark face that was more North African than Arab. The delicate features could have been those of an Ethiopian or Sudanese. Ben however was not admiring her facial characteristics but looking at the expression of absolute terror that swept across every part of her visage. He made a movement to look for a glass himself and she gave a muffled whimper, her eyes still frozen on him, still showing terror. She probably would have screamed if she hadn't been so scared but her mouth was as fixed as the rest of her face and just open enough to allow an uncontrolled passage of air to escape from her throat. As he continued to look for the glass she shuffled backwards into the corner of the kitchen, still looking at him, still absolutely terrified.

Ben decided that the best course of action would be to leave the kitchen before the woman had a heart attack or gathered the courage to scream, attracting the attention of those in the living room. It would not be seemly to be caught in the kitchen with a hysterical woman and just wearing a pair of boxer shorts. He returned to bed and Elisabetta snuggled up beside him. Lying there visualising the expression on the woman's face, he did not believe he had ever seen anybody look so frightened. The word *petrified* came to mind and he began to understand with a new realisation why it was used to describe someone so frightened that they turned to stone.

'How's my travelling partner?' asked Elisabetta.

'I only walked to the toilet,' replied Ben absentmindedly, still thinking of the scene in the kitchen.

'No, silly, the man who is going to accompany me to Austria.'

Ben smiled then said: 'I could get used to being bossed around by you.'

Chapter 17

ROBERT TURNED LEFT onto Boma Road, past the old courthouse building, which had hordes of people ensconced within its grounds, most sitting on the grass evidently prepared for a long wait. He drove down the dusty street with shops loosely packed together on both sides. Some were unoccupied, including the most prepossessing building, the former Boma Road branch of the National Bank of Commerce of Tanzania, an elegant colonial construction complete with fluted columns, which had yet to find a use after being abandoned by its banking tenants. Amongst those that were open for business were a pharmacy, general store, stationers, a travel and tours company specialising in mountain expeditions, two cafés and a shop selling car parts. The businesses appeared to do a paltry trade in Robert's eyes since there never seemed to be many people in any of them and only a small fraction of these were spending money. There was a languor about this part of town, reflected in the neglected state of the buildings, as if nobody could be bothered to apply a new coat of paint or rearrange the window display that had served them for years. At the foot of Boma Road was a clock tower set amongst a well-maintained grassy circular garden that constituted a roundabout or Kipileft as it translated in Kiswahili. Turning right here, passing the bus station on the right and the Hindu temple on the left he was entering the main shopping centre of Moshi.

Buildings of three or more storeys straddled either side of the wide road, tall concrete monuments to Indian families of consequence, the number of floors probably equalling the number of generations who had conducted business there. Tailors sat at their sewing machines competing for pavement space with sweet and cigarette sellers. There was a good crowd of people about but the vast majority did not seem in a particular hurry to go anywhere. Turning down a side street Robert parked outside a small shabby building and entered with his wife. It was eleven o'clock on a Friday morning and they were on the main shopping trip of the week. Robert had not really wanted to use his precious day off in this manner but Anna had persuaded him to tag along so that he could pick up some items he liked. Translated this meant that if he didn't join her all the things he hated would be bought. Passing through a couple of dark, narrow corridors, squeezing past the freezers that almost filled them, they emerged into the main room where the majority of goods were kept. The space was limited but within the narrow confines the shop owner had managed to ingeniously pack in a wide variety of products ranging from toiletries and tobacco to alcoholic drinks, spices and all manner of tinned goods. It was the best-stocked shop in town, with fairly reasonable prices, so had become the favoured destination of whites and middle class Africans. The owner was making a packet, though one would not surmise this from the modest and cramped environment. He could easily afford bigger and more salubrious premises but did not want to attract unwelcome interest from the Tanzanian Revenue Authority, the police and local thieves. Despite his initial reluctance Robert gradually became pleased he had come: it proved to be a refreshing change of scene and he was able to pick up a good bottle of whisky. They stopped at the bakery then went to exchange a crate of empty Tusker bottles for full ones before starting the journey home.

On the way out of town Anna requested to pass through the large catholic cathedral called Kristmfalme or Christ the King, as she needed to see one of the priests. The cathedral complex occupied a vast area of land and, as well as the large church, included commodious living quarters for the clergy, an office block and numerous other outbuildings. The many four-wheel-drive vehicles in the car park provided evidence that this religious community was very much a going concern. Robert had wanted to sit in the car as it humbly occupied a space beside such exalted company, but Anna persuaded him to go inside where it would be more comfortable.

They walked in through the foyer past photographs of the Pope and one famous African bishop, who everybody seemed to know the name of except Robert, to the office of Father Stanislaus Mpanga. He came to the door and warmly greeted Anna. Robert smiled politely out of an ingrained respect for a man of the cloth and felt obliged to enter the room following his pressing invitation.

'I have heard so much about you, Dr Williams, so much. It is a real privilege to be able to speak with you. Please take a seat.' Father Mpanga enthusiastically shook his hand and offered him a chair. 'Your wife is a great supporter of God's work here on earth, but we don't see much of you. I would be so happy if you could make it to one of our services.'

Robert remembered the last church service he had attended there some years ago. He had sat through two hours of it and, from his elementary knowledge of Kiswahili, reckoned it was nearing a conclusion when the church treasurer rose to his feet and gave a forty-five minute talk on the state of the church accounts. Despite such mind-numbing boredom one could not deny the large number of people who usually managed to fill the enormous building. A constant stream of them arrived throughout the service under the disapproving glare of the stewards who usually accompanied this look with a pointing to the wrist. Outside the church these servants of God patrolled with long thin sticks freshly garnered from nearby trees, taking a swipe at any children who were late or tarried along the way. Such chastisements never had any effect: the numbers remained the same, as did the number of latecomers.

'Well you know KCMC keeps me busy,' replied Robert.

'Surely nothing is more important than God's work,' replied Father Mpanga with a gentle smile.

Robert was beginning to realise that this was not just some chance conversation but that he had fallen into a well-laid trap. He was also annoyed with himself for the lame excuse he had just offered, it put him on the back foot and would encourage the priest to probe further to make him feel uncomfortable. A more decisive defence would have more chance of success and allow him to leave without having been totally humiliated.

'In fact I don't come to church because I am not a Christian,' he said.

'Now that is a serious business,' said Father Mpanga. 'A very serious business indeed. I am here to save souls and I am worried about your soul. You should turn to the Lord Jesus Christ if you wish to go to Heaven. Are you not worried about what will happen to you after you die?' His face looked concerned, whether he actually was or not was a more debatable matter.

'To be honest I'm not worried, because I believe I'm going to heaven no matter what happens.' It was as Mwamba had predicted: people will try to convert you through fear, and fear is the opposite of love.

'Jesus Christ is the only one who can set you free from sin and thereby give you access to the kingdom of heaven.'

'I don't believe in sin, I don't believe God requires us to behave in a certain way.'

Father Mpanga was flabbergasted. 'Look around you, see the murders, the crime, the cruelty. Look at what has happened to your own country. How can you say sin does not exist?'

'I believe in fear, I believe in weakness, most of what you call sin can be traced back to those sources.'

'God loves you and wants you to join him in the kingdom of Heaven, but he cannot accept sinners. We are all sinners but Jesus Christ will free you from the slavery of sin if you accept him as your personal saviour.'

'You say God is all-powerful but believe he cannot do something. Why can't he accept everybody into the kingdom of Heaven?'

Now Father Stanislaus Mpanga was worried. There was no carrot he could dangle in front of the doctor or stick to beat him with since he believed there were no requirements to gain eternal life and be close to God. Not only this, he had obviously thought deeply as to why this should be the case. The Father would have to think of some better strategies and arguments to convince him of the error of his ways and return his errant sheep to the flock.

'I am worried about your soul, Doctor, that's my job. I will pray for you and hope we can talk again at some time in the future.'

Walking back to the car, Robert reflected on the fact that Father Mpanga was not at all worried about his soul the previous month. A respectable atheism with an occasional doffing of the cap to the established church was somehow not as serious as a sincere belief in a God which was at odds with his own understanding.

A hostile silence occupied the car on the way out of Moshi. Everything about Anna's body language indicated that she was inwardly seething and only able to keep her emotions in check with some effort. Robert pretended to ignore this quiet before the storm and was determined not to be the first to break it, triggering the inevitable tempest. In fact he was little bothered about her mood and took it as a confirmation that he had been speaking the uncomfortable truth.

'How could you embarrass me like that?' she shouted as they

entered the house.

'What did I do?' answered Robert, trying to feign as much innocence as possible.

'Don't try to be clever with me, you know very well what you did, talking to a priest in that disrespectful way.'

'I was merely expressing my opinion, don't I have a right to do that?'

'You have no right to insult a man like Father Mpanga, a good man, a holy man like that, who is only trying to help you.'

'I never insulted him and I was not the one who arranged our meeting.'

Anna's face was becoming contorted with anger as she practically snarled at her husband. 'You, you white people, you think you're so clever but you know nothing. You believe in science, well I believe in God, we shall see who will win in the end. I will beat you through the name of Jesus Christ.'

Robert had remained calm throughout this exchange and realised nothing would be achieved through its continuation. He walked to the door, observing to Anna on the way that he had not realised before now that the two of them were engaged in a battle.

'I don't worry about anything, God knows what he will do with you, you just wait and see.'

'That's fine by me,' smiled Robert. 'Let's just leave the judging and punishing to God. I am very happy with that.'

If he had beaten his wife with a sjambok it would not have caused as much anger as that smile and the glib way he had dismissed the sincere threats of divine vengeance. She wanted to say something that would really hurt him and expose this new-found morality as nothing more than a hollow sham.

'Are you off to see your girlfriend now?' she said.

Robert stopped dead at the door and a shiver ran down his spine.

'What did you say?' he asked.

'You think I don't know the reason for all your nonsense. That Zambian tart you've been hanging around with.'

He felt sick in the stomach, sick at being found out and sick at the insensitive and crude way that special relationship was being caricatured. With an effort he remained calm and simply said: 'You know nothing about the situation, I have done nothing wrong.'

'Listen to you, you old fool,' Anna said contemptuously. 'Trying to claim the moral high ground, preaching to a priest about religion, whilst all the time carrying on with a woman half your age. You really are something.'

Robert was on the verge of making a vigorous defence of his honour, about to tell her the truth about Mwamba, but somehow managed to resist the temptation to try to exonerate himself. A phrase from the Bible came to mind: 'Don't throw your pearls before pigs' and he felt it would be painful and destructive to share something so personal and close to his heart with somebody who would merely trample it underfoot. He simply repeated, 'I have done nothing wrong,' and walked out into the garden.

How had Anna come to know about his friendship with Mwamba? A short consideration of the facts, which he had never bothered to conduct, led to the conclusion that it would not have been too difficult. How many people inhabited KCMC on a particular day, both employees and patients, and how often had he and Mwamba spent time talking together? Such a relationship between two people of different colour and ages would inevitably have led to rumour and gossip and he knew how much Africans loved their gossip. He was a man of relatively high standing within the hospital and there would be those, envious of the respect Anna enjoyed, who would have loved to tell her the salacious news. A supporter of Dr Olanya or a disgruntled student resentful of the special attention given to one of their number could have exaggerated the facts for their own ends. Unsigned letters being sent around the hospital was not an unheard of occurrence and despite those in authority claiming they never read such cowardly allegations, they always did. In fact when he took a look at the facts it would have been surprising if his wife did not know about Mwamba.

But why was he feeling guilty? It felt like being found out committing some unspeakable atrocity. Trying to find meaning in a life, investigating different religions and talking to others openly about it, was this a crime? No it wasn't, but however often he told himself this it still felt like one. Father Mpanga would love this: the opportunity to enlighten a white man on the sanctity of marriage and the importance of family life. It would be fruitless to try to convince the priest of his innocence since the issue of 'keeping up appearances' or 'being seen to do the right thing' would no doubt be raised. Robert tried to stop his current train of thought and took a few deep breaths in an attempt to take stock of his current predicament. He was experiencing guilt and fear, two emotions which he had resolved would never be permitted to take him over again. Logically there was no reason to feel guilt, but just what was it he was so afraid of? This question perplexed him for some time before he was able to follow the fear through to its root cause, by means of a painful process of self-examination. He realised that he was afraid of his marriage breaking up.

Robert walked amongst the flower beds in the large garden and examined the mango trees to see if any fruit was turning from green to yellow. Whist he was doing this he made a remarkable discovery, a discovery made all the more staggering by the fact that it was so obvious and yet had been so elusive. He realised he did not love his wife and indeed had not done so for a long time. This being the case there was nothing to be afraid of: why should he care what she thought, and if the marriage broke up so much the better. How had he managed to fool himself for months despite the evidence of his own actions? On one level of consciousness he did everything possible to avoid Anna, whilst on another he kept on telling himself he needed to be with her. The dawning of the truth of the situation was a weight off his mind leading to a feeling of liberation. Now that he was in touch with his true sentiments any actions could be directed with greater purpose. In fact come to think of it not only did he not care about the marriage falling apart he actually wanted a divorce. He wanted to tell her this immediately but through instinct recoiled, thinking matters were proceeding too hastily. This needed to be thought through carefully, but then what was there to think over? He didn't love his wife and he didn't want to be with her, that was the stark reality. Robert walked up the garden path and opened the door to the living room. Anna was sitting on the sofa reading the newspaper and ignored his presence. With as much sincerity as he could muster he said: 'Anna my wife, I want a divorce.'

Chapter 18

ABRAHAM'S SMALL BOAT sailed out of the eastern part of
Mumbai into the sea of Oman. It was a bright cloudless
morning and the water was thick with fishing boats
and other trading vessels. As they progressed further east the
volume of sea traffic decreased and Tallis looked over the edge
of the boat watching the bobbing up and down of the waves. For
probably the first time since arriving in Mumbai he felt at some
degree of peace with himself; there was no need to think about
what to do next but merely follow the course of the boat. After
about an hour on the sea they reached their destination, the small
mountainous island of Elephanta.

The boat was tied up and the two of them ascended broad
stone steps to the caves of Elephanta. On the way Abraham
explained a little about their history. Hewn out of the granite
rock between the ninth and twelfth centuries as a temple to the
Hindu god Shiva, the many sculptures and panels carved into
the cave walls depicted Shiva in a number of different roles from
gambling to dancing to showing his marriage to Parvati.

'Are you familiar at all with Hindu gods?' asked Abraham.

'The only one I've ever heard of is Sitala with her cooling
water and fan,' replied Tallis.

Abraham nodded his understanding and clapped him on the
shoulder, pointing the way to the main cave. The entrance was a
dark rectangle supported by stone columns, like the entrance to
a Roman building except that it was surrounded on all sides by
greenery and one could not see what was inside. The columns

continued inside the cave, dividing it into equal rows and aisles. A small square sanctuary had been created towards the west but without doubt the most impressive feature was a six-metre high bust, which dominated the cave.

'This is the triple-headed Trimurthi,' explained Abraham. 'It embodies the roles of Shiva as creator, preserver and destroyer. It is even said that the three faces change their expressions according to the amount of daylight in the cave.' He paused then looked seriously at Tallis. 'The question I suppose you have to ask yourself is which head are you going to put on?'

Tallis didn't answer. They walked out of the dark caves into the sunlight, and sat on a rock outside amongst the vegetation.

'What do you desire for the future?' asked Abraham. A simple enough question but one which Tallis found great difficulty in answering.

'I might try to get a job abroad, make some money, try to enjoy myself,' he muttered.

'You misunderstand me,' said Abraham. 'Where is your life leading, what do you want out of it?'

'I don't think I'm blessed with options,' replied Tallis. 'My homeland is no more, I am destined to travel from place to place in order to make a living.'

'Wandering the earth like a restless spirit?' suggested Abraham.

'What do you suggest I can do?'

'Stay here in India, you can make good business, you have money, you can invest it. I will help you. You can make Mumbai your home.'

'I don't have that much money,' replied Tallis.

'Details, details,' Abraham waved his arms in the air. 'You need a home to grow some roots to enjoy life. At the moment you are running away from a real life.'

During the boat trip back to Mumbai Tallis' head was full of confusing thoughts. For the first time in years he allowed himself to think about where his life was heading and what he needed to do. Last night he had felt like an outsider to society, but now he was being offered an opportunity to enter that same society. But was it practicable and was he ready for it? By the time he arrived back on dry land he had decided to try for one last military posting then hopefully save enough money to return to India. The time away might also clear his head and sort out priorities. He would return with a more coherent vision of what he wanted to do and the money to achieve it.

They clambered out of the boat and walked up to Mumbai's coastal streets. Abraham turned and said: 'Let me know what you decide. You are always welcome here.'

Tallis shook his hand and said, 'Thank you for all your kindness.'

As he was walking away he thought what a kind man Abraham was. A man who offers help to strangers without seeking any reward, a man who does not let the rules and conventions of society stand in the way of showing compassion.

Chapter 19

'THE PROBLEM WITH THIS MARRIAGE IS that it was not solemnised within the Roman Catholic Church,' Father Malya peered over his thick black plastic framed glasses as if to emphasise to Anna the seriousness with which he viewed this neglect of religious duty. 'You married outside the church you were born into, you didn't even ask our permission, and now you come to us for help.' He shook his head at the foolish lack of foresight of this woman and gazed at Father Mpanga who shifted uneasily in his seat. 'I really can't see what we can do. The Catholic Church has no power in this matter and as your husband has never shown any inclination to convert to Catholicism we can hardly bring much influence to bear on him. The only way you can fight this divorce is through the courts, though unfortunately I don't give much for your chances of success there either.'

Father Malya was the church's expert in theological law but despite the weighty legal tomes that occupied the shelves in his large office there was no crumb of comfort he could offer to stop the action started by her husband. Anna was tired of people saying in as many words 'I told you so' when it came to exploring the reasons for the disintegration of her marriage. Her mother was of the opinion that children were necessary to tie a man down, whilst others felt she should have kept closer tabs on what was happening at the hospital and recognised the many tell-tale signs of another woman's presence. A more traditional point of view was that he should have been given more freedom to sow his wild oats, as all men need to do from time to time, and was just rebelling against too much control.

Whatever the merit or otherwise of these arguments the stark reality remained that Robert had moved out of their large house, taken up lodgings in Moshi town centre and petitioned for divorce. He was relieved to be away from his former residence, which at times had felt more like a prison than a home and enjoyed the freedom to come and go as he pleased. Occasionally he wished for some companionship: he was no more lonely than before, it was just that his loneliness now was so much more conspicuous, to himself as well as others. When he ate out by himself or did the shopping, his solitary state could not be hidden and led to some embarrassment. He was careful not to have much social contact with Mwamba lest anyone should accuse him of leaving home to set up a love nest. During this period he began to question more and more the reasons for being in Africa, the more he thought about it the more the realisation dawned that there was really nothing to keep him there. It was surprising how few Britons lived in Moshi and certainly there had been no new arrivals in recent years, only the long-serving variety: eccentric, geriatric figures who seemed to be more in love with Africa than the Africans.

Robert drove up the long road to KCMC and, as was so often the case these days, was mulling over a religious issue. Today he was thinking about eternal life, the carrot that was so often dangled in front of his nose by those Christians attempting a conversion. He felt his opinions on this were not properly thought through and during the last discussion with Father Mpanga could not adequately explain what would happen to his soul once having slipped this mortal coil. Apart from a belief that he would not be forced to jump through hoops in this life to assure immortality in the next, the idea of eternity presented some difficulties for him. Mwamba was interested in the possibility of past lives, suggesting that the soul continues but simply inhabits a new body and set of circumstances. At first he had dismissed such notions out of hand, believing them to be a preserve of those more interested in superstition than religion. Further discussion and a reading of the considerable literature on this subject, including the testimony of many who had returned under hypnosis to a past life had started him thinking that perhaps it was not such an outlandish idea.

What would be the consequences of knowing you would come back as another person with intermittent breaks in paradise between your many and varied lives? It would mean not being so afraid of death or failure, since one could always come back and had more than one chance at getting a life right. It would mean an end to racism or sexism once a person realised they could return in the body of a person from any corner of the world. It would mean people would be less interested in storing up riches in their present life and more interested in solving the problem of world poverty, since there was no guarantee they would be born into wealth in the future. When Jesus said that feeding the poor was the same as feeding him, did he mean that quite literally? The whole concept fitted in with Robert's belief that this life was not merely a trial to see who was worthy to enter the kingdom of heaven. The purpose of people's lives would be to give meaning to them. The idea had its attractions but he would have to think about it a bit more.

Robert parked in the staff car park at KCMC and went to the gynaecology department. A conference of three nurses was taking place around the reception desk and was sufficiently animated for him to realise that some major incident had recently occurred. Upon enquiry it was discovered that seven young men had been flown to the hospital last night with terrible wounds after having been involved in some military action in Kenya. Either the hospitals there were too overwhelmed with the injured or political considerations had necessitated that they be treated in Tanzania.

Apparently one of the soldiers was British so Robert decided to walk to the Intensive Care Unit to investigate further. A special room had been set aside for them and two Tanzanian policemen in khaki trousers and shirts stood guard at its entrance. Robert was not challenged by either of these gentlemen as he pushed open the door, his white coat and stethoscope hung round the neck evidently being sufficient reason to gain admittance and convince them he was not going to do any harm. Not one person was conscious and a white sheet was draped over one individual for whom the ministrations of KCMC had come too late. They were bandaged and connected to drips but there was no evidence of any lost limbs. An eerie silence occupied the room, the only sound being that of Robert's footsteps as he slowly walked on the tiled floor looking at the victims and reading their names. When he reached the bed that was nearest the window he looked at the card hung on the white metal railing at its foot which read, 'Tallis Halliday, Custard Nights for Justice, severe shrapnel wounds, British citizen.'

Part 2

Chapter 1

KING ABRAHA SAT atop the mighty elephant Mahmood. The canopy fixed to this noble beast protected his majesty from the fierce desert sun above, but his eyes still screwed up in response to the glare from the sandy valley surrounded by rocky hills. A cloth wrapped around the mouth afforded some protection against inhaling dust but it was still possible to see the large scar on his face, the result of a duel with a now dead adversary. King Abraha was outside the city of Mecca and, for the first time on the journey from his native Yemen, was a seriously worried man. The campaign had gone without a hitch so far, as the invading force had pillaged along the route encountering little or no resistance, capturing local Arabs who became their guides to the holy city. His men however were now tired and a strange pestilence was spreading through the camp. The trophy for which he had undergone a long and bigoted pilgrimage was in sight but he now doubted whether his men even had the strength to overcome the tiny number of men defending the shrine. He privately chided himself for spending too long at this spot talking to the Quraysh family who guarded the relic and wished he had levelled it to the ground at first sight.

He thought of the magnificent church he had built in Yemen and how it had been so grotesquely defiled by visitors from Mecca who had smeared excrement on the altar. They would pay dearly for this act of desecration and there would be no religious monument left standing to rival his creation. The Ka'bah, God's temple on earth built by Adam and restored by Ishmael and Abraham after the flood would be destroyed once and for all. The caravan routes running over Arabia would no longer stop here to worship their idols al-Lat, al-Uzza and Manat but would come to his church to pay homage. The pagan cults in and around Mecca would be converted to Christianity. This would no doubt please the Abyssinian king who would be sure to congratulate him when next they met. Victory had seemed assured less than a week ago and even most of the Quraysh had taken to the hills rather than endure an apparently inevitable slaughter. But then this sickness had started: at first a headache, slight fever and nausea, nothing too unusual there, but later a rash appeared and spots developed all over the body. Twenty men had died so far and the majority of the others were suffering to a greater or lesser extent.

An assistant brought the elephant to its knees and helped the king to the ground. He retired to his tent and lay on the bed pondering this misfortune and the best course of action under the circumstances. He thought of his wife, the beautiful Raihana, who would be sleeping under guard at their large residence back in Sanaa. She was a bit like the Ka'bah, a prize tantalisingly close but nevertheless out of reach. A true Yemenite noblewoman, she despised him for having taken her by force away from her beloved husband. King Abraha had sired two sons with her but could never capture her heart for the cruelty he had shown. His generals came to the tent throughout the afternoon but the news was always bad: more soldiers had died, more had become sick, the elephants were suffering from the heat and the lack of water.

King Abraha gathered his advisors together in the tent that evening. He wanted to talk of plans for destroying the Ka'bah but was informed that the soldiers were too ill to fight and hardly any of them had been spared the effects of the contagion. Not only were they sick, they were afraid: many believed this disease to be divine retribution for their intention to destroy the Ka'bah. They were reluctant to go one step further, fearing what else God might have in store for them. The king postponed his plans and then fell ill himself. The retreat from Mecca was hastily ordered by his generals, who did not share their leader's enthusiasm for this particular military campaign, and the demoralised and depleted fighting force retraced their steps to Yemen still plagued by illness. King Abraha suffered long and painfully before eventually dying just as he entered Yemen.

The disease did not spread to the residents of the city of Mecca, but the lady Aminah who lived there was mourning the death of her husband Abdullah. Her grief was mitigated by the fact that although one life had ended another was about to start. She was heavily pregnant with Abdullah's son. The disease not only spared her life, it spared the boy the experience of growing up in a Christian city. One can only speculate what effect this may have had on him and on history, for the child was the prophet Mohammed, destined to bring the religion of Islam to Mecca. One and a half thousand years later the same pestilence that was so merciful to him would be unleashed in the name of Islam against the island of Great Britain.

On a large ship a fatal contagion is a nasty thing indeed. It spreads rapidly and there is nowhere to run to avoid infection. The only alternative to succumbing to its rampant advances is to jump over the railing to a speedy death in the water below. Nobody wants your ship to dock close to them and, if they do allow it, the passengers are not permitted to disembark. Doctors are reluctant to come on board to treat the sick and dying and once there are never allowed to leave. It is a situation with which nobody is happy.

The summer before the attack was rife with rumours of an

impending terrorist outrage. Planes were grounded at the merest whiff of something amiss or the merest whim of the Home Secretary. Security at ports and airports was tightened and visa applications to visit the United Kingdom were subject to the closest scrutiny. The 'little Satan' who had so faithfully supported the United States of America in its war against Muslim terror organisations was long overdue a day of reckoning, the only question was when and where. Politicians spoke of a real and imminent threat but were vague as to the details of the terror, partly to protect intelligence sources, partly because they did not really know themselves.

What nobody suspected was that the increased communication along the well-known channels linking the loose affiliation of terrorist groups and individuals was a diversion from the real evil being planned. Agents solicitously tracked down cells in Indonesia, Iraq and Iran who talked of making bombs, carrying out assassinations and downing aircraft. Meanwhile in a remote area in the foothills of the northern Caucasus region of Russia an underground warehouse contained a deadly cargo.

Since the cease-fire agreed between the Russian government and representatives of Chechen independence fighters, that troubled part of the federation had been granted de facto autonomy, although in a face-saving deal it was still officially part of Russia. Since then funds had poured into the region from sympathetic Muslim organisations. Ostensibly this was to help rebuild the economy, but it had the effect of creating a fundamentalist hotbed and denying ordinary Chechens civil rights. The territory had been carved up between Islamic leaders who supported the government. They were effectively local chieftains with absolute power to control their populations through Sharia law, a brutal police force and a complete absence of democracy. One of these tyrants, Bai-Ali Osmaev, had been approached by a representative of al-Qaeda to build an underground storage facility in exchange for money and arms. Bai-Ali honoured his part of the deal by asking no questions as to what the building was for and al-Qaeda fulfilled their obligations by supplying the badly needed items.

In contravention of international agreement and despite strenuous denials to the contrary, the former Soviet Union had conducted extensive research on biological and chemical weapons for decades. They had succeeded in making the smallpox virus more virulent and contagious and their production line at the Vector Institute at Koltsovo near Novosibirsk was capable of making one hundred tons of it every year. In addition to creating strains resistant to existing vaccines it had been possible to insert genetic material from the Ebola virus and the Venezuelan equine encephalitis virus into the smallpox host. Victims would not only be subject to one disease but two or three at the same time. Naturally occurring smallpox typically produces a mortality rate of about thirty per cent, but these variants were almost one hundred per cent effective as agents of death. It had been suggested that the viruses could be dropped as cluster bombs by long-range aircraft or delivered by intercontinental ballistic missiles. Whether any such weapons were ever produced is debatable but what had been produced was an aerosol spray, which could release large quantities of virus into the atmosphere.

Whilst the attention of the intelligence services was focused on following leads from South America to China, a small but dedicated group were working in almost total isolation. They were perfecting the plan that would destroy a nation. Their aim was not to scare the British government and people but rather bring about their total annihilation. It would be an act so callous that there would be no neighbours or relatives left to bury the dead and grieve for them. Bodies would be left out in the streets without even the benefit of a blanket to hide their mortality: eyes would not be closed but be left staring upward to the sky in shock and bewilderment until the birds came to pick them out.

Plastic drums containing the deadly virus were transported in secret westward across Russia and carefully stockpiled underground. The problem facing those who never left the warehouse was how to devise a delivery system which would disperse the virus over an area the size of Britain. Planes might distribute their payload too high in the atmosphere, causing an unwanted epidemic on the European mainland. It was uncertain how effective the crude missiles they had designed would be and the number required would be bound to arouse suspicion. Despite the risks it was felt that suicide bombers would be the preferable option, except that they wouldn't be detonating explosives strapped to their waist but silently producing a fatal cloud from large canisters on their back. Placing each cadre at the centre of the squares forming the Ordnance Survey grid covering the island required a number of two hundred and four. With improvements to the propellant system, making the canisters larger and restudying the map of Britain, ignoring the Isle of Man, it was possible to reduce this to one hundred and twenty. If it were possible to place two canisters each in different locations, one automatically detonated, the other manually, this would be even better. Five cells of twelve terrorists would be a manageable team to deal with. In addition five missiles were to be targeted, one each at the cities of London, Birmingham, Manchester, Newcastle and Glasgow. A fine mist reaching to all parts of the island would kill all humans underneath it. This would be a dark cloud for which it would be difficult to see any silver lining.

Chapter 2

My Dearest Maureen,

Hope you are well and have settled in at your new school without a problem. I am sure things will work out fine if you remain firm with the children and keep on top of the paperwork. Can't wait for the day when I return to marry you. I know the time we spend apart is difficult but I am hopeful of being able to start my own business back in Britain soon.

I have been in Prague for three weeks now and I must say I love the place. It is such a historic and elegant city and has been restored to much of its former glory following the neglect of the communist years. There is a real buzz in the air that things are about to take off and the business contacts I have made seem very promising. The Czech ladies are beautiful: very tall and graceful but the only woman who occupies my thoughts is you.

My brother Michael arrives tomorrow and will be staying for a couple of weeks. He is having a holiday after packing in his last job and I suppose I'm looking forward to seeing him. We normally get on fine when it's just the two of us, it's mainly family gatherings where the arguments tend to start. I haven't yet decided where to take him but hope he will be able to occupy himself during the daytime as I shall be fairly busy.

The weather here is bitterly cold and it seems to become dark earlier than in Britain. The children outside the apartment made a snowman and I generously gave them a carrot for the nose. Feels like Christmas already.

Give my regards to everyone
Love you always Ben

Ben reread the letter and then sealed it within an envelope. Although ninety-nine percent of his communication was via email, he always preferred to write a letter to Maureen. Somehow it was more romantic and personal, a piece of paper they had both touched rather than simply words on a computer screen. Maureen: he felt both happy and guilty when he thought about her. It had been three months since they were last together and the effect of this separation on their relationship was a cause of worry. Did she really understand the necessity of him being away so that he could return to Britain with the financial means to look after her properly? Sometimes he was tempted to jack everything in and go back to face a future which, although uncertain, would be with the woman he loved. He thought of his brother coming and hoped he didn't start expressing any opinions on the subject. This would inevitably be followed a few days later by his mother saying exactly the same thing, a telephonic echo bouncing from one end of Europe to the other and suitably amplified at the point of reflection. Anything he did would not meet with the approval of his family. He had long ago resigned himself to this reality and could take their reprobation so long as nobody criticised his relationship with Maureen.

Ben looked out of the window at the snow falling outside and realised it was about time to go out to meet a couple of business associates. At least nobody in Prague thought him a failure and indeed those he met appeared to be favourably impressed. He wondered why it was that he achieved greater success outside his native country. Perhaps it would be better if Maureen came to join him overseas: with some planning it could be a realistic proposition. He looked in the mirror and straightened his tie. At least his upbringing in Britain had taught him one thing: it was always important to keep up appearances and present an unruffled front to the world no matter what one was feeling inside, stiff upper lip and all that.

The plane arrived on time and Michael was one of the first to make it to the arrivals lounge. He smiled briefly to his brother and wanted to be on his way as quickly as possible. This was how they always greeted each other, there would be no lingering welcomes, no pleasant words of greeting, no physical contact, not even a handshake. It was an awkward enough moment to want to get it over with as quickly as possible.

Ben did his best to make conversation on the route back into the city. Did he have a good journey? What were his plans for the holiday? How were mum and dad? Michael looked down his nose at these attempts at small talk, as if such trivial topics of conversation were the product of an ordinary mind, and did not condescend to give them his consideration. Ben felt like asking what meaningful topics he would wish to talk about but instead maintained a purposeful silence until arriving at the apartment.

Michael expressed neither disappointment nor appreciation of his brother's lodgings but simply went to his assigned room and began unpacking suitcases.

'Drink?' asked Ben.

'After I've finished unpacking,' came the reply.

'Typical,' thought Ben. 'He'll wait until I've sat down and then expect to be served.'

Michael emerged from the room fifteen minutes later. 'Drinks are in the kitchen, help yourself,' said his brother.

'What are you drinking?'

'Listen, Michael, it doesn't matter what I'm drinking – you help yourself to whatever you want. There's tea and coffee by the kettle, beer and soft drinks in the fridge and something stronger in the sideboard cupboard.'

'I'll just have some bottled water,' came the rather miffed reply.

'Suit yourself,' said Ben, nonchalantly prising the top off a beer bottle and hoping it made as much noise as possible.

'I suppose it's not a problem keeping a house full of booze in your profession.' It was a weak attempt at humour though as was so often the case with Michael there was an underlying implied criticism. As if Ben was some disreputable drunk embezzling the products from the company he worked for.

'Actually most of that stuff was bought in the supermarket,' replied Ben.

The gentle put-downs did not continue, Michael enjoyed them far more in the presence of company. The safe setting of the Collins' family was his preferred stage where he could count on the enthusiastic support of his mother. Dad would remain quiet and try to convince himself it was all very funny but he was as much a victim of his eldest son's need to be top dog in the household as anyone.

The conversation carried on and Ben began to appreciate how amenable his brother could be when not in the mood for point-scoring. The years of growing up together had produced an emotional bond, which was always going to be there and which showed itself on such occasions. They went out in the evening for a drink and the awkwardness of the initial meeting melted away.

The days that followed were pleasant enough: Michael toured the sights of Prague during the day and the two brothers would meet in the evening for a drink or something to eat. The time spent together was congenial and Ben was beginning to think that perhaps he had been too harsh in his assessment of Michael. Everybody has their flaws and perhaps he had exaggerated Michael's in his own mind and carried grudges reaching back to childhood for far too long. All families had tensions and problems, why should his be any different?

One day Ben was delayed at a drinks factory. The manager, a portly fifty-year-old with a permanently avuncular expression, had given him a personal tour of the building. From the beaming smile, it was not difficult to predict how the tour was going to end. Here was a man who liked company, conversation and drink and so it was no surprise when an invitation was extended to sample some of the products in his office. It was a beer of some promise, which with a slight modification of the ingredients and the right marketing strategy could be successful. By indulging the old man in his passion for drink and company no harm would be done to building a mutually beneficial business arrangement.

By the time Ben arrived back home it was nine o'clock in the evening. He was happy and inebriated but Michael was fuming at this lateness, and his brother's good mood only inflamed his anger further. Ben was aware of the tension in the air, even in his drunken state, but was determined not to apologise for carrying out duties related to his job. Michael was the visitor and should fit in with his plans. He ignored the tense atmosphere and sat down with a beer to watch television.

'Don't you think you've had enough beer?' said Michael accusingly.

'This is my house and I'll drink as much beer as I want to,' replied Ben.

'You just sit there like a drunken slob then. Don't you have any plan as to how you are going to progress in life?'

'I have a plan, I just don't want to discuss it with you.'

'All you seem capable of planning is where to get your next drink from.'

'I'm running a successful organisation here in Prague and earning good money. I don't see anything wrong with that.'

'You're just drinking yourself to death in this God-forsaken part of Europe. That doesn't seem like much of a plan to me.'

'It's really none of your business, Michael.'

'Then there's that fiancée of yours who you never see. I'm sure she thinks you're being really fair to her.'

'That fiancée is called Maureen and I don't want to talk to you about her.'

'I wonder why? Could it be that you know I'm speaking the truth?'

Ben suddenly snapped: 'OK, let's speak the truth, Michael. The truth is that you've resented me ever since I was born. The truth is you bullied me as a little boy and have never been able to stand me having any success in life. The truth is you've been unpleasant and cruel all your life, and let me tell you one other truth: I'm not putting up with it any longer, so tomorrow you can pack your bags and leave Prague.'

The next morning when Ben woke up Michael had already left. There was no note of either criticism or thank-you. This did not bother Ben but at least he would have liked to have known where his brother was going. He sat at the breakfast table and felt depressed. It had seemed recently that the two of them were finally putting to rest the ghosts of the past and all it had taken were a few hours of lateness to make them reappear again. They had had arguments in the past but never as serious as this; Ben had never articulated so directly what had been bottled up for so long. If only Michael hadn't mentioned Maureen perhaps the situation would not have got so out of control.

Chapter 3

TALLIS WALKED DOWN the steep pedestrian walkways that linked the houses in the Spanish town of Nerja. The wide steps and white low walls either side of the thoroughfare, scrupulously cleaned of all rubbish and grime, made the act of walking a real pleasure. It was such a beautifully simple idea to have a system where one could walk from one house to another without the inconvenience of traffic, as well as being able to admire the gardens which flanked one on either side. Tallis paid particular attention to the plant life in each one. He wanted to walk all the way down to the beach in order to look back up at the large villa introduced to him that morning.

He was in Spain at the invitation of Sir Steven Wilkinson, whose grounds he maintained one day of every week when back in Britain. His client had recently acquired a Spanish villa but seemed to possess a peculiar aversion to dealing with native workers when it came to improving any aspect of the property. Interior designers had been flown in from London, a team of builders from Sunderland and now Tallis had been called upon to give advice on what to do with the garden. The morning had been spent plodding around studying the present layout of the plot and poring over books on Mediterranean plants. The view of the sea from the villa had been of particular interest, but now he was looking back up he realised the return journey would be far more arduous than the pleasant jaunt down. Having said that, there was nothing to stop him spending a bit of time investigating the beach before he returned.

He sat at the bar whose floor led directly onto the sand. It was quiet now in the winter, but he tried to imagine what the scene would be in the summer. No doubt the beach would be packed, and drinking and loud music would continue until the early hours of the morning. He had even heard that the bar employed flamenco dancers during that period, whilst an old man cooked paella from a small stand on the beach. He made a rough sketch of the villa, which could clearly be seen despite its distance. It was important that nothing was planted which would spoil the imposing façade. Tallis climbed down off the stool to start the uphill walk. Perhaps the night life around the beach would not be too lively at this time of year and it would probably be a better bet to explore the centre of Nerja later on. It could be more Spanish in the wintertime without the summer influx of beer-swilling Brits, eating fish and chips, tanned like lobsters and calling all the waiters *garçon*.

Sir Steven Wilkinson, for whom money seemed no object when it came to beautifying his villa, had lent Tallis a car with which to travel around during his three-week stay. He visited garden centres, nurseries and shops during this time and tried as best he could to converse with knowledgeable Spaniards as part of his grand plan for designing a garden. For once in his life he felt that there was an opportunity to produce something spectacular, a living monument which would make his name. Whilst travelling around the region he had inevitably heard of the magnificent gardens at the Al-Hambra palace in Granada. Not wishing to miss any opportunity for fresh ideas and inspiration, one day he made the two-hour drive there.

The Al-Hambra palace occupied a position on a plateau above Granada overlooking the Darro River. Built by the Nasrid dynasty in the thirteenth and fourteenth centuries it represented the pinnacle of Islamic arts and culture. The sprawling structure had been designed with due regard to the climate. Air circulated freely between rooms, which were grouped around quadrangles where water flowed abundantly in pools and fountains. Tallis visited the many doorless rooms connected to each other by elegant archways supported by slender marble columns. Although most of the interior paintwork had been erased, it was still possible to see some Arabic calligraphy on the walls and ornate, geometrically precise patterns carved into the stone.

The extensive Generalife Gardens contained all manner of plant life. Tallis made careful notes as he walked from one flower bed to another. The part that impressed the most was the Sultana's Garden. A succession of small fountains fed into a rectangular pool, which ran virtually the whole length of the garden. Flowers and trees of varied and intense colours tastefully occupied the remaining part, and arched cloisters bordered the whole. There was a seven hundred-year-old cypress under which it was said that the Princess Soraya secretly met her forbidden lover from the Abencerrage family. It was not difficult to imagine how such idyllic surroundings could have contributed to their love. The fact that King Baobdil had the amorous young man put to death in the Al-Hambra palace along with other members of his family only seemed to accentuate the emotional atmosphere of the place. 'By thee were slain in evil hour, The Abencerrage, Granada's flower.'

Tallis pocketed his notebook after writing down the name of a tree with blood red blossom. Not only had he learned a lot from the tour but now felt inspired and pleased that he would be able to create a beautiful Mediterranean garden. He had even started to rough out the plan of what he would plant where. Walking back to the entrance of the palace he bought a postcard to send to his parents in Britain. The picture side was of the font in the sixteenth century chapel, which had been built on top of the site of the palace mosque. On the reverse he wrote of how he was enjoying Spain as well as his feelings of optimism over the contracted task. No, he was not in any hurry to return to Britain and hoped they would understand if he stayed on in Spain a little longer and missed going round to their house for Christmas Day.

The year was 1492 and Kind Baobdil rushed up the staircase to the tower of the Al-Hambra palace, closely followed by his queen. On reaching the top, a sight, though not unexpected, made him feel sick to the stomach and filled him with dread. In the distance could be seen the large Christian army of King Ferdinand and Queen Isabella, who were both riding magnificent white horses. At the rear followed Cardinal Mendoza on a pony with his own army of priests. There was no way the few soldiers at the palace gates could resist such a force so the king gave the order to evacuate his family. Standing atop the hill of tears some distance from his beloved Al-Hambra palace King Baobdil took one last look at it. That he should live to see the end of his family's two hundred and fifty year occupation of the palace they had built and the end of seven hundred years of Muslim rule in Spain was a misfortune that was almost too much to bear. He fervently wished he had died rather than see this day. Cardinal Pedro Gonzalez de Mendoza had climbed to the highest tower where he had planted a silver cross. Soldiers were fanning out throughout the palace whilst priests were conducting summary baptisms of its occupants. King Baobdil turned around and headed south from where his ancestors had come so many years ago, back to Africa.

Chapter 4

THE AFRICAN SUN dawned clear out of a cloudless blue sky. The atmosphere was fresh from the overnight rain but already there were whisperings that something dreadful had occurred during the night. Dr Robert Williams had phoned KCMC to request the day off work but still felt the need to attend to his hospital duties despite the unbelievable news. That it was so unbelievable made it easier to bear, at least initially, and he was able to carry on as if anaesthetised to reality by the sheer magnitude of the horror. It was just impossible to get one's mind around the scale of the catastrophe unfolding in his homeland. First estimates of the fatalities had been in the thousands but the number seemed to increase exponentially with every hourly news broadcast. He surprised himself at the unconcerned manner in which he was able to perform routine tasks and the sympathy of colleagues, although touching, was not particularly helpful. Later in the day it was announced there would be a candlelit service and vigil in the hospital chapel. Robert did not really want to attend but realised it would look bad if he didn't, both to the living and the recently departed.

The news event was unlike any other in reporting history. Although of an unprecedented importance the quality and quantity of pictures reaching television screens were poor. British-based news agencies tried to put together a skeleton staff but this proved difficult. Jerky images of deserted streets littered with corpses and interviews with the sick and dying were about all that could be mustered. Most people had been asleep in their beds when the attack came and had died in their own homes. Pictures sent via the internet or by videophone lasted beyond the first day, by which time the television studios were inoperable. These provided little useful information, just some sick faces trying to cobble together a few meaningful words for an epitaph as their lives drifted away. Phone messages also continued as relatives said final farewells, their words laden with emotional as well as physical pain. The virus had been mercifully quick in dealing its mortal blow. Most were killed within a few hours of inhalation but a few managed to cling on to life and eke out a pitiful existence for a couple of days. By day four all communication from Britain had ceased and it was presumed nobody was left alive.

Whilst the pictures dried up quickly the theories and explanations as to who or what had caused the outrage continued unabated. The cause had been determined a couple of hours after the outbreak: passengers travelling by air from Britain were immediately quarantined and, once tested, the enhanced smallpox virus was detected. All planes and ships from Britain were sent back or anchored at sea and all British airports and seaports were closed as it was made clear that no cargo, human or otherwise, would be accepted by any other country.

The remaining facts emerged during the course of the week. Six low-flying aircraft had flown the length of Britain at night from north to south, parachuting down men and women willing to commit suicide and cause the death of many others by detonating canisters strapped to their backs. The precise and ordered location of these canisters told a chilling story of a cold-blooded, logically planned operation to exterminate a nation. The six missiles had all gone off releasing additional amounts of virus, although they were not particularly accurate: the two aimed at Newcastle and Glasgow city centres missed their targets by over twenty kilometres.

At the candlelit service in KCMC, religious leaders from different faiths had come together and each conducted a small part of the service of remembrance. There were representatives from the Anglican Church, Baptist Bible Mission, Lutheran Methodists, Hindus, Sikhs and Muslims. Prayers for peace as well as prayers for the dead were uttered in sad, hushed tones. The Imam, against a background of flickering candles, called for tolerance and no acts of retribution. Meanwhile, across the world, but particularly in North America and Europe, the mosques were being burnt to the ground. Many were not waiting for the official verdict on who had been behind the attack before starting to blame the Muslims. Surely there was no other group with the planning, finance, suicide bombers and evil intent but al-Qaeda.

Anna wore a mournful expression throughout the service and accepted expressions of condolence with good grace. She was collected enough to play her part in the proceedings perfectly, and probably enjoyed the attention that came her way. Whilst outwardly showing as much sympathy to her husband as possible, she was more uncomfortable in dealing with his emotions on a one-to-one basis. She reached out to hold his hand in a private moment. This however only had the effect of making him more upset, as the forced tenderness of the act seemed to confirm his alienation from the world. Despite the many who spoke kindly with offers of assistance he felt truly alone with no one to turn to.

Robert lay awake in bed at night, listening to Anna snoring quietly on the other side of the room, and tried to comprehend the enormity of what had happened that day. The list of people he had known throughout his life who were now probably dead was a long one, which kept growing when supplied with fresh memories. It would be impossible to grieve individually for each one and for once he felt happy that his parents had died early. He knew their exact fate and had been able to provide them with the send-off they deserved. Those he had sat beside at school, with whom he had played football, smashed conkers and climbed trees were all dead. The shopkeepers, teachers, bus drivers and policemen from his childhood were all gone forever. His fellow students from university with whom he had engaged in outrageous drinking competitions and whiled away hour-long coffee breaks between lectures were no more. The intangible threads of affection between those he had loved and who had loved him to a greater or lesser extent had been irrevocably severed and he would live on in nobody's fond memories.

It is strange what one thinks of at such times and none of his crowning achievements or special occasions came to mind. He did not think of the day he mastered riding a bicycle, came top of the class or gained a university degree. Instead the comforting routine and banality of his old life assumed a great significance: walking home from school with friends, playing cricket on a summer evening, sitting in front of the television on a Wednesday and watching the Play For Today. The security and predictability of it all fuelled a kind of nostalgia and produced a feeling of intense sadness. The ordinary life he had taken for granted in the past now seemed so special but alas it had gone forever and he could visit no part of it except in his dreams.

Chapter 5

Tallis was asleep in his room at the villa in Nerja, a fitful lie-in occasioned by a late night's drinking in the town centre with some recently acquired Spanish companions. The phone on the bedside table had already rung for a prolonged period twice and he had ignored it on both occasions. Now it was ringing for a third time and it was clear this was a persistent caller who was not going to give up. Reluctantly Tallis picked up the receiver and immediately recognised the voice of Pedro, with whom he had been the previous evening.

'Tallis you must go and switch on the television.'

'Pedro, did you really disturb me at this time of the morning just to tell me to watch television?' replied Tallis, feeling intensely annoyed at this intrusion.

'You don't understand, bad news, very bad news.'

'Bad news can wait, I'm going back to sleep.' Tallis slammed down the phone, turned over and pulled the sheets over his head. He lay there for half an hour without being successful in his stated objective, so showered then walked downstairs to the kitchen for breakfast. The house was unusually quiet and the few Spanish staff on duty seemed reluctant to talk.

'Where are the builders?' he asked the housemaid. She appeared uneasy but managed to inform him that they had travelled to Malaga to meet with a representative from the British Embassy in Madrid.

'What the hell for?' he asked, irritated at the sudden unexplained departure. She simply shrugged her shoulders and continued to wash plates without turning round.

Something was definitely wrong. It could be sensed in the uncomfortable silence, the body language of the staff, the fact that nobody looked him directly in the eye. Remembering Pedro's phone call, he switched on the television and scrolled down the menu to the British news broadcasters. The first thing that was strange was that they were not broadcasting from the usual studios, nor were the presenters the faces to which he was accustomed. He sat there in a complete state of bewilderment as nothing these people were saying seemed to be making any sense. They spoke of ten million dead, a catastrophe of unimaginable proportions, death on an unprecedented scale. This didn't seem like the news but more like a disaster movie, it was definitely closer to fiction than fact. Was this the correct channel? The unfamiliar faces and settings cast some doubt on this so the channel was changed. The news was exactly the same except that the figure was different: they were talking of twenty million fatalities. He was starting to feel the need to seek confirmation from some other source when he heard Pedro knocking at the door.

'Tallis, I am so sorry,' he said, walking into the living room uninvited.

'Sorry about what?' asked Tallis, still in a dazed state.

Pedro looked surprised for a moment then waved his hand towards the television. 'I am sorry about all this.'

'Is it true?' inquired Tallis, for the first time appearing to have some idea of what had happened.

'It is true my friend. They don't think anyone in Britain will be left alive.'

'What do you mean no one will be left alive? We're talking about an entire nation here, millions of people.'

'It is the worst act of terrorism the world has ever witnessed,' replied Pedro sadly.

Tallis was quiet for a while, the horror of what had taken place seeming to induce a state of mental inertia where all thinking was impossible. Out of the fog of this torpor one thought slowly emerged like a light, becoming more distinct as he became aware of its approach out of the haze.

'My parents, I must phone my parents straight away.'

The two of them returned to Tallis' room and attempted to phone Britain. The phone rang and rang at his parents' house but there was no response.

'Please answer the fucking phone,' he pleaded down the line, tears of frustration and worry beginning to well in his eyes. He tried and tried without any luck, the ringing continuing in his head after he put the receiver down, a rhythmical, repetitive reverberation, reminding him of his own impotency. The situation was much the same when phoning other numbers, either the line was engaged or nobody answered.

Having had no luck with this exercise, the next logical action was to find out where the builders had gone. Perhaps the representative from the embassy had some important news. Pedro insisted on driving the car the hour-long journey to Malaga, and this gave Tallis the opportunity to collect his thoughts somewhat. He wanted to return to Britain to see with his own eyes what had taken place. The not knowing was unbearable and there could still be a chance that not everybody was dead. His own safety was unimportant, besides he was not sure he really wanted to continue living if all his friends and relatives were dead and life could not continue as before.

Crowds had gathered along the beach at Malaga. Notice boards had been erected for the many British who were there. They contained no information about relatives in the UK, their purpose being to inform individuals how to register and where to go to seek assistance. Some people had had been as close to returning to Britain as being on a plane taxiing down the runway at Malaga airport when their flight was cancelled. There was a need to accommodate those without a permanent home in Spain as well as providing food and clothes. A team of counsellors had set up base a short distance away from the main group. They didn't appear to have much custom today but this was predicted to increase in subsequent days. Twenty desks were arranged in a row, each with a line of people in front waiting to register their presence. Warnings appeared on the boards instructing nobody to try to return to Britain. Although all airline and ferry operators had cancelled journeys to the United Kingdom there were still some who were determined to ignore this caution. Included in this resolute – some may say foolhardy – group was Tallis. He was already planning to travel up to France where perhaps it would be possible to get a boat to cross the Channel.

Chapter 6

BEN CAUGHT A taxi to Prague International Airport. His hands were trembling and he was feeling slightly faint from the nervous state he had been in for the last hour. Michael, all he could think of was Michael and how he hoped he had not returned to Britain. It had been four days since the morning of his departure and the disagreeable nagging sensation at the back of Ben's mind as to the fate of his brother had exploded into outright panic with the morning television news. It was impossible to sit idly at home and wait for information so he decided to make his own enquiries. The taxi made painfully slow progress and the rush hour traffic had not yet thinned out, although it was nearly ten a.m. He watched the people as they drove their cars, walked along the pavements, conversed with each other, laughing and joking. How could anybody feel anything but misery on a day like today or be able to ignore the catastrophe in Britain and continue with their daily activities? Their lack of demonstrable grief seemed like an insult to all his dead countrymen.

The taxi pulled into the drop-off area and Ben rushed into the main airport building, heading for the information desk. He had not been the only one asking about travellers to Britain and was directed to a room near the airport management offices. It was a medium sized room with a large old wooden table in the centre. Passenger lists from the last five days were sellotaped to the surface and six people pored over these in silence. Ben joined them, walking slowly round the table as he finished looking at each one, but despite two perambulations could see no mention of Michael Collins anywhere.

This discovery did little to alter his state of mind. He hadn't really expected Michael to leave the Czech Republic on a plane. It would be more his style to use the train or bus and see something of Europe on the way back to Britain, if Britain was where he was headed. Would it be possible to travel from Prague to Britain in four days? The answer was yes, easily. Ben's hopes now had to rest on a couple of days' unscheduled stop somewhere or the train or bus breaking down. The bus and rail companies did not keep good records but what they had showed no trace of Michael. There were so many transport companies operating out of Prague it would be impossible to track them all down and he could always have hitched a lift.

Ben returned to his apartment in the afternoon feeling deflated. All the running around had exhausted his nervous energy and he sat down in front of the television. The announcer was saying nobody would survive the biological weapons that had been unleashed on the British mainland. The word *nobody* struck him with a grievous force and a concern that had been kept uneasily in abeyance at the back of his mind whilst he searched for his brother now came to full prominence. Nobody – that meant Maureen, the woman he intended to marry, the reason he was out of the country, the person he loved above all others. Everything he had been working towards for the last two years was worth nothing, it had all been a waste. Tears ran down his face as he mourned the loss of the love of his life. Was there ever a man more miserable than he? Separated from the land of his birth, his fiancée was dead and now responsibility for the possible death of a brother lay on his conscience.

He lay on the bed whilst memories of Maureen mingled with those of Michael and a number of other friends and relatives. He remembered the first time he had kissed Maureen in her living room, how he had felt so shy and awkward and how she had quietly reassured him with her unconditional love and affection. He remembered how Michael had stood up for him in a fight and got into trouble for it, the games they played as children before the perverse teenage years turned a little brother into an annoying encumbrance and they drifted apart. Even during those times there were occasions when the two of them could reach across the divide and share a few minutes of fellow feeling. Looking back he began to realise he was also responsible: he had not behaved as well as possible and had not made the effort to keep up ties when they were both adults.

Ben felt guilt as he had never felt it before. Guilt for leaving Maureen in Britain and all the tender moments they must have missed over the last two years. Why hadn't he thought to bring her out with him so much sooner? They could have enjoyed Eastern Europe together. Why had money been such an issue with him? And Michael: he could say some cruel things but was that reason enough to condemn him to an unpleasant death? Had he acted differently they could both be alive today. Two people who occupied different parts of his heart had left a void there and he realised it was all his fault. He must find out what had happened to Michael.

Chapter 7

A N EMERGENCY SESSION of the United Nations Security Council had taken place without one of its permanent members. Although the British ambassador to the UN was present in New York, he couldn't be said to be representing any government and had diplomatically turned down an invitation to attend to avoid causing unnecessary procedural difficulties. In any case the Council was not really the appropriate place to discuss the kind of action the Western powers had in mind. Words of condemnation were predictably issued but the argument was not with any one government, rather a terrorist organisation operating out of many countries. The response necessarily had to be on a variety of fronts and most of it would be secret and dirty. The deliberations of the Security Council were therefore by and large irrelevant. The important discussions were being held in small side rooms at UN headquarters, by phone between the major capitals of the world and within the command structure of the leading intelligence agencies.

The United States took the lead in organising the reply to the threat. The first stage was to prevent further attacks just in case Britain was not the only country to be targeted. A well-rehearsed plan of sealed borders and restricted travel from the Department for Homeland Security came into force in the United States and was followed in European countries. In an effort to stem the rising tide of panic, the President made a speech the day after the attack promising to keep his nation free of biological attacks and massively increasing resources to find and root out this new menace. He made it clear that total cooperation was expected from every country in the world and that he was prepared to use force to get his way. European governments were less bellicose but no less determined to find those responsible, and gave full support to the Americans.

Apart from the defensive measures immediately put in place to prevent another attack there was something of a lull before it was possible to see any signs of the response. There was no major military engagement but a gradual shift in the way governments and law enforcement agencies conducted their business. Detention without trial, assassinations, bombings and torture were all whispered about as necessary evils, and even the media felt constrained in what it could report. These were not deeds sanctioned by some tin-pot dictator in Africa or a life president in South America who had come to power through a military coup. These acts were promulgated by the country that had enshrined the rights of man in its eighteenth century constitution and the continent that prided itself on being the cradle of Western civilisation, where democratic governments had hailed human dignity and freedom for generations.

The United States President made many speeches stressing that terrorists would not prevail nor be allowed to alter the freedom and way of life of ordinary Americans. The paradox was that in fighting the terrorists these privileges had already been compromised. Al-Qaeda was not going to enslave the American people by running the machinery of government from the White House with the President being turfed out of the Oval Office by a bearded fanatic wearing a white robe. The real threat to freedom came from Americans themselves and how they responded to the danger posed to them. Every act of cruelty and intolerance on their part was a small victory for the men and women of evil.

One throwback to a more idealistic time was the second amendment to the US Constitution, contained in the Bill of

Rights. This had always been much favoured by gun owners and advocated to all and sundry on the premise that society was a static entity and that solutions at one period in history would remain solutions forever. Now it seemed to many that the founding fathers of the American state were speaking directly to the present generation from beyond the grave and showing them the way forward: 'A well regulated Militia, being necessary to the security of a free State, the right of the people to keep and bear Arms, shall not be infringed.' Organisations sprang up to accommodate the number of willing fighting men and women who could not be absorbed within the increased ranks of the army. More people were prepared to part with their money than their way of life so these became well armed and well funded. They formed a mutually beneficial loose alliance with the defence forces of other nations.

Chapter 8

TALLIS SURVEYED THE outline of his dream garden, marked with wooden sticks, twine and containing piles of freshly dug earth. The plan to create a living testament to the beauty of nature lay in tatters as an irresistible force, which he didn't fully comprehend, was pulling him back to Britain.

'You don't have to go Tallis,' said Pedro who was standing beside him on some recently laid paving stones. 'Stay here in Nerja.'

'And do what?' asked Tallis in an expressionless tone of voice.

'Finish your garden for a start, then we try find something for you here in sunny España.'

The attempt at humour did nothing to lighten his friend's dark mood. He was not thinking of flowers and sunshine but a cold small flat in Nottingham where his parents would be lying – dead.

'I'm sorry Pedro, I can't stay here, I don't belong here, my place is with my friends and family.'

'But it is madness to return to Britain, you die for sure.'

'I really don't care any more, all I know is that I have to return.'

Pedro pointed to a collection of potted plants and trees standing in a shady corner waiting to be planted. 'These plants, what you say if I plant them on the beach?'

Tallis shrugged his shoulders.

'I tell you what you say. You say it is crazy, you say they

die, you become angry. You think you less important than the plants?'

'Last week I would have cared if you'd planted them on the beach. Today I'm really not bothered if you throw them in the sea.'

Tallis was troubled to see how upset Pedro was. The Spaniard was blinking from the water collecting in his eyes, and shaking his head in a despairing manner.

'Goodbye Pedro,' said Tallis holding out a hand. Pedro ignored the proffered hand and threw his arms around his friend's shoulders in a sorrowful embrace.

'I pray to God we meet again,' he sobbed and with that walked slowly out of the unfinished garden in the villa of Sir Steven Wilkinson.

Tallis looked at the villa that was still undergoing repair, then thought of his boss. Poor old Sir Steven would never see this completed. He who had dreamed of a Mediterranean dotage would never be able to sample the delights of Spain again. Whilst not exactly counting on sun, sangria and sex in his declining years, the warm air and Spanish wine would have been most agreeable. For entertainment he would have contented himself by watching the sea rhythmically pounding its bulk upon the soft golden sand, creating white surf as it did so. Having divided his time equally between Britain and Spain, it was his bad luck to be in the wrong half when the attack came. One could imagine Sir Steven saying in his understated upper class way something like, 'I backed the wrong horse in a two-horse race,' or 'Lost the toss on a sticky wicket old boy.' Not that the domestic staff seemed aware of his permanent absence, they continued to clean the villa and press his shirts as if nothing had happened. For Tallis however the abandonment of the garden project was made easier by knowing that the one who had commissioned the work could no longer care about how it progressed.

Tallis started to think of his travel plans. Plane travel was unpredictable at the moment but there was sure to be a bus travelling northwards. He wasn't sure what the train service was like or whether one even existed but that could be another option to check out tomorrow. He just had to get through a frustrating evening of inaction on his own with no doubt a sleepless night to follow. There was no way he could occupy himself in Nerja town centre as he had the previous evening and the company of others would simply be irksome. He thrust his hands into his pockets then had an idea on feeling the warm metal and plastic of the car keys. He would drive up to France and start that very afternoon. Sir Steven had entrusted him with the safe-keeping of the car but was hardly going to complain about its use anymore. Besides, when set against a likely death in Britain the crime of car-jacking did not seem particularly significant. He drove along the coast road with its many twists and turns as it followed the contours of the coastline. The late afternoon sun provided wonderful views out to sea, which on any other day would have caused him to slow down and appreciate. There was a satisfaction to be gained from doing something rather than just hanging around kicking one's heels. If he were able to make good progress it would be possible to be in Barcelona that night. Tomorrow the journey would continue on to France.

Chapter 9

THE PLANE FROM Prague touched down at Charles de Gaulle Airport around lunchtime. It had been thirty-six hours since the attack and there was still much confusion and panic. Apart from the disruption caused to schedules by no planes going to or coming from Britain, a large number of travellers from that island were being kept in quarantine. Relatives and friends anxiously paced the large shopping malls and lounges waiting for their loved ones to be given a clean bill of health whilst the airport chapel was full to the point of overflowing. Into this scene of turmoil stepped a young man of thirty-five, tall with short black hair. Benedict Collins was just one more person with emotional problems joining the many, another drop in this pool of anguished humanity.

He did not tarry at the airport but passed through it as quickly as possible. There was only one object in mind and upon exiting the airport building he directed the waiting taxi to head straight for the offices of the ferry companies. If Michael had not used the plane it stood to reason that he must have crossed the Channel by boat. In contrast to the fruitless afternoon spent tramping around Prague, Ben quickly found the information he was looking for in Paris. Walking into the offices of the largest ferry company that came to mind, he explained his predicament to a woman, one of a row of people sitting behind computer screens at identical desks. She obligingly typed in the name Collins then turned the screen around so that Ben could see it. Three names appeared: Caroline Collins, Edward Collins and Michael Collins. They had all sailed from Calais to Dover two days before the attack. The sight of his brother's name produced a cold feeling in his arms and stomach and he could almost feel the blood draining away from his face. It also produced a curious sense of relief, confirming what he had really known in his heart all along, that Michael was dead. As expected, no information other than the name was forthcoming, but it was all Ben needed to close this troublesome chapter of his life.

A printout of the information was requested in case he doubted his eyes or memory in the future. Checking into a hotel he sat down on the bed and took out the crumpled piece of paper from a jacket pocket. The words 'Michael Collins' were read again and again and the date and destination were also checked with equal frequency. Staring at this sheet of paper, the reality of what had happened sank in: his older brother was dead and he was responsible. He curled up on the bed in the foetal position, immobilised by grief. Now the truth was known there was no need to be chasing around town any more. His head was hurting and a sudden feeling of tiredness swept over the entire body as if the exertions of the last day and a half had finally caught up with him.

When Ben woke up the room was dark. It took him a while to get his bearings and locate the light switch. The clock on the wall was showing five-thirty p.m. Though he still felt depressed the sleep had been beneficial to his mental state. After taking a bath and changing out of the creased, slept-in clothes he was ready to venture outside in search of something to eat and drink. Walking around the Paris streets he eventually settled on a small, quiet restaurant and sat down at a simple wooden table. Tomorrow he would travel to Calais just to see where Michael had left France. Somehow he would be sharing in the experience of his brother's last hours, witnessing the scene that would have greeted him just hours before death visited in a viral fog.

The waitress brought a tall glass of French lager and set it down on the table. 'Enjoy your drink, I hope it improves your mood,' she said haughtily in French.

'Merci,' replied Ben, not really listening to what she said. In his broken French with an English accent he started to go through the menu and order a meal. At once the offhand mood of the waitress began to change.

'Excuse me, I didn't realise you were English. I am sorry for what I said.'

Ben pardoned the slightly sarcastic remark, which he hadn't even noticed, and attempted to complete the order.

'I am so sorry about ...' she paused to try to find the appropriate words, 'about what happened to your country.'

'Nobody is more sorry than me,' replied Ben thinking of his dead fiancée and brother.

Ben found himself watching her as she returned to the kitchen to hand over the order. She had a pleasant figure, which although slim still had curves in all the right places and suited the white blouse and black skirt she was wearing. She had delicate, refined facial features and long black hair. In fact she was probably too attractive for her own good and this had probably contributed to her over-proud and remote bearing. Upon returning to the table she made the effort to smile and he involuntarily experienced a strong attraction. As a token of his appreciation of her sympathy he asked if he could buy her a drink.

'Not here, later,' she said conspiratorially as if the offer was one to be taken with the utmost seriousness and loaded with meaning. 'I finish at ten o'clock. Where will you be?'

'Hotel Boulevard,' replied Ben automatically, not really thinking about what he was saying.

'We meet in the bar,' she said.

Ben sat in the bar of the Hotel Boulevard and wondered how he had got himself into this situation. He tried to convince himself that the waitress would not turn up, that she was as uninterested in him as he was in her. But then if he wasn't interested what was he doing sitting here? He really should have had an early night in preparation for the trip to Calais tomorrow. He attempted to analyse the complex and contradictory thoughts and emotions that occupied his mind and affected other bodily organs. He felt guilty about Maureen, for her death and for thinking about what he wanted to do with the French waitress. Was this logical though? Maureen was dead so how could his actions affect her in any way? He was ashamed of himself, his fiancée had been dead for less than two days, how could he consider such a thing? With an effort he tried to put all these thoughts out of his head through the belief that the woman from the restaurant would not turn up and no moral dilemma would be faced. He would not face a moral dilemma if he got out of his seat and went to his room. Why was he still sitting there?

To his surprise and unexpected pleasure the French waitress walked into the hotel bar and made directly for the table where he was sitting. With a self-assurance which belied the turmoil and guilt he had been feeling five minutes before, he ordered a drink and attempted to start a conversation. Her name was Nicole, she was twenty-five years old and from the Basque region of France. She had lived in Paris for two years, had one brother and one sister but lived alone. The conversation continued and bored them both though Ben felt it was somehow necessary. Nicole was the first to rail against the tedium of it.

'The attack was terrible. Those Muslims deserve death, every single one of them.'

The veneer of unimportant, inconsequential discourse was broken and Ben's composure was ruffled as he was reminded of Maureen and Michael.

'It is just terrible. Words cannot describe how I feel.'

Nicole saw she had got through to him and leant over the

table to hold his hand.

'Will you show me your room here?' she asked and without waiting for a response got up from the table. Ben followed her lead and in a grief-induced trance walked up the stairs to the first floor with her following.

Nicole was lying on the bed naked, Ben was walking from the bathroom naked. As he clambered onto the bed he wondered for the second time that evening how he had got into such a situation. Still, it was too late to change things now and he had to go through with what had been started. Maureen was the only woman he had ever had sex with before that night and he wondered how similar the experience would be with a different woman. He no longer tried to analyse his actions and thoughts, but simply asked for forgiveness and understanding from his dead fiancée as he entered Nicole.

Chapter 10

T ALLIS HAD REALLY underestimated the length of the drive to Barcelona. His late arrival in that city, however, did not prevent him from making an early start the next day. He crossed the border an hour later and by lunchtime was in the French town of Clermont-Ferrand. It was here in 1095 that the Council of Clermont had initiated the first Crusade at the prompting of Pope Urban II. Exhorting the faithful to participate in a holy war in the Holy Land he had promised remission of sins and automatic entry into Heaven for those who took up arms. One thousand years of history hadn't changed much, as no doubt the suicide bombers anticipated much the same reward for their role in the extermination of Britain. *Deus vult* – God wills it – had been the cry of the first Crusaders as they set off to do battle. Something similar had probably been said by the equally zealous sixty as they parachuted down onto British soil. Tallis sat in the car munching on a baguette, unaware of the town's role in the conflict that was continuing to the present day. Perusing a map he plotted a course which would skirt Paris to the west and then continue north towards the port of Calais.

It was night-time and despite the cold raw wind coming off the sea, the beach at Calais was crowded. Some had come to be as close to their loved ones as possible, whilst others were looking for passage to the island beyond. Fires were lit on the sand as well as candles in impromptu services of remembrance. Ben stood above the beach on the pavement of the coast road, leaning against a railing and gazing out to the black beyond where nothing was visible. His brother and fiancée were out there in that blackness somewhere and there would never be any light in his life again. Tallis was on the beach, mingling and talking with the boat owners. Like standing on the black poisonous waters of the river Styx he was looking for a modern day version of the ragged old boatman Charon to ferry him over to the other side. The payment however would not be the coin in the mouth favoured by the ancient Greeks. Tallis needed someone who would accept the car of Sir Steven Wilkinson as payment for this one-way journey.

Chapter 11

DR ROBERT WILLIAMS sat on the verandah of his house in Moshi. He was alone with the sounds of nature, trying to determine whether a high-pitched fluttering, which had been repeated three or four times, originated from a bird or insect. The intermittent pleasant shrill cries of small birds were rudely interrupted by the raucous call of a black and white crow, whilst from a distance a dog could be heard barking. There was scarcely any breeze but the odd white butterfly still flew a wayward path from bush to bush. The afternoon sunshine glistened off the unwavering waxy leaves, whilst it put others in the shade. Dr Williams contemplated the grandeur of the tall trees and looked up at the white wooden beams supporting the tin roof of the verandah. He began to feel small and insignificant, as if he were a mouse in the corner. The chair was too large for him, and his elbows squeezed against his chest and his buttocks tightened, producing a thrill in the stomach. He was like a baby finding comfort in inconsequentiality and helplessness. He wanted to bring his knees up to touch the chest and bow his head, blocking out reality. He pushed his back against the chair, he did not matter anymore.

Robert was disturbed from this reverie by the sound of Anna calling his name. As she came closer his heart sank as it became obvious she was not alone. There had been no end of long-faced sympathisers visiting the house since the day of the attack. Africans appeared to have no concept of private grief or leaving anyone alone in their misfortune. In fact, to the contrary, the belief seemed to be that the greater the number surrounding the unfortunate party the more comforted he or she would be. The Reverend Josiah Mchome, accompanied by two men and four women from the Apostolic Church of the Sacred Heart, slowly made their way to the verandah where they each in turn reverently shook the doctor's hand. Such an occasion was not a time to talk but to share wordlessly the pain of the grief-stricken victim. It was as if they could absorb some of the pain and illuminate the dark cloud of sorrow through their proximity. Robert found their presence irksome, though out of consideration for his guests' feelings did not let it show. This was despite a suspicion that the visit had more to do with satisfying curiosity and fulfilling religious duty than any concern for his well-being. It was therefore with some relief, after half an hour of this silent gathering, that he accepted the phone his wife brought out and finally had an excuse to leave. Dr Schuster, his German colleague, was extending an invitation for a sundowner at six p.m. and without a lot of effort was persuaded to bring this time forward to five p.m. Robert made his excuses to the visitors, pleading a medical emergency which required his expert attention. The group was obviously disappointed, probably hoping for another couple of hours of silent vigil, but hardly felt in a position to complain if a fellow human being was in physical distress. Driving along the dusty roads of Moshi's premier residential area he reflected on how useful it was at times to be a doctor, allowing one to leave any engagement at the drop of a hat. A shopkeeper could not claim to have an emergency sale, just as a teacher could not make a hasty exit on the pretext of urgently helping a student solve a quadratic equation.

Dr Schuster was sitting with his visitor's gin and tonic already poured out and gestured to him to take a seat on the verandah. One feature of the expatriate life that Robert always appreciated was its informality and refusal to stand on ceremony. Dr Schuster was wearing khaki shorts and a short-sleeved pale green cotton shirt, unbuttoned to the sternum to allow air to freely circulate within. His leather sandals had been locally made and the only sign that he was expecting a guest were a bottle of gin, numerous cans of tonic water and a jugful of ice cubes placed on the table. There was no small talk on meeting each other, Dr Schuster merely looked at him sympathetically and raised his glass.

'Tough times,' he said.

The way this was phrased it wasn't clear whether it was a question or a statement. Robert simply nodded his assent and replied: 'The worst.'

They both took a sip from their drinks and looked at the view. People were walking or cycling home along the roads and paths. Fields were ploughed in anticipation of the planting season, whilst banana trees shot up like fountains from the earth, their large green leaves cascading downwards from a single stem. Behind all this Mount Kilimanjaro oversaw and dominated the landscape.

'I don't know how to feel about the situation Hans,' said Robert after a long pause.

'You don't have to feel anything, your feelings are your own, only assume responsibility for your actions.'

'That's easy to say but all my family and friends are dead. I do feel bad about surviving but most of all I feel guilty about not experiencing more pain. I sometimes wonder what kind of person I am.'

'I have known you for over twenty years my friend. You are a very good person, a principled person, do not doubt that.'

Robert sighed, 'Whatever the case is it will take a long time to come to terms with this loss and sort it all out in my mind.'

'Time is what we have in Africa,' said Dr Schuster smiling and refilling his glass.

There was another long pause. Robert decided to change the subject but not the sense of loss at a disappearing way of life.

'You know Hans, things aren't the same as when we started here.'

'They certainly aren't. What do you miss the most?'

'I've always wanted to see a more compassionate world and thought I'd found it when I came here, but people are no longer the same.'

'You believed in the noble African, that tribes and communities would pull together for the common good and it seemed to be true for a while. Now people are more grasping, ruthless and envious than in the West.'

'Did it have to happen like this Hans?'

'We saw a lot of what we wanted to see in those days and believed in a lot of myths. There never was a perfect world here and the arrival of the free market only widened existing divisions. We just happened to be around when people still believed in dreams.'

'I've witnessed human suffering and death for years but for the first time I really feel scared about the future.'

'Yes,' said Hans. 'This attack will change the world forever and its effects will even reach our far-flung little plot here.'

Dr Schuster placed his glass on the table.

'There's something else I need to tell you Robert.' There was a silence as he tried to form the next sentence in his head as diplomatically as possible. 'I'm going to be leaving KCMC and Tanzania. Heading back to Germany.'

'But why, whatever for?' asked Robert, alarmed at this unexpected news.

'If I don't go now, I'll never go. I've been thinking about it for a while and you're right, it's not the same job it used to be.'

'You could maybe find another job,' protested Robert. 'Talk to your organisation, set up a consultancy, work for yourself.'

'It would never work. Besides, my organisation cannot go on funding me forever. They say African doctors should be doing the job and I can't say I really disagree with that.'

'But you will be the last white face to leave KCMC.'

'Second last, Robert, you will be the last. We are both in the same department anyway, you will be able to carry on the good work.'

'There's never any shortage of African women producing babies. There's still plenty of work to be done.'

'You will be able to cope and will probably end up running the department in my place.'

'No way, I'll never have any part to play in the management of KCMC.'

A silence of five minutes followed as Robert digested the news of his friend's departure. At last Hans spoke, smiling just before he did so at his own reminiscences.

'Can you remember when we had over twenty expatriate doctors in the hospital?'

Robert returned his smile and sighed. 'I was talking to the Headmaster at International School Moshi a few weeks ago. He was telling me how the student roll has halved in recent years. Used to be the case that it was full of Swedes, Finns and Norwegians, the children of all kinds of aid workers. Nowadays these projects just don't take place and it's just Indians and wealthy Tanzanians who send their children there.'

'Maybe it's all for the best in the long run. One needs to be an optimist in our line of work.'

'Maybe, but I'm ashamed to say I feel more saddened by your departure than by the destruction of my homeland three days ago.'

'The future is going to be difficult Robert.'

'Let's not talk about the future on a beautiful evening like this Hans. Let's talk about the past, let's talk about all the good times we've shared over the years.'

Chapter 12

THE UNITED NATIONS Security Council was meeting to discuss an emergency motion tabled by the United States. The world had watched with horror as hundreds of Britons had crossed the Channel to a certain death. There was no legal way to stop them as they were not committing any crime, nor were they subject to the laws and law enforcement agencies of any nation that could restrain them. Of course the major ferry companies and airlines had discontinued trips to the island but an armada of small and medium sized boats and a fleet of light aircraft were still making their way across. It had even been rumoured that some people had swum to British shores from France or walked the length of the Channel Tunnel. Apart from the appalling waste of life, concerns had been raised that these human conveyances might be touching British soil and returning with viral material to infect mainland Europe. A total blockade of the British Isles was being proposed and Western nations already had ships and submarines heading to the area to enforce this in anticipation of a favourable vote in New York.

The flurry of diplomatic activity at UN headquarters had precipitated a flurry of activity on the beaches of Calais. Tallis had spent the third day since the attack in negotiations with any number of shady characters and had finally arranged himself a sailing. The *Whitsuntide* was a family sized boat, designed for about six people but would probably be carrying at least twice that number. It left at midnight from a small cove to the north of Calais. Though there was nothing illegal in what was being planned, none of the boat owners particularly wanted to draw attention to themselves.

The owner of the *Whitsuntide* was a small, slightly built Frenchman with a thin moustache and short black hair, which was greasy enough not to move in the stiff sea breeze that was buffeting the coastline. Despite his nationality he spoke English rapidly, accompanying the words with a piercing stare into the eyes of whoever was being addressed. There was only a slowing down as an important point was being emphasised, when he would squint suggestively at those around, searching for any signs of reaction. He dominated his small sphere of influence and two much larger Frenchmen who walked one pace behind responded in haste to any signs of displeasure, when he would wave his arms about or stand shoulders slumped with hands on hips. Tallis had been impressed by his apparent seriousness and no-nonsense manner. He did not ask for payment in advance of the midnight rendezvous and the thoroughness of the preparations actually provided some hope that the boat would probably make it to Britain. This man, Alain, would not be sailing in the boat, having entrusted that task to one of his burly henchmen. Tallis would deposit the keys to the car with Alain before boarding and disembark with the other passengers some two hundred metres from the British shoreline. They dared not go any closer and the human cargo would have to swim the remainder of the journey. Alain thrust his hand out to Tallis on sealing the deal, shaking it vigorously, all the time fixing him with a beady-eyed look.

Ben hadn't moved from his position on the wooden bench overlooking Calais beach all afternoon. From there he had observed the comings and goings of the band of grievers, travellers and those who just wanted to see what was going on. A couple of large ships were tethered about five kilometres out to sea and a dozen smaller vessels were bobbing up and down in the water closer to shore. It was a clear afternoon and the faint outline of the Dover cliffs could be made out without too much effort. He had been playing a kind of game with the people below him on the beach, observing their behaviour and demeanour and trying to guess their stories. The couple in their sixties staring out blankly towards the water for over an hour had probably lost a son or daughter in the United Kingdom. The pair sauntering along the beach hand in hand looking at all the other faces were probably French and had just come out of curiosity. The man in his twenties had a desperate look on his face, whilst it was clear that the man with whom he was shaking hands was there to conduct a business transaction. One didn't have to be a perceptive student of human behaviour to realise that the man was British and arranging to sail to Britain.

Ben thought of his brother and then looked at this young man. The needless loss of another human life appalled him and he began to feel angry with this person about to throw away his existence on earth when he would have done anything to bring back his brother Michael. He might not be able to bring Michael back now but perhaps he could do something to save this man's young life. Ben waited until Tallis had moved away then approached Alain. The Frenchman seemed disconcerted that enquiries about passage to Britain were being made so directly but deigned to answer Ben's request for a berth on his boat. Alain shook his head slowly, pursing his lips.

'Sorry full, no more room.'

'I have money,' replied Ben holding out a few hundred dollar bills. 'Four thousand dollars to take me over.'

'We leave at midnight,' replied Alain. 'Don't be late or we go without you.'

Ben followed Tallis at a discreet distance as he returned to his car and surmised from his dishevelled appearance that he probably wasn't staying at a hotel. He would be sure however to be eating a last supper somewhere and Ben watched as he drove off towards the town centre. It was likely he would go no further that evening, probably whiling away the hours in some bar or restaurant until midnight came. The registration number of the car was noted, then Ben returned to his wooden bench overlooking the sea to consider the next course of action. If he could save just one life, that at least would be some compensation for causing the death of Michael.

By eight o'clock it was a cold wintry evening. A fine mist had rolled in from the sea and all but the hardiest or saddest of souls had deserted the beach. In a way the weather suited Ben as it was unlikely his prey would be mobile in such conditions or far away from his car. Starting at one end of Calais he slowly walked the length of the main shopping street, checking the parked cars along the way. The smell of freshly baked bread still wafted from the pâtisseries and estate agents continued to carry house advertisements in English for customers on the other side of the Channel. He had been slowly and methodically walking for half an hour before arriving in what looked like the town square. There was an island of cars parked in rows in the middle of the large paved expanse, which separated two rows of shops some distance apart. He made sure he walked along each aisle between the vehicles then suddenly felt a thrill of excitement when Tallis' car came into view. Remaining calm he squatted down on his haunches and slowly opened a pocket knife. This was not going to be a crime of passion: being out of emotional control had already cost the life of Michael and he would not make the same mistake again. There was simply a calm but resolute determination not to let this young man throw his life away. With as much force as he could muster he stabbed the pocket knife into the thick rubber tyre. The knife jarred and closed producing a cut along the knuckle of the little finger, which began to bleed. Next time, instead of trying to pierce the tyre with the point of the blade, he pressed the sharp side against the rubber, moving it backwards and forwards in a kind of sawing action. This technique did not produce much success either, he had never before realised just how thick and difficult to penetrate a car tyre was. What was needed was a kitchen knife, not necessarily large but strong enough to withstand a forceful impact without breaking or buckling.

Ben walked into a nearby liquor warehouse. At this time of year it would normally be full of British customers stocking up for Christmas and New Year. Numerous signs in English advertised special deals and extolled the virtues of an inebriated festive season with red-nosed and ruddy-cheeked Santas holding up glasses toasting good cheer and good health to all. The twenty-four-hour opening hours had not changed despite the downturn in custom and the aisles which were normally full of people pushing trolley loads of booze were remarkably quiet. Although alcohol was its main stock in trade it was possible to buy a knife. The shop assistant sold it with no questions asked despite Ben's wild-eyed look and his bandaged little finger, which was now staining the white handkerchief crimson.

There was no mistake this time as he returned to Tallis' car and crouched down beside it. A large stainless steel blade with the capability to carve up an ox produced a collection of deep gashes in each tyre. That would be bound to at least slow him down, thought Ben as he crossed the road to an Irish bar opposite. He ordered a drink and something to eat at a seat by the window, keeping an eye on the vandalised vehicle and tending to his wounded little finger.

At eleven o'clock Tallis approached the car. The headlights were switched on then it jerked backwards before coming to a sudden stop. Ben observed the driver get out, inspect the tyres and without a moment's hesitation start to walk towards the sea. Ben stood up from the table at the Irish bar and immediately rushed to follow him. 'I've been through too much trouble to save your life tonight to give up now,' he thought as he began to stalk his quarry.

They eventually reached the point where it became necessary to leave the road for the beach. The lights of boats could be seen in the distance, though people were going about their business noiselessly. Ben wanted to talk to him but realised no words would stop him from this suicide mission. The desire to cross arose from a deep-seated emotional need, however irrational, and no forceful, eloquent argument would deter him from satisfying this craving. The first Tallis became aware of Ben's presence was with a punch to the kidney area, which doubled him over in pain. A succession of blows then rained in on his head, forcing him to the ground. There was no time to react or register what was happening, he just experienced a painful throbbing sensation in the blackness of the Calais night.

When Tallis came to he was lying on the beach. It was still dark and cold but at least somebody had thrown a blanket over him and stuffed a jacket under his head as a makeshift pillow. The first thing he became aware of on trying to get to grips with reality was a fire crackling some three metres away. Suddenly he remembered Alain, the boat, his passage to Britain, and struggled to get to his feet.

'It's too late,' came a voice from the darkness. 'The boat has already gone.'

'Jesus Christ,' groaned Tallis. 'What happened?'

There was a soreness around his temple and cheeks and his mouth hurt when he spoke, from the congealed blood around the lips. The voice from the darkness began to assume a physical reality as Tallis recognised a human form sitting near the fire, which now rose to its feet.

'Let's see if we can get you cleaned up,' said Ben.

'Somebody attacked me, punched me from behind, the bastard.' The sequence of events was now coming back to him.

'That bastard was me I'm afraid,' replied Ben calmly.

Tallis looked at him in complete bewilderment and didn't know whether to be angry or grateful. This man who had recently pummelled the living daylights out of him was now talking kindly and trying to be helpful.

'You! What the fuck for?'

'It was for my brother,' replied Ben.

'Your brother! What the hell did I ever do to your brother?' His ire was beginning to rise as he sensed the beginning of some unjust allegation.

'It's not what you did, it's what I did.'

This conversation would have confused Tallis at the best of times, but in his punch-drunk state no sense could be made of it at all. He surmised this friendly assailant must be some kind of weirdo and just told Ben to leave him alone as he staggered off into the night.

The next morning a swollen and bandaged Tallis walked the full length of Calais beach two times. He was looking for Alain, but the Frenchman was nowhere to be seen. Neither could he find any of the other hawkers who had peddled passages to Britain in recent days. On the horizon a collection of large American warships could be seen. The United Nations had passed the resolution enforcing a blockade of the British Isles. No one would be permitted to make the journey there any more.

Chapter 13

STEPHEN DE CLOYES was born in the year 1200, and in the year 1212 he was twelve years old. A tall thin boy with bright blue eyes and bushy brown hair, he walked barefoot and was dressed in rags. Having been orphaned at the age of five he made a living of sorts as a shepherd near the city of Orleans. It was in the year 1212 that, whilst standing in the middle of a field of sheep, he had a visit from no less a personage than Jesus Christ. The saviour of the world explained to the awestruck boy that the Crusaders had failed to regain the Holy Land because their hearts were impure, and gave an assurance that Christendom had tasted defeat for the last time in that part of the world. The young Stephen was given a letter instructing him to lead a Crusade, which was duly delivered to King Philip II. The French King hesitated to act on the instructions but the determined youth could not be deterred and refused to take no for an answer. He started preaching in the town of Vendôme and soon rumours spread that he had performed miracles of healing. Before long he had a considerable following and was able to set out on the divinely appointed mission.

So began the Children's Crusade with the ex-shepherd boy herding and driving his new flock across France. Like the pied piper Stephen travelled through villages collecting children on the way. Their families were powerless to stop them joining up and, when asked where they were going, the answer invariably came back, 'To God'. Crowds carried homemade wooden crosses, candles and the Oriflamme, the blood red three-pronged crusader's banner. Most were on foot though Stephen rode in a special cart with a crimson and gold canopy, flanked by some of the wealthier children who rode on horseback. He slept in a fancy red and white tent outfitted with a throne on which he would sit, wearing a golden crown, and bestow holy knighthoods.

The sight of these brave youths shamed their elders, whose zeal for religious warfare had waned over the years. Like the young freedom riders being bussed through America's south as they fought against racial discrimination in a different time, it reminded the older generation of their own failings. Pope Innocent was heard to say: 'These children are reproaching us, for they are hastening to recover the Holy Land while we slumber.' Not one of the youngsters was armed: they believed that the Muslims would be afraid when they saw such noble and pure hearts arriving and immediately convert to Christianity, simultaneously delivering the holy city of Jerusalem into their hands.

The march was long and many gave up or died along the way. With each new town or city they entered the children asked the inhabitants if this was yet Jerusalem. By the time they reached Marseilles only about five thousand of the once thirty thousand travellers remained. It was expected that the waters of the sea would part and they would carry on with their march as before, walking along the seabed of the Mediterranean. Stephen sat on the beach with the faithful but bedraggled band of followers and stared out to sea. One day passed, then another but there was no sign of the waters dividing. Hope was beginning to be lost when two ships offered the remaining numbers free passage to the Holy Land. Believing this to be a gift from God in his hour of need, Stephen gladly accepted the offer and they all set off to continue their journey.

Chapter 14

Tallis sat at a table in the Café Promenade not far from the beach at Calais. The large cafetière, designed for two coffee drinkers, was doing its job of returning warmth to his body. Through handling the glass casing, his skin was warming up and a welcome glow spread out from his stomach with every sip of the hot liquid. Perhaps there was some tissue between the inside and outside, which hadn't completely thawed out as he had been standing on the beach exposed to the icy elements for a considerable period of time that morning. The coffee alleviated his physical discomfort to some extent but his head still ached from the assault received the previous night. What had that lunatic had in mind? It was by no means the first time Tallis had been hit over the head, but the reaction of his attacker was just plain weird. What was his racket? Was he a thief who had a sudden pang of conscience mid-battering or a repressed homosexual who didn't know whether to beat or befriend him? What was that reference to his brother about? No explanation seemed to make any sense.

The coffee was almost finished and thoughts turned towards the next course of action. He had no idea how to spend the rest of the day, never mind what to do with the rest of his life. If only it had been possible to make it across to Britain, there would be no more problems. He would be dead by now. This realisation struck with an unexpected force. But for the incident on the beach he would be no more and would not be experiencing the cold of a winter's day or the heat of a cup of coffee. Isolated from time he would have no comprehension whatever of the present moment. For the first time since the attack, the journey to Britain seemed less important: he could do away with himself on French soil and achieve much the same outcome. Paradoxically, thoughts now turned to survival. He was in pain, feeling cold and funds were running out. It seemed there was no option but to report to the organisations helping British refugees and, at least temporarily, rely on the kindness of strangers.

A large warehouse by the ferry terminus at Calais docks had been set aside to accommodate British refugees. It had probably been used at some time for storing commodities for import from or export to Britain. Either way there was clearly no such purpose for it now. Plywood boards partitioned the cavernous space into dormitories, a canteen, recreation area and a small clinic. The only facilities, which were not inside, due to a lack of plumbing, were the ablution blocks. Temporary toilets, showers and sinks had been constructed but these were far from ideal and were too far away to be able to run the gauntlet of winter weather with nothing but a towel wrapped around oneself. Although Tallis was living there of his own volition, he hated the place and he hated the people even more. The patronising attitude of those who doled out food, clothes and cash was bad enough but the abasing gratitude and forced optimism of his compatriots was almost unendurable. It was how he imagined it must have been during the Battle of Britain when Londoners spent nights in underground train stations trying to keep spirits up. The crucial difference, however, was that they were not relying on handouts from anybody else and still had their pride.

Tallis didn't want to keep his spirits up and shunned the company of most. Neither did he have time for grief counsellors or the whole paraphernalia of people and organisations trying to get him back on his feet in a positive frame of mind with which to embrace the future. As soon as he received a small monetary allowance he was off to spend it at the nearest bar. The wine with the greatest alcohol-to-price ratio was purchased and consumed rapidly with a gleeful disrespect for those who said they wanted to help him.

He could not, and did not wish to, continue to live in the warehouse by the Calais docks. As weeks passed by his existence became more hateful and the numbers of inmates decreased as Britons willing to cooperate were rehabilitated back into a society somewhere with jobs and a home to go to. Remembering the words of Pedro, he toyed with the idea of returning to southern Spain but was unsure as to what kind of living could be made despite the assurances of his friend. Gardening skills were not the most marketable, especially in the middle of winter, and his stubborn refusal to cooperate with the staff at the warehouse made him one of the most difficult cases to place. He had gone through the sheets of possible vacancies, without great enthusiasm, a hundred times and had found nothing suitable. Then one day a member of the placement staff took him aside and unfolded a piece of paper from his pocket. This showed a vacancy which had never been included in any of the job files.

WANTED
Young men to defend Western Civilisation
Excellent rates of pay
Opportunities for travel
Opportunities to make a difference with your life

'What's this all about?' enquired Tallis.

'One of many organisations that have recently sprung up,' said the man behind the desk. He put his pen down, looked around then bent over the desk and whispered: 'They want to get back at the people who destroyed your country.'

'What? How?' replied Tallis, still confused by what was being said.

'You would be fighting against the people who killed your relatives,' the man continued with his hard sell. 'It's not the kind of employment we recommend but I can see we are going to have major problems placing you in any regular job. You are not doing anybody any good hanging around here. I thought it might appeal to you, instead of getting mad get even as they say.'

'Where would I be sent? What would I have to do?'

'Haven't the foggiest, you'd better phone the number on the advert.'

'Can you help me arrange a meeting with these people?'

The man behind the desk for the first time seemed displeased by the request.

'I shouldn't have shown you the advert. In fact I never did show it to you and this conversation never took place. Just write down the phone number and bugger off. I think we'll all throw a party when you finally leave this place.'

'You think I don't want to leave this fucking hell hole?' snarled Tallis.

Although it shouldn't really have come as any great surprise to him that his presence at the warehouse was not particularly welcomed by the staff, the man's tone of voice had annoyed him. He was definitely living there on sufferance and did not want anyone to think he was scrounging off them. Yet the longer he stayed, the more it appeared to others that this was indeed the case. For Christ's sake, he had never wanted this to happen and it wasn't his fault his country had been destroyed. Maybe it was, however, time to get out of there and attempt to make it somewhere else. He dialled the number written down on the scrap of paper.

After a succession of brief phone calls with nameless individuals who always insisted on phoning him back, an appointment was eventually made to meet with a Mr Sachs from the recruitment agency of Goldmeier and Sachs. Tallis spoke his name into the intercom beside the polished brass plate bearing the names of the company's two founders. The smart doorway was located in a quiet Calais street and the door noiselessly unlocked allowing him to enter. The secretary ushered the agency's hopeful new recruit into the large modern-looking office of Mr Sachs. He was a short man of about forty, well dressed in a grey pin-stripe suit and red tie. There was something of a middle-eastern look about this well-groomed person and it was fairly obvious that he must have been of Jewish extraction.

'Hello Mr Halliday, please take a seat,' he said in a businesslike manner.

He finished writing a letter on the desk, gave it to his secretary and watched her as she left the room. When the door closed his gaze fell on Tallis and for the first time the disciplined demeanour of Mr Sachs slipped and he appeared a little disconcerted. Pressing his lips together and pushing out the skin between them and the nose, where a mature black moustache had established itself, he said:

'Rather irregular this meeting of ours, Mr Halliday, I'm afraid. I'm not recruiting for one of our regular clients but doing a favour for an old friend. Hope you don't mind if I never make any mention of you being recruited,' he stopped to correct himself. 'Rather, having passed through this company of ours.'

'That's fine by me,' replied Tallis.

'Good, nothing personal you understand, just so long as we understand each other from the outset. Now tell me why would you like to work for this particular organisation?'

'In fact, sir, I know very little about it and was hoping you could fill me in on a few details, regarding what my duties would be.'

Mr Sachs' uneasiness increased at the direction this conversation was taking. If he had been instructed to conduct a full-length interview with this young man, the plan was immediately aborted. Totally ignoring Tallis' last enquiry Mr Sachs continued:

'Tell me, Mr Halliday, are you physically fit?'

'I think so, sir.'

'How do you feel about the Muslim world?'

Tallis sensed this was the key question that would determine his acceptance or otherwise. He wanted to convey some of the animosity he felt but also believed an emotional outburst would show a lack of discipline and count against him.

'How do you think I feel, having just seen my country destroyed by a Muslim terror group?'

Mr Sachs smiled. 'I think you could be the kind of person we are looking for. Let me arrange a meeting for you with someone who would be in a position to explain things in a bit more detail. What I can tell you are some basic terms and conditions: five thousand dollars a month into your bank account, three months on duty one month off. Is that acceptable?'

'Yes sir, it is,' replied Tallis, feeling pleased that he could at last be earning some money. 'Would you like to see my CV?'

'Oh don't bother with that,' replied Mr Sachs, waving a pin-striped, cufflinked arm. 'Just leave your contact details.'

Tallis returned to the dockside warehouse. He continued a cantankerous lifestyle as before, complaining at everything smiling at no one, but he did so now with a greater air of confidence. Knowing that his stay there was drawing to a close removed any last vestiges of behavioural constraints. He had set himself the goal of annoying everyone as much as possible before leaving and relished each small triumph. It was three days later when he received a call from Mr Sachs.

'Can we meet tomorrow for a chat?'

'Certainly,' replied Tallis. 'What time shall I come round?'

There was a pause at the other end of the telephone line, then

Mr Sachs said: 'Tell you what, Mr Halliday, why don't we meet in the morning in town? Where would you like?'

Tallis mentioned the only café that came to mind. 'Café Promenade.'

'Splendid, see you there at ten a.m.'

Tallis sat looking at his large cafetière at the Café Promenade, but felt a good deal more optimistic than last time he had done so. Christmas and New Year had passed and his wounds had completely healed. His prospects were looking up and even the weather seemed a bit brighter though it remained bitterly cold. Ten a.m. arrived but there was no sign of Mr Sachs. At 10.15 a young man much the same age as Tallis walked into the café. The two exchanged glances and for a moment this newcomer seemed unsure as to whether or not to approach the Englishman. In the end he said in an enquiring tone of voice, 'Mr Tallis Halliday?' and the named individual nodded to signify his correct identification.

'I have a letter from Mr Sachs,' he said, producing from an inside jacket pocket a white envelope with Tallis' name typed on the front.

'Did Mr Sachs have any other message?'

'My instructions were simply to deliver this letter to you.'

From a cursory appraisal of this young man's demeanour he was probably the most junior member of Goldmeier and Sachs and would not have been entrusted with anything but the simplest of tasks. Having performed his duty he appeared anxious to leave and Tallis did not attempt to delay him further.

One thousand dollars in hundred-dollar bills and a one-way ticket to Atlanta, Georgia were discovered on opening the envelope. There was no other explanation, just the ticket and money. Upon closer inspection of the ticket Tallis discovered that the flight was set for tomorrow evening. He resolved to pack up and leave for Paris that day. The United States of America seemed so far removed from his present situation, it would be a totally new experience and probably exactly what he needed. The possibility of starting a new life, instead of commiserating the loss of an old one started to take shape in his mind. For the first time since the attack he felt real excitement about what the future could hold. A last act of revenge was planned for the staff at the Calais dock warehouse. He would park Sir Steven Wilkinson's car in front of the entrance to the building, before exchanging a few unpleasantries and catching the train from Calais to Paris, with the car keys in his pocket.

Chapter 15

THE NEWS OF the United Nations blockade of the British Isles had been Ben's cue to leave Calais. Now that no other person would make it across the Channel to infected soil, he at least had the consolation of having saved one life. His heart was still heavy as he thought about those who had perished in the attack. Grieving for all of them was impossible and one hardly knew where to start. His mourning lacked focus and direction and the result of this was that he just constantly felt depressed without fully comprehending all the reasons why. As the days passed, Maureen gradually began to assume a pre-eminent position in his thoughts. Her death had the greatest effect on his present life: he was not only mourning her passing but mourning the passing of the life he had dreamed of sharing with her. A happy secure home, the love of a woman, children, all the ingredients that made for a satisfying and worthwhile life had disappeared overnight. In mourning her he was not only mourning the past but the future.

The festive period had been spent in Prague. Despite the best efforts of everyone to make his time there as enjoyable as possible he was unable to appreciate much of what was going on. The more he tried to be happy, the more guilty and depressed he became. What was most upsetting and what he could not understand was why he had started sexual relations with so many women. The morning after a night of moderate passion he felt so guilty and low-down, he would make every kind of sincere promise to himself to change his ways. At night-time however he would trawl the bars picking up whoever caught his eye and felt powerless to stop going all the way with them. Sex became like a drug with cravings, pinnacles of ecstasy and feelings of worthlessness and low self esteem. The only source of comfort was the huge amount of alcohol he had become accustomed to drinking, which numbed the mind and temporarily made him forget the pain he was experiencing. When his company was taken over and he was offered a new job in Paris, this seemed to be an ideal opportunity for a fresh start. He would be away from the people and places of temptation that he knew and who knew him. He would put aside the aberration of his Prague Winter but had no real vision of what kind of life he would lead in Paris.

Chapter 16

DR ROBERT WILLIAMS waited for Dr Hans Schuster and his wife Annette in the latter's large garden in Moshi. A small gathering of domestic staff and others from KCMC were assembled there to bid farewell to the couple who had been such a major part of their lives. Dr Schuster had been bequeathed the title 'Mzee', literally 'old man' whilst his wife was referred to as Mama Schuster. This was despite Dr Schuster still being in his fifties and the couple having no children. There was nothing so worthy of respect in Swahili culture as being old or having children and so even when neither of these applied they were conferred as honorary titles. Robert looked at his watch then anxiously at the group of people assembled. It would be the height of bad manners and extremely hurtful to rush such important farewells. Nevertheless the KLM plane to Amsterdam would wait for no one. He went inside the house to hurry his old friend along and insisted on putting the luggage in the car whilst Hans was saying his farewells in order to save a bit of time. In the end Dr Schuster conducted the whole proceedings with the assurance of an old pro. Robert admired the sensitive way he dealt with each and every individual and realised he would be sorely missed. It made him wonder if he would command such respect and sorrow when he eventually left Tanzania.

Robert drove the forty-kilometre stretch to Kilimanjaro International Airport, which was out in the middle of a flat grassy plain about half way between the towns of Moshi and

Arusha. They had agreed they would say their farewells as soon as the Schusters were safely escorted inside the terminal building. There seemed to be little point in hanging around whilst they checked in, it would only diminish the dignity of the occasion.

'Well my old friend, I suppose this is it,' said Hans as he turned to Robert.

'You will be missed more than you realise,' replied Robert.

'Keep up the good work, you are doing a fine job.'

'You are always welcome here Hans.'

The German gripped his hand firmly and said: 'We will meet again Robert, that is for sure.'

Robert kissed Annette Schuster goodbye then returned to his car without looking back.

Driving along the road from Arusha to Moshi, Robert knew so well the landmarks that lay in front of him. What his future held was something altogether more uncertain and worrying. The only certainty was that things would not be the same. Benedict Collins, meanwhile, was making arrangements to leave Prague and start a new job in Paris, with a determination to lead a better life. Tallis Halliday was on a plane from Paris to Atlanta, thinking what kind of postcard he would send to the director of the Calais warehouse to cause him maximum embarrassment. Of this threesome he was the most optimistic about the future but also the one with the least idea of what it would be like.

Having accepted the two ships as a gift from God, Stephen de Cloyes enthusiastically continued his journey to the Holy Land. Unfortunately the ships had no intention of sailing anywhere near that part of the world but instead headed to Algiers. There the captains sold their youthful human cargo into slavery. Stripped of his gold crown, fine clothes and the admiration of all around, the boy Stephen was paraded around the hot and dusty slave market and examined as a piece of merchandise. Sold for a paltry sum of money he resumed the kind of humble life he had been accustomed to just a few months before and cried like a twelve-year-old boy.

Part 3

Chapter 1

ROBERT LOOKED AT the man with closed eyes lying on his back on the simple iron framed bed in the now unguarded ward at KCMC. He wondered what his story was. It was fairly clear what act had driven him to sign up as a mercenary but the degree of pain he had experienced was a mystery preserved behind the impassive eyelids. Robert guessed he was some kind of labourer and a cursory glance at the rough hands confirmed this theory. Those with good qualifications or money had had the means to set themselves up somewhere. Unemployed, depressed, with no home to go to and a burning hatred of the destroyers of his homeland, he would have been an easy recruit for any paramilitary organisation. Still, despite the obvious hardships endured, there was a look of innocence about his face and an abiding impression that he didn't really belong in a military uniform.

Robert's eyes rose and he gazed, as he had done so many times before, out of the window to Kilimanjaro rising majestically above the tranquil countryside. Why was it that no human life seemed to capture the peace of Mother Nature? Looking at the tableau presented, life seemed so easy: you live, you work, you die, and if you are lucky you find a little love along the way. It was only man who made things complicated, ugly and painful. Complicated? Yes, that was a good word, simplicity was the requirement to be in harmony with one's surroundings. 'To see the kingdom of God it is necessary to become like a child again.' Perhaps the kingdom of God is all around us, we have just attuned ourselves to not seeing it. Robert looked at the patient who was still not stirring and who hadn't stirred now for two weeks. He left word to be notified should the patient regain consciousness and returned to the Gynaecology Department.

At lunchtime Robert drove out of the gates of KCMC and to Lutheran Uhuru Hostel at which place he was due to meet Mwamba. Lutheran Uhuru Hostel was probably the most morally respectable place in Moshi for a man to be seen with a woman. Frequented by Methodist clergy of all ranks and from all places, it was the preferred meeting place of people who desired sex and debauchery to be as far removed from the agenda of items they had to deal with as possible. No alcohol was sold and no room was rented for the afternoon. For these reasons it was an ideal place for Robert and Mwamba to have lunch since nobody would accuse them of getting up to anything of a scandalous nature on the premises. The food was reasonable and cheap and in keeping with the religious sentiment the surroundings were clean and adequate without the decadence of excess luxury. There was a smell of polish from the manually burnished dark wooden floors and the staff gave the impression of serving God first and the customer second.

Mwamba was sitting outside on a paved concrete area under the shade of a Jacaranda tree reading *Conversations With God* for the umpteenth time but no doubt gaining some new insight about her own life from its pages. A thermos flask of tea stood on the white painted wrought iron table in front of her and a brown piece of half-eaten rock cake was lying on a saucer. Robert sat down on one of the white iron chairs and waited whilst Mwamba finished what she was reading. On concluding a page she carefully placed a bookmark in the book, looked up and smiled.

'You should be revising for your exams,' said Robert in mock seriousness.

'With you marking them I should be OK,' she replied.

'Don't even joke about such things,' said Robert trying to reduce the humour of the situation. 'That's exactly what most people are expecting to happen. I'm still not sure how to handle the situation.'

'Anyway I'll be glad when they are over,' said Mwamba, her voice filled with relief as she tried to imagine that stress-free time.

There was a pause as they both realised that this would mean her leaving Tanzania and returning to Zambia.

'I won't,' replied Robert mournfully.

'I'll be sad to leave you here, you have been such a good friend.'

'Yes,' replied Robert, the praise leaving an empty feeling inside. He chided himself for having any other expectations that things would ever have worked out differently. She was thirty years his junior, he should be glad of at least having her friendship. Why should she want to be tied down to an aging medic like him? Mwamba noticed the look of disappointment on his face and decided to change the topic of conversation.

'How was your morning?'

'Oh fine, my British mercenary still hasn't regained consciousness.'

'I hope he does so soon, if only to keep you company.'

'I hope so too, but he will eventually leave like everybody else I've known.'

'Perhaps it should be you to leave next time,' suggested Mwamba.

Robert did not answer, he was thinking of something else, something that would sound daft as soon as he said it but Mwamba was the one person he knew who could be trusted not to laugh.

'Mwamba, do you think we have met in a previous life?' He braced himself, not knowing how she would answer this.

'I am sure of it,' she replied calmly.

The simple affirmative answer to the question was the one he probably least expected.

'Why?' he asked, amazed at her coolness.

'Because we get on so well and understand each other's feelings. I felt it about the second or third time we met, that deep empathy, the way our souls communicated.'

'Why didn't you say something?'

'Why should I have said something?'

Robert wasn't about to start an argument on this point, but wanted to explore this past but newly discovered life.

'What do you think was the connection between us?'

'We were husband and wife.'

This simple truth stunned him but he felt compelled to ask one more question.

'Were we happy?'

Mwamba smiled. 'I am sure we were very happy together.'

Robert felt a warm glow of affection for this woman now that this truth had been unmasked. It was as if the vessel containing his conception of their relationship had suddenly been shattered, creating rivulets of revelation, which flowed rapidly and uncontrollably in all directions. He unsuccessfully tried to make sense of this much larger picture before coming back down to earth.

'But you are leaving.'

'Yes,' replied Mwamba.

'Why do you leave knowing what you do about the two of us?'

'Has anybody asked me to stay?'

It was such an absurd idea that he wanted her to leave he had never bothered to ask her to stay, simply assuming she would remain if she wanted to.

'Will you stay here with me, Mwamba?'

'Of course I will.'

'I really don't know how to handle this. I've never even kissed you and now I learn we used to be husband and wife and who knows could be destined to repeat this union in this lifetime.'

'You can start off by kissing me.'

Robert felt guilty and elated at the same time. It was a long time since he had kissed a woman in any romantic way and the experience was so strange it was difficult to believe it was actually happening. He tasted the tea from Lutheran Uhuru Hostel as Mwamba unexpectedly pushed her tongue into his mouth. It was a relief they were seated alone and thus spared the disapproving looks of more morally upright customers.

'You make me feel as if I'm sixteen again,' said Robert.

'You make me feel very happy,' replied Mwamba.

The waitress came with the bill, placed it with a thud on the table then abruptly turned to go back to the kitchen.

'Next time I think we'd better not meet at Lutheran Uhuru Hostel,' said Robert.

Chapter 2

THE FOLLOWING DAY a note was delivered to Robert in his office at KCMC. The young Englishman in whom he had taken such a keen interest was beginning to return to consciousness. Apart from a curiosity to hear the mercenary's story, Robert wished to reassure his compatriot at what was probably a bewildering time for him. An African doctor was just leaving the ward as he arrived. To the enquiry as to how his charge was faring this man shook his head.

'Don't know why we bother looking after the likes of him,' he said in a tone of disgust.

Robert entered the room and saw the man lying on the bed with his back towards him.

'Good afternoon,' he said.

The patient turned and looked startled for a moment at the presence of the Englishman. He soon regained his sullen composure however and contemptuously asked: 'What do you want?'

'I don't want anything,' replied Robert, ignoring the venom in his voice. 'I've come to see how you are.'

'Well my welfare is none of your concern so bugger off.'

'OK,' and with that word Robert began walking towards the door.

'Wait,' exclaimed Tallis. 'What's someone like you doing out here?'

'What I am doing out here is not relevant. What is important for you to realise is that I am the only Englishman at this hospital.

I'm the only one who can help you, nobody else will bother.'

'I don't feel like talking now,' said Tallis.

'See you tomorrow then,' and Robert continued his brisk exit of the ward without waiting for a reply.

He returned to his office and was sorting through papers on the desk when there was a knock at the door. Following the invitation to enter, his wife Anna walked in. It was one of only a few times she had visited her husband at work and he found her sudden unexpected presence disconcerting.

'Hello,' he said, feeling rather foolish at the ordinariness of the remark.

'Hello,' she replied quietly, walking carefully to the settee, where she sat down.

'I didn't expect to see you here,' said Robert.

'Well since you never come to our home these days it's the only place I can find you.'

'What can I do for you?' The question sounded cruelly formal and impersonal but it was the only way he could think of framing it.

'I've been doing a lot of thinking,' said Anna, then she took a deep breath, signifying the imminent delivery of a prepared speech. 'I've been talking with Father Mpanga from the church and it is a good idea if we go together to see him.' She continued quickly before her husband could raise any objections. 'We need to sort things out in our marriage. First we get it blessed in the Catholic Church so it is sorted out with God. Second, we need to try hard for a baby. I know it would make your heart happy to have a son. We need to stay like a proper family, not just like boyfriend and girlfriend in the same house. Thirdly I need to get a job. It is not good that I am relying on you for money all the time. It causes a lot of problems in our marriage and I need to sweat to bring something into the family home. I am your wife forever but we need to sort things out so that we can live happily and peacefully together.'

Anna's monologue depressed Robert on a number of levels. Firstly the resolve not to let go of their marriage and admit that it could never work. She was trying so hard to keep things together and it was obviously painful to contemplate the possibility of divorce. Secondly she had misread the situation so badly. Neither money, children, nor religious approbation mattered in the least to Robert. That she failed to even come close to understanding the reasons behind the divorce only confirmed how far apart they were and how little she knew him. He could say nothing to give her the slightest hope of a reconciliation, but the gulf between them was so wide it was futile to start any argument.

'Our marriage is over,' said Robert sadly. 'There is nobody who is more sorry about that than I am, but it's something we both have to accept.'

Anna looked determinedly at her husband. 'What do you want me to do?' she asked in the vain hope of receiving some instructions that would save the marriage.

'I don't want you to do anything. It's not your fault, it's neither of our faults, it's just that we weren't meant to be together.'

'We shall see who will win this fight,' declared Anna angrily as she stormed out of the office.

Robert sat in his chair and thought about that last statement. The words 'win' and 'fight' stuck in his mind. How could such terms be applied to what they were both going through? Thinking about his marriage a new word thrust itself into his head. The word was 'pain': pain for him, pain for Anna, pain seemed destined to follow them both at all times. He thought of the young man in the ward. It was pain he was feeling, pain that directed his actions, pain and fear and each of these fed off the other.

The afternoon passed with Robert being depressingly preoccupied with his current predicament. He felt a need to revisit the young Englishman: perhaps through a mutual sharing of each other's pain it might be lessened. The hospital was less busy now, with only a skeleton staff on duty for the evening shift. A quiet began to descend around the place as the evening sun set. Robert sat down on a chair by Tallis' bed after drawing back the curtain so they could both have a view of Kilimanjaro. The time just before dark was when he considered the mountain to be at its most serene. Tallis looked out of the window for ten minutes, until the reddish tinge of the scene turned grey and night arrived. This view might have the ability to achieve what no amount of words could and quieten this angry young man's disposition.

Another period of silence followed as Tallis lay on his back looking up at the ceiling, then Robert said: 'Tell me about your family.'

'My parents lived in Nottingham, my mother was a nurse, my father was a plumber.'

'Did you have any brothers or sisters?'

'No, I was their only child. They were good to me. I should have been with them when the attack came.'

'What good would you have done? You couldn't have saved their lives.'

'I could have been there for them as they were always there for me.'

'Is that what they would have wanted? Would they have wanted you to die with them or be alive today?'

'I feel so guilty about surviving.'

'That's how you feel. Have you ever thought about how your parents felt? When the attack came and they knew they were about to die, I am sure it was a great comfort to them to know that their only son was alive.'

'I wish I had died.'

'Don't be so selfish, don't be so weak. You have been given

a chance to make something of yourself in this life. Nothing happens by accident, there is a reason why you were saved.'

'What reason could there be? So that I can live through this hell on earth?'

'It is for everybody to find the meaning of their own lives. Yours is obscured at the moment, but if you let the pain, fear and hatred subside for a moment you will begin to glimpse it.'

'I know you're trying to help but I think you're wasting your time with me.'

'Don't let your parents down, don't let yourself down. There is always hope no matter how dark and desperate the situation may seem. Anyway you try and get some sleep now, we'll talk again tomorrow.'

'Thank you, doctor,' said Tallis and for the first time, in those two words, the façade of bravado seemed to be cracking as the gratitude appeared to be heartfelt.

Robert was encouraged by this evening bedside talk and the possibility of relieving someone else's emotional pain had indeed eased that of his own. With more of a resigned than a worried air regarding his own situation he drove back to the small flat in Moshi town centre.

How would Dr Schuster have dealt with Dr Olanya? The question had run through Dr Williams' mind on numerous occasions. Although he could not think how he could have acted differently, Robert found it almost inconceivable that the former head of the Gynaecology Department would have been treated with the amount of disrespect that Dr Olanya reserved for him. Nowhere was this exhibited more blatantly than with the new customer care initiative that Robert was trying to introduce. Patients' rights, greater accountability and an emphasis on carrying out medical procedures to the highest standards were treated with derision and he refused to show any cooperation with the new system. Moreover there was a ready audience of nurses, medical technicians and other orderlies who were only too eager to lap up any criticism of the new regime. Each one could see extra work and extra questions being asked and didn't like it one bit. The idea of being answerable to patients and pandering to their needs was simply anathema to most. Were they running a hospital or a hotel?

Dr Williams' work at KCMC was becoming increasingly unbearable. He was receiving little support from his colleagues and the situation regarding Mwamba was being used by some to undermine his authority. He would have caused much less of a scandal had he just picked up the occasional prostitute from one of the bars along the dust road that ran parallel to the border of the hospital grounds. There seemed less and less reason to stay, but where could he go? In the past Britain had always been a viable if unwelcome proposition but now that avenue of opportunity had been closed no other country really appealed. If Dr Olanya wanted his position he was welcome to it and if the hospital authorities were happy with that then so much the better. Perhaps Dr Schuster was right that African doctors should be running the hospital and finding African solutions to African problems.

His thoughts turned to Mwamba. What would happen to her after finishing her exams? They must definitely live together, but doing so in Moshi would only add to the problems at work and with Anna. He might be able to endure the pressure but feared the distress that would be visited on his partner. There was no other option: he had to seriously put his mind to moving away from KCMC. Robert looked out of the window: it was a bright sunny morning and he had just finished consulting with his patients. At least they seemed to appreciate his presence at the hospital and perhaps would be sorry to see him go. It was not quite time for lunch so he reckoned there was enough time to pay a visit to his injured compatriot in the ward upstairs.

Tallis was in a slightly brighter mood, occasioned by the arrival of a number of personal effects from Kenya. Of much the greatest interest was a laptop, but as his hands were still bandaged it was not possible for him to access the information it contained. Robert was able to offer assistance and the conversation began easily, centred around this A4 sized piece of technology.

'Are there any new emails?' asked Tallis.

'Apart from the usual junk there doesn't appear to be anything,' replied Robert, scrolling down the list.

'Who would contact me?' said Tallis in a defeatist tone of voice.

'You have one unopened email here that looks of interest.'

'Who's that from?'

'From Pedro Hernandez, but it's so old, over two years.'

'Don't bother opening that.'

'Shall I delete it?'

'No!' The suddenness with which Tallis replied surprised Robert.

'But if you don't want to read it, why not just delete it?'

'I don't want to read it and I don't want to delete it, OK?' Tallis raised his voice for the first time and seemed angry.

There was a pause, then Robert said in a calm voice: 'What is it you are afraid of, Tallis? You have risked your life, fought battles and now seem afraid of opening an email. What do you think is the worst it could do to you?'

Tallis could see he was sounding increasingly ridiculous.

'Do what you want,' he said reluctantly.

'I will,' replied Robert with a mischievous smile on his face.

My friend Tallis,

I am sending this email in the hope that you have been unsuccessful. I pray to God that your car broke down, you were stopped at the border or had a change of heart about returning to Britain. What happened to your country was a tragedy, but there is no reason to add to this tragedy. One more life may not alter the statistics very much but everyone's life is special. No scale is capable of weighing it, no person able to place a value on it. Your life is special to me, I hope it will become special to you before it is too late. I hope this reaches you while you are still alive to read it. I meant what I said about you coming to live in Spain, but even if I never see you again, please just email to tell me you are alive and my heart will be full of happiness.

Always your friend Pedro

'It sounds as if there is at least one person who feels it worth contacting you,' said Robert.

Tears were running down Tallis' cheeks and he clumsily tried to remove them with his bandaged hands.

'I'm sorry,' he said.

'Sorry for what?' replied Robert. 'I bet you haven't cried in a long time and you have plenty to cry about.'

'I don't know what to do with my life,' he blubbered through the sobs.

'Take things one day at a time. The first thing you have to do today is to reply to Pedro.'

'Will you help me?'

'It would be my pleasure.'

Chapter 3

AFTER LUNCH ROBERT returned to his office only to find a note from Dr Fidelis Massawe on the desk, requesting a meeting at his earliest convenience on a matter of great concern. The usual phone calls were made and an appointment was set for three p.m. the same day. He picked up the note again: its brevity and absence of any first names did not bode well and he spent no little proportion of the time before the meeting thinking what it could be about.

Robert sat in Dr Massawe's waiting room mentally reviewing his actions of the last few days until he was eventually called in. The mood was altogether more formal than the last visit and it was clear from the hospital administrator's implacable face that a serious issue was under consideration.

'Good afternoon Dr Williams, please take a seat,' said Dr Massawe peering over his glasses.

'Good afternoon,' replied Robert.

The chief of KCMC had a letter in front of him, which he had read many times already but was now reading again. After finishing, he paused, exhaled to signify the commencement of the unpleasant duty his station demanded he perform and looked Robert in the eye.

'Are you aware, Dr Williams, that as well as being a hospital this is a Christian organisation? Not only do we tend to the sick, we do our best to promote God's work through what we do and how we behave.'

'I am very much aware of that,' replied Robert.

'That being the case, any extra-marital relationship, particularly with a woman much younger than yourself, over whom you are in a position of authority, would therefore be viewed very seriously by the hospital management.'

'If you are referring to my relationship with Mwamba Phiri, sir, I can assure you it is an entirely innocent friendship.' Robert remained calm and conveniently chose to forget about the tea-flavoured kiss.

'Perhaps you can explain this then.' Dr Massawe leant over the desk to hand over the paper he had been perusing earlier. It was a simple handwritten note, requesting Mwamba to meet Robert in the hospital cafeteria. There was nothing damning about the message at all except that it began, *To my wife Mwamba*, and ended, *From your husband Robert*.

'Is that your handwriting?' asked Dr Massawe.

'Yes it is,' replied Robert, reddening.

'Perhaps you could explain why, if this is an innocent friendship, you are calling this student your wife.'

Robert could see the hopelessness of his position. Any talk about past lives would be greeted with incredulity and, besides, he didn't really want to share this personal secret with anyone.

'It is something you wouldn't understand and I therefore can't explain but I can assure you I have never had sexual relations of any kind with this woman.'

'I don't really want you to explain this to me, I just want it to stop,' said Dr Massawe, treating the protestations of innocence with disdain.

'I will discontinue my teaching role and avoid all contact with her in the hospital, but what I do in my own time is my own business.'

'You will stop seeing her altogether,' the hospital administrator's voice rose for the first time. 'There are enough women in Moshi to choose from if you find it impossible to be faithful to your wife.'

'I have told you my position, I will make sure none of my actions cause the hospital any embarrassment.'

'Let me tell you my position. If I hear any more reports of you with this girl, the matter will be taken further and could end in your dismissal.'

Robert walked out of the office feeling angry and humiliated, like some thirteen-year-old schoolboy who had just had a lecture from the headmaster after being discovered masturbating behind the toilet block with a copy of *Penthouse*. The assumption that he was involved in a sexual relationship, that his contact with Mwamba compromised his performance as a doctor and teacher, along with the implication that she could be replaced by any young tart from the local bars, showed just how little Dr Massawe thought of him. The strategy of trying to supplant Mwamba was destined to have about as much success as the headmaster advising the boy to take up cricket or learn to play a musical instrument to take his mind off such matters. 'What the hell if I do lose my job,' he thought. It was looking more and more like the best thing that could happen to him.

The following evening Mwamba visited Robert's apartment for the first time. They talked easily about the life they wanted to share together. Nothing fazed Mwamba as she took the news of the interview with Dr Massawe, Robert's desire to leave Africa and the plans for a quiet registry office marriage with an equanimity that was nothing short of astounding. It became more and more clear to her former husband that this was demonstrably the effect of a belief in a God who always planned things for a reason and who never judged.

Robert found the physical part of their new relationship difficult to handle. It wasn't that he did not desire her, it was just the transition to the new role of lover that was not easy. He had mentally partitioned her in a space encompassed by red and white striped plastic tape with big signs which clearly said 'Danger: do not cross this line'. He now had to overcome the self-made defences so conscientiously and elaborately constructed. He nervously removed his trousers whilst Mwamba pulled her T-shirt over her head revealing a pair of perfectly shaped, smooth, dark brown breasts cupped in a black bra. Her scanty underpants of the same colour resembled an eyepatch more than an item of clothing. She had a beautiful body and the skin was so soft to the touch that his fingertips tingled on caressing it. He clumsily clambered on top of her, kissing her on the lips whilst running a hand underneath the string of the underwear that girded her hips. Slowly rubbing against her, searching for an opening, he was evidently looking in the wrong place as she grabbed hold of his erect member and pushed it downwards. It had been so long since he had had sex, he could feel the excitement surging through his lower body and he had scarcely entered her when he exploded.

Robert rocked off her and lay on his back in bed. He was satisfied but conscious he had hardly done the job for Mwamba and felt something of a failure.

'I'm sorry, it's just been such a long time and you get me so excited.'

Mwamba now climbed on top of Robert, her eyes full of acceptance and a gentle smile on her face.

'Don't worry my husband. We have the rest of our lives to get it right'

Chapter 4

THE TRAIN SMOOTHLY pulled out of the station at Rosenheim and made its way east towards the German-Austrian border. Ben had not been over-enamoured of Munich: though admittedly he had only stayed one night, it had the feel of just another large European city. The journey from there, however, had been pleasant enough, travelling through the countryside of the foothills of the Alps. It was now autumn and reddish brown hues diffused throughout a landscape which was only weakly illuminated by a sun yet to pierce the grey clouds. He glanced at Elisabetta, who was reading a book. What memories and feelings the familiar scenery brought to her mind he could only guess at, though she didn't appear to be in a particularly wistful mood.

He returned to a story he had been reading repeatedly since having bought the *Daily Telegraph* in Munich. It was possible to buy a number of English language dailies in the major urban areas, not as good as the originals from Fleet Street but they satisfied a linguistic and cultural need for the refugees living on the European mainland. Three men had made it across the North Sea in a power boat, dodging the UN blockade and the mines that were rumoured to have been planted. Reaching just north of Hull they had stayed on land for two days, taking photographs and video footage, which was then emailed back to France. Although Hull was not particularly renowned for famous landmarks, some good shots of the Humber Bridge were taken and they remembered to include a current edition of *Le Monde* on them as proof of the date. None of the three had had the courage to venture into the city centre or enter any houses. Whether it was through fear of contagion or the horrific scenes that might await them, the dead were given a wide berth. On their journey back they had been picked up by a UN vessel and placed in immediate quarantine.

The illegal expedition re-ignited a debate which had been smouldering ever since the attack had taken place. Just how safe was British land? So far none of the men had suffered any medical complications so they clearly had not come into contact with the most virulent of the viruses, which would have killed within hours. Smallpox had an incubation period of about two weeks, so the men would be kept in isolation and under observation for at least a month before being released back into society. Of course the fact that they might not contract any illness was not sufficient proof that the whole island was safe for human habitation, but the sight of the three healthy men walking around would be a powerful image, sure to be exploited by the British refugee community.

Scientists discussed at length whether the virus could still be active and pose any serious health threat. The smallpox virus was capable of surviving for years in the soil but it was theorised that this new chimera created in a laboratory was probably more unstable and could break down much more quickly. In truth no one really knew and it was such an emotive issue that reliable, impartial, quality research was difficult to come by.

Ben looked up from his paper and sighed. He had a feeling that the final decision as to if and when to recolonise Britain would be dictated by political expediency rather than scientific fact so the whole argument was somewhat academic. With this sentiment in mind it was with dismay that he read, a few pages on from the three men in a boat story, the *Daily Telegraph*'s account of Ken Louis' recent one man expedition to Gibraltar. The self-appointed representative of the British community had addressed an ecstatic bunch of Union Jack-waving Gibraltarians near their border with Spain. He declared them to be the brothers and sisters of all Britons, making reference to a special indissoluble bond that would forever tie the two groups together. Looking at the photograph of the former member of the House of Commons declaiming to the masses in the warm sunshine whilst the wind ruffled his hair, Ben received the distinct impression that he was enjoying the role of rabble rouser. Certainly the manner in which he was provoking the Spanish government only made a return to Britain more difficult. Perhaps Ken Louis didn't want a return to Britain? Without doubt he would never have enjoyed this much fame if the attack had never taken place. Ben wondered if he was alone in thinking an argument over a rocky outcrop of the Spanish mainland completely idiotic given his country's current predicament. He looked at Elisabetta, who was lightly dozing, then checked the time on his watch. Taking out his laptop he reckoned he had just enough time to write to the *Daily Telegraph* before his train journey ended. It was the first occasion in his life he had ever written to a newspaper and he viewed the process more as an exercise in catharsis, rather than holding out any real hope that his effort would be published.

> *Dear Editor,*
>
> *I have watched with growing alarm and incredulity as you have covered Ken Louis' recent 'tour' of Gibraltar. It seems that both he and your newspaper assume he is speaking for all British refugees. Let me assure you he does not speak for me. I suffered as did so many thousands of my compatriots from the loss of family and friends when the attack came. It has not been an easy task to try and rebuild a life and like so many others I yearn for the day when it will be possible to return to the land of my birth.*
>
> *What Ken Louis' hysterical stubbornness has to do with*

moving this day forward is beyond me. Instead of addressing the real issues, which might lead to an early return home he seems more intent on stirring up trouble and making their solution more difficult. Why concentrate on a small stump of rock in the Mediterranean Sea when our own land lies deserted? If the Gibraltarians really were our brothers and sisters they would be doing all in their power to help us rebuild our island and planning to come with us when the day of return comes. As it is they are enjoying their own comfortable brand of patriotism in a warm sunny climate no doubt enjoying a glass of Spanish wine with Ken Louis.

Yours Sincerely
Benedict Collins

The train had crossed over the German-Austrian border without Ben noticing it. He clicked the mouse button, confirming he wished his views to be sent to the *Daily Telegraph* and felt better for giving vent to the frustration he had been experiencing. Soon afterwards the domed roofs of Salzburg with the imposing Hohensalzburg fortress overlooking them came into view. The former Hapsburg capital, which had stood as the stronghold of Christendom against the forces of Suleiman the Magnificent in the sixteenth century, still retained some of its old charm, at least from a distance. Elisabetta began to perk up a little at the sight of her hometown and Ben began to feel nervous for the first time at the knowledge he was soon to meet her family.

Chapter 5

THE TWO OF them were met by Elisabetta's older brother Eberhard, who took Ben's hand in a vice-like grip and wouldn't let go until he had completed a rehearsed two-minute speech of welcome. Thinking of his recent advertising project, Ben visualised him as being the ideal candidate to advertise a beer manufactured by the Nazi Party. Tall, broad-chested with blonde hair and pearly white teeth: they could have branded it Aryan Superman. A few generations earlier it would have gone down like a house on fire in the Bavarian beer-halls.

'Elisabetta has talked much about her English boyfriend,' he said, glancing in a knowing kind of way at his sister. 'We will become great friends.'

The thought of this made him suddenly stop on the platform and put down the collection of suitcases he was carrying.

'Please think of me as your brother,' he then said, flinging his arms around Ben's back and holding him in a bear hug.

Ben felt relieved when brother and sister began a discussion in German as it allowed him some time to take stock of his ebullient welcome. Would it be like this with the rest of the family and how would it affect his relationship with Elisabetta? Having happily contrived to make the relationship with her as serious as possible, he began to feel disconcerted as to just how serious it may have become. The meeting and evening meal with Elisabetta's parents did nothing to dispel this uneasiness and only confirmed the impression that he had suddenly got into a situation rather too deeply. The mother went as far as to say that since he no longer had any parents he should consider them for that role and fussed over him at the dining table as if he was the prodigal son returning home. Elisabetta's father, a man of few words, simply smoked his pipe, nodding and smiling at his new English son in a contented manner. The domestic scene was one of almost uninterrupted joyful and banal banter, where nothing was said to offend anyone and harmless indulgent jokes flew back and forth across the dining table. Ben was reminded of the saying that happy families are all alike whereas unhappy families are each unhappy in their own way. It was easy to imagine such a spectacle being repeated by families worldwide. On the other hand, he had never come across and could not conceive of ever coming across a family like his own.

It was a relief to discover there was no issue over where the newly arrived couple would be sleeping. Ben had been dreading an embarrassing scene where he would state his preference for inhabiting the same room as Elisabetta. Without even asking, Eberhard had taken all their luggage to a room at the back of the house the instant they had arrived. It afforded a view of a green hillside dotted with detached houses at different levels. The room even had its own en-suite bathroom for greater privacy and enhanced love-making. As it appeared to be one of the larger rooms, Ben wondered if the parents had moved out to make way for them, but thought it prudent not to pursue this line of enquiry even with Elisabetta.

The fact that they were having sex in her family home proved to be a tremendous turn-on. It was as if they were engaging in some kind of illicit activity, which only added to the thrill. One moment Elisabetta would be the dutiful daughter, respectfully listening to her parents' conversation, the next she would be a sweating, squealing, quivering sexually charged woman underneath her English boyfriend.

Every morning her mother cooked a large breakfast for the

two lovers, which sustained them during most of the rest of the day spent touring Salzburg or visiting friends. At all times and in all places Ben was greeted amicably and it seemed that everyone had their favourite British remembrance, be it a village, a person, a song or a film. Most of the days were easily forgotten, their events merging into a fog of comfortable pleasure. The exception to this was the fourth day after their arrival. They were scheduled to see the Dickens exhibition which had toured throughout Germany to great acclaim and had now come to Austria. What had been expected to be a dry literary review of Britain's most famous Victorian novelist turned out to be an intense emotional experience capturing the very essence of Englishness.

A large building had been partitioned into rooms, each with its own scene. The tour lasted two hours and began in a brightly lit room complete with artificial trees and green grass. Dappled light hit the country lane on which Mr Pickwick and entourage were walking on their way to watch the cricket match at Dingley Dell. Augustus Snodgrass' abortive duel was played out by actors trying to reconcile this gentleman's personal honour with his own fear of dying. In the next room the light was weaker, indicating a day's late afternoon, and the late afternoon of the life of Miss Havisham. Imitation wisteria grew on the creaking iron gates and stone walls of Satis House and one was left to wonder what ancient secrets and stories lay behind the forbidding entrance. Outside Pip was walking with Estella, his intense and enduring love for her being returned with as obdurate a defence as the high stone walls. In another room Nancy was meeting with Oliver Twist's grandfather under Blackfriars Bridge on a dark London night, whilst the noises from a rough tavern could be heard in the background. The country inn where horses and people rested for the night could have belonged to a number of novels. A big bowl of punch was being warmed in front of a log fire, whilst the atmosphere crackled with lively conversation.

Throughout the rooms were men wearing top hats, pure and virtuous ladies, pompous public officials, simple honest peasant folk and eccentrics of all types celebrating the diversity of the human spirit. Snuff boxes were in great use, oil lamps lit and horse drawn carriages the principal means of travel. Of the myriad of characters peopling the exhibition were Mr Jaggers, David Copperfield, Samuel Weller, Trabs boy, Little Nell, the fat boy who was always sleeping, the sick boy who spent his days gazing out of the window and the red-nosed gentleman who was the object of everybody's reprobation. The Cheeryble brothers lived in a quiet London square where it was always sunny, whereas the town containing Oliver Twist's workhouse was cold and dismal. It celebrated a period when Queen Victoria and the empire were young and the biggest problem for most living at the time was to figure out their own social standing.

Ben came away from the exhibition feeling depressed. It had really brought home the cultural legacy of a nation that no longer existed. Would he and his compatriots become absorbed into lives on the European mainland, forgetting what it meant to be British? Would his descendants view the destruction of Britain in the same way as that of Atlantis? A way of life that had become idealised through centuries of dreaming so that it became little more than a myth, which was forever unattainable. He began to see why it was imperative that there was an early return to Britain and his anger with Ken Louis grew even more. He needed to get away from the throng of well-meaning people who invaded every hour of his day and took a solitary walk along the banks of the Salzach River. What in fact was he doing here? In his efforts to build a new life for himself had he forgotten the country of his birth?

He and Elisabetta were eating out the same evening at one of Salzburg's top restaurants. It was a comfortable establishment with red velvet chairs and the inevitable portraits of Mozart, the city's most famous son, hanging on the walls. Elisabetta sat across from Ben and he looked at her. 'Is this the woman with whom I want to spend the rest of my life?' he thought to himself. Things had developed so quickly since his arrival in Salzburg he felt as if he was on a runaway train beyond his control heading straight for the altar and matrimony.

'Your family are very pleasant, they have been so good to me,' said Ben.

'They are your family now,' replied Elisabetta. 'And I am all yours.'

There was a pause as Ben thought of his parents, his brother Michael and his younger sister. They may not have been the happiest collection of people the world had ever seen but they had had their moments and there probably was some affection behind all the posturing. To substitute another family for them was not going to be an easy task, to replace Maureen with Elisabetta would be even more difficult. Elisabetta seemed to sense his uneasiness and the subject of his thoughts.

'You should never forget your own family and you should never forget Maureen. You must continue to love them all. I am not here to take away your memories but to help create new ones filled with happiness.' She took his hand and looked lovingly into his eyes. At that moment he could see she was sincere and felt as if their relationship was becoming so much deeper.

'There are so many thoughts and emotions in my mind, clashing and contradicting each other, I don't appear to know what I want anymore.'

'Have you got over the guilt about your brother?'

'I've been thinking a lot about that in recent days,' admitted Ben, 'and have realised that despite everything I never stopped loving him for one day of my life. It's a strange thing but knowing that helps me deal so much easier with his loss.'

Elisabetta smiled. 'You need time. I'm sorry if things have

been a little overwhelming these last few days.'

The two of them walked hand-in-hand through the streets of Salzburg until they reached home, where they enjoyed a night of intense and sensitive love-making.

Something had definitely changed in their relationship. There was a much greater closeness, which neither of them talked about but they both sensed. Elisabetta's ability to empathise over the loss of his family and Maureen made it so much easier for Ben to express his feelings and bring out into the open emotions that had been suppressed for so long. The sex had always been good with Elisabetta but now they could connect intellectually with such sensitivity he began to think that perhaps she was everything required in a woman. He realised that the numerous women whose bodies had provided him with physical gratification since the attack had only provided a short-term dulling of his emotional pain and he had been unhappy during that period. Those relationships were so unlike the one he had enjoyed with Maureen they had allowed him to put off thinking about her. Now that once again he was experiencing tender feelings for a woman, the times he had spent with his former fiancée came flooding back to mind. Being able to talk about them, however, meant they were at least bearable and he could begin to make sense of them.

Now that this change had taken place, the actions of Elisabetta's family did not seem so loaded with meaning. He was able to enjoy their company more freely without fear of how his words or actions would be interpreted. The letting down of the guard also resulted in him appreciating them so much more. Of her two older brothers, Eberhard was the talkative one whereas Andreas was quieter and the one to whom Ben found it easiest to relate.

After one week it was time for Ben to fly back to France. He was sorry to leave Elisabetta and her family in Salzburg and it would be three weeks before the two of them would meet up again. He would miss her very much, especially as he had only recently recognised what he possessed in her. He was also worried that without a woman to keep him company in Paris he might slip back into his old ways. Like a junkie attempting to give up drugs it would require a superhuman effort to remain clean and stay away from places of temptation. For the first time since the attack, however, he had found a relationship with which he was happy. He recognised just how valuable this was and did not intend to throw it away needlessly.

Chapter 6

'WHEN YOU CONSIDER THE LAWS OF probability, the chances of meeting up with you, my former wife, are extremely remote.'

Robert was finally giving voice to a question that had perturbed him more and more in recent weeks. Was he believing what he wanted to believe or was there some evidence behind it? Numerically speaking their confluence was about as likely as winning the old National Lottery.

'When one considers the numbers, you are exactly right,' said Mwamba smiling. 'In fact it is so statistically unlikely it can be dismissed as a possibility.'

'Why don't you dismiss it then?' asked Robert.

'Because my darling, our meeting was not a chance encounter, it was meant to be and planned by a higher authority. When you look at it from that perspective you begin to see that it was a virtual certainty.'

'Yes, I can see that. Do you think God plans everything in our lives?'

'I think he plans some things,' replied Mwamba, thinking about the question. 'In my opinion he plans opportunities for us, but he always gives us a choice. We are free to ignore the opportunities.'

'It seems to me that we will have to make some important choices fairly soon,' said Robert in a tone of voice that indicated he did not really relish this prospect.

It had been two weeks since Mwamba had moved in with

Robert and for him it had been the happiest two weeks of his life. When people had spoken, written or sung of love in his many years on earth he felt as if he knew what they were talking about, but now realised his knowledge had been only superficial. Like a sailor who thought he knew about icebergs from seeing them floating on the surface of the sea, he didn't realise there were deeper layers waiting to be discovered when one came into contact with them. The two of them were descending further and further and it appeared as if this love was unfathomable. They were so bound up with each other, exploring the spiritual, emotional and physical side of their relationship, that the outside world did not seem to matter much. But of course the outside world did go on and was marshalling its forces for one last stand against their union.

It was only a matter of time before Robert would have to leave KCMC, and he realised as much himself. He had lost all authority within the department and his patient care initiative lay in tatters. Mwamba moving in with him had been the justification for which many had been looking to ignore their new duties. A perceived moral weakness in their boss had emboldened a more open defiance. Whilst this did not bother him too much from a personal point of view it was clearly not a sustainable position and in the long run it would be the patients who would suffer. Mwamba had been ostracised by her fellow students and had failed the medical examinations. Robert knew only too well the reason but did not even want to question the marking procedure as it would lead to claims of favouritism and wouldn't get them anywhere. Anna was scheming with priests, lawyers and anyone else who had the remotest chance of helping to stop their divorce going through, but was not having a lot of luck. It would have been so much easier for her if there were children involved or property that Robert cared about. It was expected that Mwamba's family in Zambia would be contacted at some stage to bring pressure to bear but so far that hadn't transpired.

Tallis had recovered well since coming to KCMC. His bandages had been removed and he was able to walk, albeit fairly slowly. Not only had his physical condition improved but a much more positive attitude had also developed, due in main part to the daily discussions held with Robert. The doctor's thoughts and advice provided the raw material to better see personal failings and construct the hope of a better future. Stuck in bed with only your own company almost forced reflection about one's life: there was just no way you could get away from yourself. For Robert this patient had become his only friend at the hospital, someone with whom he could talk freely and who was not part of the conspiratorial atmosphere which pervaded the rest of his working hours. He was due to be discharged from hospital soon and that caused a dilemma for his daily visitor: whether or not to ask him to stay at his place. Much as he liked Tallis, perhaps three was a crowd and it could disrupt the harmonious and magical atmosphere created with Mwamba. If he was entirely honest with himself there were also probably some feelings of jealousy at leaving the two of them at home all day whilst he went to work in the hospital. It was a personal weakness to have such unjustifiable fears and he hated to have them but could not deny their existence. Still he felt some responsibility for Tallis' welfare and did not want to see the young man end up in the kind of trouble which he seemed to have a talent for attracting. It would be some time before he had properly planned his exit strategy from Tanzania and a lot could happen in that period.

From their discussions Robert was now familiar with most of his compatriot's history: how he had been working in Spain and had tried to return to Britain after the attack, only to be beaten up by some lunatic on the beach at Calais. He had then flown to Georgia, USA, for basic military training before travelling to Afghanistan, India and Kenya or Sudan (it had never really been clear what side of the border he had been during the latter adventure). All he remembered about the incident which had brought him to KCMC was that he was sitting in a small roughly built wooden building having something to eat when there was a loud bang and everything went black. As in Afghanistan he had taken part in no real fighting and just spent most days battling boredom. The closest he came to pointing a gun was when assigned to guard duty. Why did they call it fighting? They should call it hanging around doing nothing waiting for something bad to happen, that would be a far more accurate description of what actually happened. He would have had more shooting practice if he had gone to Africa on a hunting safari.

Tallis was definitely fed up with the military, confiding in Robert that the training in Georgia had basically involved a lot of shouting, running around and not much else. At night each new recruit would try to outdo the others with tales of bravado and displays of intolerance. Would soldiers become obsolete in the years to come? Unmanned aircraft were now a reality and it didn't take a huge stretch of the imagination to envisage robot warriors as in *Star Wars* coming soon. The defence forces of the future would sit in rooms behind computer screens and its heroes would be overweight couch potatoes who had honed their skills through years of twiddling knobs on their PlayStations. Tallis for one would not mourn the demise of the proud cock strutting around with chest puffed out, who was only concerned with trying to improve his position in the pecking order.

One incident from the American part of the adventure had stuck in his mind and he had related the story to Robert. The camp had been situated just outside a small town where two hundred and fifty years previously Elias Souter had been an upstanding member of the community, running one of the village stores. One day he had fallen into an argument with two tax collectors sent by the British colonial authorities and felt honour-bound to seek retribution. This pair were caught, had their feet and hands tied with rope and were stripped of all clothing whilst they awaited their punishment. Elias Souter was a methodical man, who had already prepared a pit full of chicken feathers and was carefully stirring a vat of hot tar until it had reached the correct temperature. He did not intend to kill them but the tar had to be hot enough to teach them a severe lesson. To the astonishment of all who were watching what was going on, one of the gentlemen about to gain a new coat of feathers had the temerity to protest at his treatment and went on to knock the container of boiling tar all over the village storekeeper. Elias Souter screamed in pain as the black liquid flowed over his skin causing it to erupt in boils. The old man eventually succumbed to his injuries and died within two days but not before his friends had done something for him. Trying to decide what would be the best way to cheer him up they carried his bed outside so that he could watch the two tax collectors being hung by the neck from the large oak tree in his back garden. On Souter Day, the townspeople held a big feast to which the men from the military training camp were invited. All regretted the passing of Mr Souter but cheered his friends on for being so kind.

'What did you find strange about that?' asked Robert.

'Here is this terrible act of violence against a fellow human being, yet two hundred and fifty years later everybody treats it like a joke and even respects those involved.'

'I can remember when I was a choirboy,' Robert recalled. 'In the Abbey where I sang was a skull preserved in a glass case. It had a hole in it made by the end of a spear. The unfortunate victim, whose name I never bothered to read, was killed in some battle in the thirteenth century. I used to think as I walked past it that nobody cared or even knew what he had been fighting for any more, and would be hard pressed to remember the name of the battle. At some point in time, however, nothing in the world would have mattered more to that soldier than the cause for which he gave his life.'

Robert was in a mood for reflection and continued: 'The passage of time does strange things, sometimes it lessens or even erases a problem: at other times the problem becomes worse. If only we could pinpoint what causes the increase or decrease we would be on the way to making the world a better place.'

It was now March and the long rains had already started. A freshness filled the air after the hot and dry weather, and dust had coagulated to form mud. There was an excitement about a heavy downpour, which Robert still enjoyed. From the small verandah of the flat he sat riveted by the vertical rain, which bounced off the metal roofs and ran in small rivers down the roads creating the occasional lake. Something about the uncontrollable force of nature and its ability to impinge on people's well ordered lives produced a thrill. Tallis sat on a chair in the ward, unaware of the darkness and slight wind outside that signalled another storm was on its way. He was itching to leave the hospital and the impending arrival of that day had raised his spirits. The final payment for his mercenary duties had also reached his bank account, providing the freedom to do what he wanted after being discharged.

'Why are you so happy?' asked Robert on entering the ward.

'Because I've finally decided what I'm going to do when I leave this hospital,' replied Tallis. 'I'm off to Spain.'

'When?'

'As soon as I'm out of this place. I've been busy sending out emails and I can stay with Pedro and look for a job on the Costa del Sol.'

'That's great,' said Robert.

He was experiencing a peculiar mixture of emotions: he was pleased for his friend, though sad about the company he would lose. He felt ashamed at his reluctance to offer Tallis accommodation and the unfounded suspicions that had been harboured. Most of all though he felt envy that someone else was moving on with their life, whilst his was just stagnating. Tallis observed the look of disappointment that the doctor was trying hard to cover up, then said:

'I want to thank you for everything you've done, you've given some meaning again to my life through our daily chats.'

'I'm pleased I was able to help you,' replied Robert, smiling weakly.

'What's the matter, Robert? Is there anything I can do to help you?'

'Nothing really, I just feel a little envious of you starting a new chapter in your life and wish I could do likewise.'

This was no good, he needed to be much more positive: 'Things will sort themselves out, it'll just take a little time to get myself out of the hole I've dug for myself here.'

'One thing you've taught me is that things do get better, but not on their own. You have to decide how you'll make them better.'

'You're sounding like me now, just who is the patient here?'

Chapter 7

ROBERT'S HEART WAS not in his job that day and he felt a depression as he went about his duties. Even thinking of Mwamba did not improve the situation, in fact it made it worse. A new chapter of emotions and possibilities had been opened as a result of the relationship with her, but the current lifestyle hadn't kept pace, creating an undeniable tension. The situation could only be resolved by moving away from Moshi, but the divorce was dragging and would not be granted in a hurry, meanwhile he had no other job to go to.

'Everything is arranged!' said Tallis with a triumphant smile on his face as Robert entered the ward for his regular conversation.

'What do you mean, everything is arranged?' replied Robert with a quizzical look.

'I mean everything is arranged,' repeated Tallis with an even broader smile than the first time.

'Perhaps you should explain to me just what you've arranged.'

'I've arranged your future.'

'That's nice, do I get a say in this?'

'Afraid not my friend, the plans have already been made and can't be changed.'

'I think it's about time, Tallis, that you started speaking the same language as me and tell me just what you're up to.'

Tallis was tempted to keep the doctor waiting a bit longer, but could hardly contain his scheme for a minute longer.

'Next Tuesday you, me and Mwamba will board a plane from

Kilimanjaro International Airport bound for Amsterdam, from there we'll get an onward connection to Malaga, Spain.'

'What are we going to do in Spain?'

'We're going to live there. I'll arrange accommodation for all of us, whilst you look for a job as a doctor. I'm assured that there are plenty of opportunities for a man of your talents.'

'Are you serious?'

'Never been more serious about anything in my life.'

Robert took a deep breath and looked at the former mercenary lying in bed grinning from ear to ear. There had certainly been a wondrous transformation in this young man in the short time he had been at the hospital, and indeed he felt privileged to have been a part of it. His offer was more than generous and there was certainly something tempting about leaving all the rubbish he had to put up with here. For a fleeting moment he almost agreed then a whole stream of reasons as to why it would be impossible for him to leave came flooding into his mind. There was the divorce, his patients that he couldn't leave at a moment's notice, his car, his house, his belongings, he had been in Tanzania for over twenty years. Next week was only five days away ... no, it would be impossible for him to join Tallis.

'It's very kind of you Tallis, but I'm afraid ...'

'Stop right there,' interjected Tallis, 'You're just about to give me a whole list of reasons as to why you won't be able to make it.'

'Yes, I think that's exactly what I was about to do,' admitted Robert.

'Well I'm not interested in listening to them. You told me once that we had to decide what we wanted in life and grab those opportunities with both hands. You're unhappy here and want to build a new life somewhere else with Mwamba. I'm offering you the chance to achieve this, don't tell me you're scared of this opportunity.'

Robert was touched by Tallis' words and began to wonder if he was actually practising what he had preached. No, he also advocated responsibility, and running away in the middle of the night would be to neglect certain obligations.

'I promise you I will think very carefully about what you've suggested,' he said to Tallis, looking him in the eye to signal his serious intent.

Robert was pacing the small living room of his flat, then suddenly stopped to address Mwamba.

'Do you know what infuriates me the most about you?'

'Go on, tell me.'

'Your inability to express a simple opinion when I ask you a question. I've promised Tallis that I would give serious consideration to his proposal but when I try to have a discussion with you about it, you can't say whether or not you think it a good idea.'

'I want you to tell me what *you* think.'

'I don't know.'

'Well in that case I don't know either.'

'Let's just forget the whole thing.'

'OK.'

Robert resumed his walk of frustration, whilst Mwamba returned calmly to reading a book, apparently oblivious to his inner turmoil. At times she could be exasperating.

'We need to consider what we both want out of life,' stated Robert, trying a different tack.

'I agree. Tell me what you want.'

'I want to be with you, I want to be in a place where we can both live happily. I want to start a new life with you.'

'Now that you are clearer about what you want, what do you think is the right decision to make?'

'We should leave Tanzania with Tallis.' Robert could hardly

believe he was uttering those words.

'Fine, let's start making the arrangements.'

'Do you think it's the right decision?'

'What I think, my darling, is that you should have a bit more confidence in your own judgement.'

'But it affects you as well, are you happy with it?'

Mwamba smiled at Robert: 'I'm very happy with it.'

It was Saturday morning and Robert and Mwamba were on their way to KCMC to visit Tallis. Robert had felt a huge relief at having made the decision and was now even looking forward to leaving.

'We've decided to come with you on Tuesday,' said Robert.

'I knew she'd talk you into it,' replied Tallis, nodding in the direction of Mwamba.

'There are just a few arrangements that need to be made,' continued Robert, trying to be businesslike about the journey. 'I've noticed that you aren't due to check out of here until the Wednesday, so what do you propose to do the day before?'

Tallis pointed to his bed. 'You see these sheets. I tie them together then around the bedpost, climb out of the window, then shimmy down the wall. In the meantime you two are outside with a change of clothes and a mattress on the ground.'

'It's like an escape from prison,' laughed Mwamba. 'How exciting.'

'Will the pair of you stop it,' said Robert, irritated at the levity with which they were treating this momentous occasion.

'Whenever I go on a trip, there are three things I check on,' said Tallis: 'Tickets, passport, money. I have the money and tickets, you just come with your passports on Tuesday and we'll be on our way.'

There were more details that Robert wished to discuss but he could see that now was not the time or place. He allowed Tallis to paint the picture of what life would be like in Spain, until he became quite carried away with what the future had in store for him and Mwamba.

Chapter 8

ROBERT DID NOT want to feel guilty but could hardly help it. Leaving Anna behind, without even the benefit of living in the same town should a need arise, was not an action of which he felt very proud. He had long since reconciled himself to the fact that he no longer loved her and probably never had, but still felt bad at abandoning her completely. She had never done him any real harm and their disastrous marriage was as much his fault as hers: he showed great weakness and dishonesty in telling himself it would somehow work. Her greatest crime was in believing that lie, a lie that they loved each other. It wasn't fair to punish her too severely for that. He needed to see her before he left, to tell her that he was sorry, that he attached no blame to her for what had happened. At the same time it was imperative that no indication be given of the 'escape', as Mwamba had started to call it, that would shortly take place. It would be only too easy to for somebody to put a spanner in the works and ruin it for them all.

On Monday evening, just before the intended departure, Robert drove into the large driveway he had entered so many times in the past. There was no feeling of nostalgia, however: he had never really belonged or enjoyed himself here. It was surprising to observe just how much the garden had changed in the short time since he had taken up residence in Moshi town. The former dry and dusty grounds now had grass growing and there was a cooler, fresher, greener feel about the place. A light was on in the living room and he entered from the verandah without knocking. Anna was sitting on the sofa watching some mindless South African soap opera. She did not register any surprise on seeing him, but merely carried on with her viewing.

'Can I get myself a beer from the fridge?' asked Robert.

'It's your house,' came the reply.

Robert sat in silence studying his golden drink with the foaming white head. In some ways it resembled the shape of Kilimanjaro itself. As the froth slowly subsided he thought even this was analogous to the slow recession of the glaciers that had been taking place ever since he arrived in Tanzania. The soap opera finished, Robert picked up the remote control and switched off the television.

'I am very sorry at the way things have worked out, Anna. I realise that a lot of it was my fault but I can't change what occurred in the past.'

'What rubbish are you talking now?' She looked at him angrily straight in the face.

'I don't expect you to agree with our divorce. I just want you to know that I have no bad feelings towards you.'

'What is it you are saying?'

'I am saying,' continued Robert slowly, choosing his words with great care, 'I am saying that suppose something happened to me, I want you to know that I am sorry for how you have been treated and that I have no bitterness in my heart towards you. If I suddenly wasn't around, all my possessions in Tanzania belong to you.'

'Do you think I want your things?' said Anna, raising her right cheek in disgust.

'I think I have said all I wanted to say,' said Robert, raising himself out of the chair.

'Are you OK, my husband? You seem confused, I think I need to pray for you tonight.'

'Goodbye, Anna,' and with a heavy heart he walked to his car and drove back into Moshi where an understanding Mwamba was waiting for him.

It was no problem for Tallis to discharge himself from KCMC a day early. It seemed that everybody was happy to see him go, although the hospital had made a tidy sum of money by charging his organisation exorbitant medical fees. It was late afternoon and he and Mwamba were waiting for Robert to return from work. Two large suitcases had been packed containing all the indispensable items the doctor possessed. It was fortunate that much of the accumulated detritus of the many years he had spent in Tanzania was still at the old house. Not only did it make packing simpler, it would be easier to give them to Anna. At five o'clock the doctor returned and sat down with the two of them. The feeling of sadness at leaving this country, which had been so much a part of him, overwhelmed the excitement at starting a new life elsewhere, and however hard he tried he could not rid himself of it.

'I find empty houses so depressing, we can't stay here until it is time to leave,' said Mwamba.

'I agree, let's go out somewhere to eat,' added Tallis, trying to sound cheerful as he seemed to sense the turmoil his friend was going through.

'The plane flies at nine so we need to leave Moshi by seven, it's about a half-hour drive to the airport,' said Mwamba. 'Come on, let's go and put the suitcases in the car now, then we can go straight there afterwards.'

Robert drove the two kilometres to a restaurant just out of town called the "Golden Flower". Tables were set out in a garden filled with banana trees and brightly coloured bushes, where the three of them sat and ordered their food. Whilst Mwamba and Tallis tried to make optimistic, inconsequential conversation, Robert was remembering a time when he had first brought Anna here. He remembered the shy young lady who could hardly speak English and how he had had to encourage her to utter a few words. She was unable to understand the menu and he had ordered for her a dish which she hadn't liked. Probably because conversation was so difficult the relationship had progressed more quickly than was prudent to a physical one and then he felt obliged to marry her. It was he who was responsible for causing her so much unhappiness: had he allowed her to marry an ordinary Tanzanian no doubt her life would have been so much more satisfying. What kind of life would she have when he had gone? At least it would be easier for her to forget about him, knowing he was in a different country.

Kilimanjaro International Airport somehow looked different when you knew you were probably seeing it for the last time. There was nothing to be admired in its design: it was straight out of the east European architect's manual, with large amounts of concrete and steel enclosing huge cavernous spaces, put together with little regard to aesthetics. What was noticeable were the little things: the slow friendly pace of being checked in, being asked by a customs official whether you were taking animal skins out of the country, the entirely predictable curios on sale which hadn't changed in generations. All of this and more Robert observed as he made his way to the departure lounge. The plane taxied to a stop and they were called through for boarding. At the gate a poster of Kilimanjaro hung on the wall and he thought back to the time when he had first come to Tanzania and witnessed it with his own eyes. It was only when the plane was airborne that he began to think of Spain and what awaited him there.

Chapter 9

BEN SAT AT the small airport in Salzburg and waited to be called for the plane that would fly to Paris. He had enjoyed taking his time on the outward journey with Elisabetta but now he was alone the only priority was to return as speedily as possible and consequently he had opted for the quickest mode of travel. Besides, it was time to return to work: the promotion of the company's products was a highly personal knack and could not be left in the hands of junior staff for too long. Sipping a cappuccino from a paper cup and observing that the quiet airport was not blessed with an abundance of shops and other means of entertainment to pass the time, it seemed like an opportune moment to take out the laptop and check on recent emails. There was one from Frank Oates, which was temporarily passed over as it probably didn't contain anything more newsworthy than a notice of the next meeting of the British Refugee Society or some invective aimed at a group that had offended him. He was struck by a message from the *Daily Telegraph*, thanking him for his submission and stating that it had been published two days previously. Ben had never expected this recognition and was wondering whether it was worth his while to walk to the kiosk to see if they had retained an old copy of this newspaper. Weighing up that it was probably not worth the effort he returned to the message from Frank Oates to see what the old windbag was saying this time.

Dear Ben,

Heard you were out of town, otherwise would have dropped round at your place. Lot of anger at the society over a letter written in the "Daily Telegraph" purporting to be from a Benedict Collins. Told the boys at the club I would just check a few details before everybody starts getting hot under the collar. Couldn't believe you would have written it. Was somebody using your name or is there another Benedict Collins out there somewhere? Reply soon so we can sort this out before it is blown up out of all proportion.

Best Wishes,

Frank

Ben emailed back immediately to confirm that he was indeed the one who had written the letter and couldn't understand what all the fuss was about. Didn't they once plan to have a pint at Frank's local by the village green when the day of returning came? Why all the furore over a point of view that would bring that day closer? Ben sat back in his chair and wondered what awaited him in Paris.

Although he felt as if he might be returning to a storm, the arrival at Charles de Gaulle airport had gone smoothly enough. He had already resolved not to deny anything but also not to be provocative. With any luck he would be able to sit this turbulence out and it would all blow over in a few days.

Sitting in his apartment that evening he realised just how empty his life was without Elisabetta. During the ten days they had travelled across Europe and stayed in Salzburg they had been virtually inseparable. Even when she wasn't around, the house had echoed to the sounds of her parents, brothers and the many visitors who came. His flat now felt quiet and empty and he experienced a bored restlessness. The change of environment also scared him: would he be able to while away the evenings in this location until Elisabetta's return or would he slip back into the old haunts and girlfriends? Cold turkey was not going to be an easy option but he prayed for the strength of character to carry it through. What drove people into situations that made them unhappy? Being a junkie, alcoholic or sex addict was not a pleasurable existence and everybody knew it. Still, unseen forces propelled one forward along the road to ruin as each person struggled against the irresistible wave. Ben thought back to the Dickens exhibition and began to appreciate that there could have been good reasons behind the social conventions that prevented women baring all on a first date. He imagined Joe Gargery, Pip's once much admired brother-in-law, sitting in front of the blacksmith's forge on a cold wintry evening with just a pipe to keep him company. What a contentment and inner peace he must have possessed.

Still, a strategy for the evenings was needed and a pipe was hardly sufficient. Something to keep him occupied besides the television with which he easily became bored. After the email he wanted to give any acquaintances from the British Refugee Society a wide berth. Company that would not lead to romantic or sexual entanglement, kept him busy and only resulted in a modest amount of alcohol being drunk was what was required. It was not an easy task, even joining the local church choir didn't exactly fit the bill. Which woman could he least imagine having a fling with? The straight-haired, sullen-faced Angela from Amsterdam disliked him with a passion, as would any member of her entourage. Did he really want to spend miserable evenings sitting cross-legged on her living room floor listening to how bad the British were? There was no reason to punish himself, the television and a bottle of wine would have to suffice for tonight until a better plan came up.

Although Ben had tried to keep a low profile since returning to Paris, he realised it was only a matter of time before he bumped into Frank Oates. Sure enough, after three days the doorbell rang at six p.m. and the security camera showed the impatient face of the chairman of the British Refugee Society waiting to be let in. There was little point in trying to ignore him: he would only come back later, and besides Ben felt he had done nothing of which to be ashamed.

'Caused a bit of a rumpus you did, old boy,' said Frank, studying his generously poured glass of malt whisky, which had just been handed to him.

'I never realised it would cause such a sensation,' replied Ben.

'Course you didn't, I know you didn't upset everybody on purpose. We are all British, all on the same side.' Ben smiled wanly, he knew Frank had come to try and gloss over the whole incident. He was just waiting to see what colour paint he would use.

'We're all frustrated, we all want to return, but let's not forget what made our nation great.'

'What's that, Frank?'

'Principles, justice, standing up for what is right, heritage. We are not going to abandon these and be part of some European fudge which gives us back our land and takes away our identity.'

'What are you trying to say?'

'Gibraltar,' he thumped a hand on the table. 'We must not abandon Gibraltar.'

'Have you ever been to Gibraltar, Frank?'

'No, why?'

'Neither have I. If the Gibraltarians want a piece of Britain they're welcome to it when recolonisation takes place. We can give them an area ten times the size of Gibraltar, but to delay our return to Britain just seems crazy to me.'

'I haven't come here to argue and of course you're entitled to your opinion. The thing is, Ben, we must present a united front. Divide and rule, that's the way the bureaucrats want to handle us.'

'You talk about principles, surely one of the principles our country adhered to was free speech, the right to speak one's mind.'

'Ordinarily yes, but these are extraordinary times, you're just making things difficult for us if you start making controversial pronouncements.'

'Difficult for whom?'

'Difficult for the British Refugee Society. Governments begin to think we don't represent your views.'

'Surely another quality that made Britain great was democracy. Has anyone ever elected you to your office, has anyone ever consulted me on what kind of policies should be adopted? How can your organisation even remotely be claiming to represent my views, much less Ken Louis?'

'I'm just a volunteer, pushed into a chair because nobody else wanted it; there are moves afoot however to make the society more organised, with Ken Louis as its leader.'

'You do what you want, Frank, but don't think you're speaking for me.'

'In the meantime, Ben, if you could tone down any criticisms you may have it would be greatly appreciated.'

'I have no desire to enter politics, but I'm also not going to be silenced by a man like Ken Louis, especially if he's planning to delay my return to Britain.'

Frank got up out of his seat and smiled at Ben. 'We're all working to the same end, but it's best to leave the politics to the politicians.'

With those words he drained the remainder of the whisky and went towards the door.

The sound of the door banging after him drew attention

to the silence that occupied the living room after he left. Like an exclamation mark after a declamatory statement it was best followed by a moment of reflection. Ken Louis heading the British Refugee Society? The idea seemed crazy to Ben: the man was only seeking to promote himself. If he could see that so clearly why couldn't others? Let those fools do what they wanted: no government would take them seriously. The whole situation in fact was depressing: nothing looked like being resolved in a hurry and the day of return kept being pushed further and further into the future.

Pouring himself an equal measure of whisky to that consumed by Frank Oates, Ben turned his mind to happier items like his relationship with Elisabetta. He had not really imagined their future together on British soil. What would they do and what kind of life would they lead? He knew the ideal place, just outside Peterborough, where it would be possible to run a country pub. A tiny village with a brook running through its centre, composed of stone buildings and leafy lanes. Would the genteel world he imagined suit Elisabetta? Would they be happy together? He picked up the whisky bottle and TV remote control. It was to be another night in. At least for the moment he trusted they would be happy.

Chapter 10

BEN AND ELISABETTA were in daily contact both by phone and email. Short messages of love, pledges of affection and snippets of news flew back and forth between Paris and Salzburg and brightened up both their lives. One email, however, produced a feeling of mild annoyance. A petition was forwarded through Elisabetta, which had clearly started with Angela. The protest was at the new rules being brought into French schools. Not only were headscarves banned, students would not be allowed to cover their legs during PE lessons. Christian worship was compulsory for all and no provision for halal meat was to be made at any food outlet associated with a school. No, he definitely did not want to become involved in promoting the interests of the Muslim community, and felt irritated that Elisabetta had become involved in this. He immediately emailed Angela, telling her to keep him and Elisabetta out of her problems.

The old film had been surprisingly good, though the amount of whisky he had got through was alarming. He thought again about the petition. Maybe some of the new regulations were a bit extreme and so what if Elisabetta wished to add her name to the list of protestors. He began to regret his hasty action: the best course of action would have been just to ignore it. No doubt he was in store for a furiously irate email from Angela.

The following morning a brown envelope embossed with the logo of the UN British Affairs Department arrived through the post. It contained papers saying that his British citizenship had been confirmed and that at some stage in the future he would be granted a piece of land. Where this was located, how big it would be and when it would happen were questions which remained unanswered. He was also requested to visit their department and pick up one of the new identity cards, complete with biometric information and who knows what other secret encoded messages.

To say this package came as a complete surprise would be an accurate way to describe how Ben felt. The media had not indicated that identity cards were being given out, neither had he heard of any of his compatriots receiving one. It was therefore with a feeling of curiosity that he made his way to the same large building as he had done some months before for initial registration. He was directed to room 502, which oddly turned out to be somebody's office. Would all the new identity cards be issued from this twelve feet by ten feet rectangular enclosure by one man sitting behind a desk? Something didn't quite add up about the situation.

'Mr Collins, please have a seat,' said the man with a Canadian accent and white hair whose nameplate read "Dr Bolden".

'Mr Collins, I am pleased to give you your new identity card. If you would be so kind as to sign the paper acknowledging receipt, that would be most helpful.' Dr Bolden carefully took the signed piece of paper and placed it in a drawer of his filing cabinet before locking it.

'Will that be all?' said Ben, admiring his identity card and altering its angle to the light to gain a complete view of the holographic image of himself.

'Not quite, Mr Collins,' said the gentleman who must have been in his fifties and now leant back in his chair to study him intently. 'I have been requested to ask you what your feelings are about returning to Britain.'

'I want to return as quickly as possible,' replied Ben.

'At any cost?' said Dr Bolden, raising his eyebrows.

'I can't think what would cause me to delay.'

The man from the UN smiled. 'It is no accident that you have been called in. We are aware of your views as published in the "*Daily Telegraph*", and think you are a man we can work with.'

'I'm not sure I understand.'

'Mr Collins, the three men who made it over to Britain will be released from quarantine very soon. I'm not saying that British land is safe to inhabit, but as time goes on it appears this is the case. Moreover it is becoming more and more difficult to enforce the blockade, not to mention the expense.'

Ben began to become more interested in what was being said.

'What I am saying to you is entirely confidential, if you repeat it I will deny it. A recolonisation of Britain could be on the cards sooner than anticipated, but it definitely won't happen until the Gibraltar situation is resolved. Are you prepared, as a British citizen, to give up any claim to land outside the immediate borders of the British Isles?'

'If that's the only stumbling block to returning to Britain, of course I would.'

'What are your feelings towards Ken Louis?'

'I loathe him with a passion.'

'Good, so do I. He will take over the British Refugee Society, but don't take any orders from him.'

'What do I have to do?'

'Just wait for further instructions if you want to see your homeland again.'

There was one more question that was bothering Ben. 'Why me? I'm no politician, not even a leader.'

'Without wishing to appear rude, Mr Collins, we don't have a great choice. Once you eliminate the troublemakers and those who don't care one way or the other, you'd be surprised how few we have left.'

Ben thanked Dr Bolden and walked towards the door. 'Oh, and one other thing,' said the man behind the desk. 'Don't go showing that identity card to anyone, they're not due out for another three months.'

When Ben reached home he carefully put the identity card and all his papers into the safe. Checking the laptop for emails, he found the usual daily one from Elisabetta and just as predictably one from Angela of Amsterdam. He wondered what expletives she would call on in her message of vitriol. 'Scum of the earth', 'British racist pig', 'Muslim babykiller' could well be among them. If he opened her message first he would at least be returned to a good mood by Elisabetta's assurances of everlasting love. He moved the hand with outstretched first finger up the computer screen until Angela's name was darkened then selected her with a single click of the mouse. A simple one-line invitation to Elisabetta's and Angela's house was all it contained. No condemnation or bad language, she had even addressed the message 'Dear Ben' and ended it 'Best Wishes, Angela'. The email contained no indication what it was about, merely stating the date, time and location. Ben thought that today was a day full of surprises.

It had been almost one week since Ben had ventured outside at night. He did not trust himself in certain situations and with certain people but felt the onset of cabin fever. He decided that a night out on his own at a quiet restaurant would be perfectly in order and probably beneficial. As he sat at the Taj Mahal restaurant he was reminded of the solitary meal he had eaten in Paris two days after the attack. Thoughts inevitably turned to Nicole, the attractive waitress who had started his descent into debauchery. Replaying the evening in his mind, he realised for the first time how strange it was that she should share her body with him so easily. She could have picked up just about any man and initially had shown no interest in him, only changing her behaviour when discovering his nationality. *She* had acted strangely? What about himself? Only a matter of hours after learning of the death of his fiancée he was in the arms of another woman. It was good to be reminded of how quickly he had gone down the slippery path to infidelity, although it was simultaneously remarkably scary. At least he would be on his guard this time. Not that there was much in the way of temptation at the Taj Mahal. In keeping with the majority of Indian restaurants, the attendants were exclusively male and the business run by members of an extended family. They kept their women well and truly under lock and key.

After the meal he drove home. It was a cold and damp December evening, the bright yellow street lamps reflecting diffusely from the small amount of moisture that had collected on the roads. It was not an evening where one would choose to drive for pleasure but Ben decided to take the long way home and out of interest drove along a road renowned for its collection of prostitutes. Despite the cold they had plenty of midriff and leg on show and seemed to have no protection against the damp conditions. He wanted to see what kind of women were plying their trade at that time, though even in his more promiscuous moments he had balked at the depravity of picking an unknown woman from the street and paying her money for sex. His heart was pounding, what was he doing here? What would happen if he were arrested for kerb-crawling? He increased the speed of the car then slowed down again on noticing a particularly tall attractive woman. She walked to the road in an attempt to flag his car down. Ben then pressed the accelerator pedal hard and did not look in her direction in order to make good his escape. He was afraid of her but more afraid of himself and what he was capable of doing.

Chapter 11

THE THREE MEN in a boat were duly released from quarantine, as predicted by Dr Bolden. They were immediately lauded by the British Refugee Society and paraded around with Ken Louis at every possible opportunity, who urged all patriotic Britons to defy any law that prevented them returning to their homeland. An invitation to attend the next meeting of the British Refugee Society, where these men would talk about their experiences, appeared on Ben's laptop. For a number of reasons, but principally the sight of Ken Louis embracing this trio, he decided not to attend. The hypocrisy was sickening: three men who broke the law to go to Britain were being applauded, whilst it was frowned on for him to express an opinion that might hasten the day of return. He would rather go and meet Angela. Yes, he could hardly believe he was admitting it to himself, but he would rather go and meet Angela.

Ben sat in the living room of Elisabetta's house, a room he had sat in so many times before but never under these circumstances. There was no Elisabetta, just her Dutch housemate. Two men were sitting on a sofa and on the other side of the room two women were sitting on the floor with a little girl who was not quite two. She clung nervously to one of the women, who was obviously her mother, and fixed Ben with an unwavering stare which he found unnerving. Angela sat on the floor a short distance from the two women, which allowed Ben the use of the remaining chair, much to his relief. She introduced them as two Muslim families living in Paris, whilst Ben was introduced as a British citizen. One of the men sitting on the sofa was the first to speak up.

'I am so sorry about what happened to your country. I lost a cousin and his family who were living in Leicester. Our pain was very great when the attack happened, so I am sure we share something in common.'

Ben felt uncomfortable at this opening remark but tried not to show it, merely nodding his acknowledgement of what had been said. Angela opened up the discussion with the main item of business.

'We are here today to decide what to do about a group of youths who have been terrorising the apartment block where you live. Sahil, perhaps you would like to start off by telling us exactly what is the problem.'

The other man on the sofa cleared his throat and with an effort tried to talk slowly and rationally about the situation.

'Our family was chased away from our home. The neighbours at best ignored us and at worst insulted us, the final straw came when a cloth soaked with petrol was pushed through our letterbox and set alight.' The man paused as he remembered the horror of that moment. 'With the help of your organisation a group of families got together and moved into our own apartment block. At first everything there was fine and at least we were living amongst friends and didn't feel so exposed. Recently, however, a group of about twenty young men has been visiting our area on a regular basis. They throw stones at windows, let down car tyres and spray offensive graffiti on the walls.'

'Have there been any incidents of physical violence?' asked Angela.

One of the women spoke up: 'Two days ago they fired on my son with a catapult and I dare not let my daughters out of the house.'

'What do the police say?'

'They say there is nothing they can do. As soon as they show up the young men disappear.'

'Have you considered a private security firm?'

'It would be far too expensive, besides they would just guard a building, they wouldn't be able to protect us as we go about our normal lives.'

There was a pause then Angela turned to Ben. 'What would you recommend, Mr Collins?'

'I really don't know,' said Ben, turning red and feeling embarrassed by his inability to say anything meaningful. 'I thought we were going to discuss the new school rules introduced by the government.'

The woman who had just spoken suddenly lashed out at him: 'My children haven't even been to school for six months. It is impossible for them to go without being insulted or bullied.'

Ben felt even more uncomfortable and was regretting having come to this meeting at all. He hadn't wanted to do or say anything, but observer status was becoming increasingly difficult to maintain. How he wished he could get out of his chair and leave the room, but that would almost be an admission that he was running scared of what they had to say.

'I'll come round to your flats and see what can be done,' he said.

'That's settled, then,' said Angela with a smile, the first smile Ben had ever seen her with. 'Mr Collins will investigate the matter and we will discuss it at a later date pending his report.'

The man with the relatives in Leicester rose to his feet and walked over to where Ben was sitting to shake his hand. 'It would be an honour to have you over at our flat tomorrow evening for dinner.'

Ben accepted this invitation, though he made his excuses to leave shortly afterwards before he was involuntarily roped into anything else.

Two curries in five days was not a bad ratio, Ben considered as he sat down at a table in Bilal's small living room. Sahil was also there and another man, Faisal, who inhabited the adjacent flat. An assortment of dishes all but covered the table and Ben placed a sample from each on his plate.

'We can't fight these people on our own,' said Bilal as he put his spoon in a dish overflowing with Basmati rice.

'I really can't see what I can do that you can't,' replied Ben

'That's where you're wrong, very wrong. People will listen to you if you make a complaint. We might even stop this.'

'How do they harass you?'

'They stand around swearing at us and once we're inside the flats they throw stones at our windows. If anybody goes out they say it wasn't them and just laugh.'

'Is it the same people who come every night?'

'There are a hard core of about ten regulars, the others just come for an occasional bit of fun.'

Ben continued with his meal, immersed in thoughts as to how he had got himself into this situation. Whatever possessed him to accept Angela's invitation in the first place? Just then there was a thud as a large stone hit the wooden shutter that was protecting the glass of the window. Without that shield he could well have been picking glass splinters out of his biryani. A coldness starting in the shoulders ran quickly to the tips of his fingers and his senses suddenly became heightened in preparation for whatever was next to come. Some obscene shouting was all he became aware of but he was in no mood to finish the plate of food in front of him. There followed something of a lull and Bilal suggested they venture outside to see what was happening. The two of them walked out onto the first floor passageway of the apartment block. On the ground below an open fire was burning fiercely and about ten men dressed in dark thick clothing were warming themselves by its flames. They appeared to be in a good mood, exchanging jokes and laughing whilst they clapped their hands and moved from foot to foot in an effort to fight the cold. It was surprising to see how openly they showed themselves and how they appeared to be just your average guys out on a cold night. One could have transported the scene to a Guy Fawkes' night celebration and it would have seemed perfectly normal.

How best to deal with the situation though? Ben felt as if he could just go up and talk to them but doubted whether there was any chance whatsoever they could be talked out of their present activities. It was worth a try and he could think of no other strategy at the time. Together with Bilal he approached the huddle around the fire.

'Look, here comes a traitor with his friend wearing a white dress. What's the matter with you, are you queer or something?'

Ben did not deign to answer the insult directed his way but simply said, 'I've come to ask you to stop harassing these people, they've done you no harm.'

'Fifty-eight million British people wouldn't agree with you,' said a tall youth who must have been in his early twenties with a sallow face and eyes that weren't afraid to look at you but which did not look into you. He could have been French or Belgian but was definitely not British.

'I repeat, these people have done you no harm, if you want revenge look elsewhere.'

'They're all the same,' came a voice from the huddle. 'Don't think he wouldn't stab you in the back given half a chance.'

'I am asking you to leave this place and stop bothering those who live here,' said Ben.

The tall youth who had spoken first took one step closer to Ben, whilst keeping his eyes fixed on his face. 'Now listen, you, nobody tells us where to go and what to do. We are simply here minding our own business and will not move for anyone.'

It was clear Ben was not going to get anywhere with any arguments, so he turned and went back to the apartment block.

He hadn't walked five paces before experiencing a sharp pain on the back of the head. Somebody had thrown a stone with real force. Ben automatically moved his hand to where he had been struck and although he could not see the colour red in the dark he could feel the stickiness and warmth of blood oozing out of the newly created wound. He turned and looked at the group again.

'Who threw that?' he said with anger in his voice.

'Nobody here,' they laughed. 'Maybe it was one of your Muslim buddies.'

Ben had the wound treated and dressed at a clinic. He was particularly touched that Bilal and the two other men insisted on coming with him and wouldn't leave until he had been safely escorted home. 'There is far more danger at their place,' he thought. 'How can they leave their families with those yobs outside for my benefit?' He phoned to check they had got home safely and there had been no more trouble at the apartment block that night, which to his relief there hadn't. Blood was a bugger to get out of the hair. He stood in front of the bathroom mirror and tried to soak it as best he could without getting water on the plaster that had been recently applied. The comb hurt as it became stuck in the matting and he realised more water was required. At least one problem had been solved tonight: he knew now how he would occupy himself in the evenings. They were not going to get away with this.

Chapter 12

I T WAS NOT the first time Tallis had travelled the road from Malaga to Nerja in the bright Spanish sunshine. He had barely looked at the passing scenes the last time the journey had been made, so numb was he from the enormity of the tragedy that had just taken place. So much had happened since that fateful day it was difficult to believe it had been just over three years ago. Now he had an opportunity to observe at leisure what passed for everyday life in the Costa del Sol, as Pedro was driving the car and Robert and Mwamba were on the back seat. It had been a bit of an effort to fit all the luggage in and they had ultimately failed; another trip would be necessary a bit later. Pedro had been delighted to see them, stating that some divine intervention had unquestionably led to Tallis' return. He would definitely offer up a prayer of thanksgiving when next visiting church.

It was with some dismay that the three new arrivals to Spain discovered a reception in Pedro's garden, with tables strewn with food and drink, and about twenty people there to welcome them to their new home. The journey from Tanzania had been long and tiring and none particularly relished the prospect of a party. Still it would be churlish to disappoint those who had put so much effort into preparing a celebration for them. Tallis recognised most of his old drinking partners from the last stay in Spain but it was good to also meet their wives and girlfriends for the first time. The female contingent had a mollifying effect on the gathering, ensuring it did not become too noisy or boisterous, which helped the trio's nerves not to fray any further. That said, the sincerity of the greetings, combined with the effects of not having had a good night's sleep, was almost sufficient to drive Tallis to tears. He had no idea he had been missed so much and felt ashamed for having wanted to take his own life and then keeping everybody in the dark when he was alright. He had not attended a meeting such as this since the attack and the warmth of the friendliness brought back memories of times spent with family and friends back in the United Kingdom.

Robert and Mwamba were happy not to be the centre of attention, realising this was more Tallis' homecoming party than theirs. They did however start to put out a number of feelers with regard to the opportunities for medical practitioners. As the tourist season was starting there could be a few new openings. There would have been plenty of opportunities had the traditional influx of British holidaymakers been present. Robert pondered on the fact that he would probably have required no more than a good supply of sun cream, paracetamol and penicillin to deal with ninety per cent of the cases that would have presented themselves in those days.

The high-pitched resonance of a teaspoon being struck against a wineglass was the signal that Pedro wished to say a few words.

'Ladies and gentlemen, señoritas and señors, friends of Tallis and new friends to Robert and Mwamba, today is a day like no other. We had given up hope of ever seeing Tallis alive and now he stands before us fit and healthy. It is a miracle similar to the raising up of Lazarus from the tomb. Not only is his body alive, but his spirits have been lifted, due mainly to our other two guests at this party. That a tragedy so horrific as the attack on Britain should contain a story of such hope is a wonder indeed. We pledge ourselves to continue the miracle and will do all we can to help our friends. In the meantime let us give thanks to

God for the happiness he has bestowed upon us all and continue the party.'

Cheers went up from all around and Tallis felt it behoved him to respond.

'My friends, I am truly overwhelmed with the welcome you have prepared and on behalf of the three of us I would like to offer our sincere gratitude.' Robert nodded his head as Tallis spoke. 'I feel truly ashamed when I see such kindness from such good people. I know I am not worthy of it for the way I behaved after the attack, but will do whatever I can to make amends for the way I treated you all.'

These words of contrition had a sobering effect on all present, though they did nothing to reduce the affection in which Tallis was held. Robert understood for the first time the enormity of the burden of guilt weighing down on his friend's shoulders and how it would be necessary for him somehow to get over this for a happier future.

They were all accommodated in the modest yet comfortable home of Pedro. Though the first days were spent happily enough it was clear, at least to Robert and Mwamba, that this could only be a temporary arrangement and at some time soon they would need to find their own apartment. Pedro and Tallis were good friends and the medical couple already felt a little like outsiders. Shortly after their arrival the four of them went on an evening walk along the streets and footpaths of Nerja. Pedro directed their course towards the villa that once belonged to Sir Steven Wilkinson and was now owned by a wealthy Spaniard. Tallis picked out the rooms where he had once stayed and was surprised to discover the garden had changed little since the sunny evening he had left it to drive to Barcelona.

'The man who owns this villa knows your story and wants you to finish the garden,' said Pedro.

'Listen, I know you mean well,' replied Tallis, 'but I don't need charity from anyone.'

'It's not charity,' protested Pedro, raising his voice. 'You would be working for money.'

'Why me? Why can't he get somebody else?' Tallis shrugged his shoulders.

'Because only you know how it's supposed to look. It's your creation, nobody else would be able to do it justice.' Pedro was warming to his topic but Tallis cut him short.

'I don't really know. What would be the point?'

'What was the point three years ago?' asked Robert, joining in the conversation. 'What makes it different now?'

'Let me think about it,' said Tallis, trying to extricate himself from the discussion on seeing that his reluctance was becoming the minority viewpoint.

'It certainly has a wonderful view,' stated Robert and they all paused to admire the blue Mediterranean Sea below them.

'Why don't the three of you continue down the hill to the little taverna?' suggested Pedro. 'I need to return home now.'

A waiter brought three tall glasses filled to the brim with golden lager. They were sitting outside and although it was becoming late the stones seemed to be exuding a warmth of their own which maintained a comfortable temperature.

'Here's to our new life,' said Tallis, raising a glass. They all joined in the toast, then there was a pause as if each one was trying to figure out what this new life would personally entail.

'Are you really enjoying yourself here?' asked Robert.

'Of course I am,' answered Tallis, seeming surprised that anyone could ask such a question. 'What could be better than all this?' He waved his arms out to draw attention to the drinks and the surroundings.

'I'm not talking of external things, I'm talking about how you feel inside.'

'I feel just fine.'

'You're still feeling guilty. You felt guilty for surviving the attack, which resulted in your attempted suicide, and now you feel guilty about that. Guilt drove you into disastrous military adventures and now you feel guilty for those. No matter how desperately you try to run away from guilt it follows you about at all times.'

'What do you suggest I do about all this guilt?' asked Tallis in a matter-of-fact way.

'Cease the self-punishment from reminding yourself how unworthy you are. You will only be able to enjoy the life God has offered you by learning to freely accept his gifts without the requirement of a payback.'

'Don't you start talking about God, I had Pedro trying to convince me to go to church yesterday.'

'Which you naturally refused.'

'Of course I did, I can solve my own problems.'

'So you now admit that you have a problem?'

'I admit nothing, just leave me alone.'

'I'm afraid I can't leave you alone since you refused to leave me alone with my problems. We are forever bound by a bond of interference in each other's affairs.'

Tallis smiled. 'I suppose that's fair enough.'

Mwamba, who had been quiet up to now, began to speak. 'Tallis, I would like it very much if you would accompany me to church tomorrow.'

Tallis smiled in a resigned manner, which expressed the difficulty he would have in doing that, whilst recognising the kind-hearted gesture she was making. 'That's very good of you but I'm not really a church-going person. Besides, the service would be in Spanish and I wouldn't understand it.' That last excuse had come to him in a flash of inspiration and he was rather proud of it.

'I'm not intending that we attend any service, and if you are not comfortable with going to a church we could always visit a mosque or somewhere else.'

'You see, Mwamba, I've done some bad things in my life, some things that even God would find difficult to forgive.'

'There is nothing to forgive since you haven't committed any sins. Jesus made no requirement of the criminals crucified beside him when he promised them they were going to paradise.'

'It seems to me you're running out of excuses,' said Robert, smiling.

'OK, anything to keep the two of you quiet,' said Tallis finally in exasperation.

It was now dark and the temperature had turned cooler. In the distance they could hear the noise of revellers from the bars that bordered the beaches. Tallis reflected on how he had changed since the last time he was in Spain. Then he would have wanted to party until the early hours and drink inordinate amounts of alcohol. Now he was content to walk the moonlit streets in comfortable silence with his two friends. The only unsettling weight on his mind was the appointment at the church tomorrow.

Chapter 13

Tallis' daily routine in the morning was to switch on his laptop after showering and changing. This day was no different and, perched on the edge of the bed, he methodically went through those electronic communications that had collected in the inbox since yesterday. Amongst the emails was one from the Crusading Knights for Justice. Just seeing the name sent a shudder down his spine as he remembered some of the unpleasant experiences endured in their name. The message consisted of the usual diatribe against the Muslim world, replete with impassioned reminders of the suffering of the United Kingdom. The Western leaders were castigated for not doing enough to counter the menace of Islam and there were campaigns to be fought in Indonesia, Serbia, Albania and North Africa. Tallis was surprised that at one time he had been taken in by all this, then a thought occurred to him. Try switching the words Muslim for Christian, Palestine for the United Kingdom, Western leaders for Arab leaders, and the article could probably appear on an al-Qaeda website. Was this all it came down to in the final analysis? The logic of a football supporter who preferred Chelsea to Manchester United and then fanatically followed his team?

Pedro was only too happy to take Tallis and Mwamba to the church after lunch. Mwamba had collected a bunch of flowers of different kinds from the garden started by Tallis. She wanted a tangible expression of something close to his heart that would aid meditation and bring him closer to God. As they walked towards the entrance of the church, however, a steward stopped her from taking them inside.

'These flowers are very special to us. They are a reminder of something living and beautiful that we once tried to create.' Mwamba's gentle protestations fell on stony ground, however, and they were forced to leave them at the entrance.

Tallis' anxiety at this appointment had if anything increased and he began to wonder what form the prayer session would take.

'What part of the church should we head for?' he asked.

'Let's see if there is a prayer corner we can use.'

'How do you normally pray, Mwamba?'

'I generally prefer to sit cross-legged on the floor.'

'Mwamba, you can't just sit down on the floor of a church and start to pray to God.'

'Why not?'

'Mwamba, I don't feel comfortable here, can we please go somewhere else?'

'Whatever you want.'

During the course of their conversation Tallis' cheeks had gone through several shades of red just thinking about the embarrassment of being found out in the church with the desire to pray. He wanted to vacate that building as speedily as possible and encouraged Mwamba's sluggish progress towards the exit. She stopped to pick up the flowers, then, as they hit the bright afternoon sunshine, said: 'You are not getting away with it that easily Tallis.'

Mwamba sat cross-legged that afternoon on the floor of Tallis' bedroom at Pedro's house. Tallis was sitting opposite her in the same position and between the two of them was the bunch of flowers and a candle. The curtains were drawn to keep out the sun and there was total silence while the two of them tried to calm down. Mwamba was the first to break this.

'God, we are not here to ask you for anything, but to thank you for everything you have done for Tallis. We know you are all around us every moment of the day and seek only to become more aware of your presence.' After a pause she addressed herself to Tallis. 'Tallis, I want you to just concentrate on your breathing. Try to empty your mind of all thoughts, all desires, remember you are not looking for anything but simply making yourself more receptive for God to enter your soul.'

Tallis obeyed the instructions and for five minutes simply relaxed his body, breathing in and out slowly.

'Now concentrate on a point in the middle of your forehead, a light will appear. Now let the light of God fill your whole being.'

Tallis sat for another fifteen minutes and experienced the total calm, peace and love which could only come from being touched by God. He eventually rose to his feet as Mwamba drew back the curtains, but continued to feel a lightness in his chest as though there was a gentle burning beneath the rib cage whose warmth pushed ever upward. Without saying a word he went out of the house for a walk down by the sea.

Robert had spent the afternoon watching television. The state funeral of Queen Elizabeth II had been showing. Liveried footmen, soldiers wearing ceremonial dress, horse-drawn carriages and a collection of world leaders not seen since the death of Pope John Paul II were all in full view. It had been the last state occasion before the attack, a time when the British nation had come together to commemorate the life of this great monarch, admired most for her fortitude, staying power and devotion to duty. Crowds thronged near the floral tributes outside Buckingham Palace and all along the route to St Paul's Cathedral in a sombre and silent mood. In the cathedral all ranks of British society were represented, from Knights of the Garter to

Lords, Viscounts, Earls, Field Marshals, Members of Parliament and the odd member of the general public. She hadn't quite managed to beat Queen Victoria's record but it had been a long reign and for the main part a happy, peaceful and prosperous one. Watching the event it was almost inconceivable that all this would come to an end afterwards. The hundreds of years of tradition and ceremony, however, would offer no protection against the viral cloud that would engulf the island of Great Britain. One wondered what the old queen would have made of it all and in a sense it was good that she had died when she did so she was not a witness to the horror. Having overseen the peaceful dismemberment of the British Empire, it surely would never have occurred to her that the very existence of the nation at its heart could be in jeopardy. It would have been a cruel death indeed to see everything you had dedicated your life to go up in smoke with your last breaths.

It was the first time Robert had viewed the entire funeral; edited highlights were all he had seen in Tanzania. His feelings were peculiarly mixed however: although he felt nostalgic at seeing the tradition of British society, he also felt distanced from it. It was undoubtedly his heritage but not a heritage he felt able to embrace fully. The old question kept nagging away at the back of his mind: just where did he belong?

When Tallis returned home late in the afternoon he looked different. There was nothing you could put your finger on, no external features had been altered, in fact there were no material changes whatsoever. The transformation had been internal and spiritual but it was real and it was noticeable.

'What have you been doing this afternoon?' asked Robert.

'I was just sitting on the beach looking out to sea and thinking.'

'That's good, I can see you look a lot more at peace with yourself.'

'Yes,' replied Tallis absent-mindedly as if this insight had not yet occurred to him 'Yes, I think I am. Have you ever had a significant moment in your life, Robert?' he asked.

'I'm not sure I know what you mean.'

'I don't mean being at some prestigious event or witnessing some dramatic occasion. Maybe nothing out of the ordinary was going on around you at all but something monumental was going on inside you. In that moment it's like time stood still and you felt the touch of a divine being.'

Robert put his newspaper down and thought about this for a while. 'I remember one evening, one cold November evening when I was a teenager. I can't recall why but I'd been dropped off in the centre of a small Cumbrian village with a group of other young people. As we shivered together in the night air I looked at a row of cottages. They each had their curtains drawn to the outside world but soft lights could be seen coming through them. I sat and looked at those lights and thought that the people inside had no idea of my existence just a few yards away. I wondered what stories lay within those thick stone walls and what kind of lives the inhabitants led. I don't know why but I kept telling myself I had to remember this moment. The scene couldn't have been more ordinary, but the moment felt important. I can't explain it, it was just a feeling I had. Years later at university I met a man who had lived in that village. Further questioning revealed that he had lived in that row of houses at the exact time I had sat outside.'

'How did you feel when you discovered that?'

'I felt scared. Looking back, I probably felt scared because I sensed the presence of God.'

'And how did you react?'

'I turned my back on the incident and attempted to block it out of my mind. You know, I haven't thought about that in years. I think I've learned something about myself today.'

'I too was scared today,' admitted Tallis. 'In fact I've been running scared for a long time. Today I finally had the courage to face God and accept him into my soul.'

Within a short period of time Robert was offered a job at the first aid hut set up near the beach tending to holiday-makers, principally suffering from sunburn or the change in diet. Tallis resumed the gardening project he had aborted three years earlier. Although the plans for it had not changed, the intent behind its design had. Whereas at one time Tallis had sought approval and admiration from others, now the work of beauty was intended to give meaning to his life. Although the wages for both of them were fairly modest they were sufficient for their needs. Through a friend of Pedro, Mwamba and Robert had been offered a flat close to the beach at a negligible rent. Tallis preferred to stay with Pedro, although the threesome from Tanzania met up at regular intervals. Mwamba stayed at home and integrated well into the new culture of housewives. In short it was the kind of existence they had all dreamed of, though Robert felt it was only a temporary arrangement and some other home was ultimately planned for him.

Chapter 14

BEN HAD COME to feel rather uncomfortable with all the praise heaped on him. The Muslims at the apartment block treated him with an indebted reverence for having helped them and he had even gained Angela's grudging acknowledgement. This all paled into insignificance, however, when set against the fulsome adoration received from Elisabetta. Since her return to Paris she had revelled in tales of how he had unselfishly stood up for justice and the downtrodden, never losing an opportunity to embarrass him by recounting these. His uneasiness was caused by a sincere belief that he had done nothing extraordinary to deserve this limited celebrity status. He had never even wanted to be a hero, not this kind anyway, and wished he could just return to his ordinary life.

Driven more by the desire for revenging the cut on his head than the welfare of others, Ben had set up surveillance cameras and gathered intelligence on those who had been terrorising the apartment block. It had not been a difficult exercise: the young men freely showed their faces and made little attempt to hide their identities. Their confidence in not being held to account for criminal acts was amazing and even when confronted with all the evidence they did not seem too bothered. There was no way, however, the police or the courts could ignore it and the majority had received short custodial sentences. Ben's relief at sorting out that particular problem had been tempered by the knowledge that they or others were likely to return at some time in the future, only with increased caution and ferociousness.

Now he was an outcast but happy to be one. The British Refugee Society would not have approved of his recent quest for justice and there was still the controversy over the email sent to the "*Daily Telegraph*". Ken Louis had recently been elected leader and Ben could think of no other person he detested more. To go to a meeting and hear that man pontificating on the sensitive subject of what it meant to be British would be sheer hell. His circle of friends had taken a distinct shift away from those with a narrow nationalism to others with a wider perspective and a greater degree of tolerance. Elisabetta had many contacts through Angela, of which Ben had never before been aware, and they began to move in more culturally diverse company. The conversations tended to be more interesting and nobody seemed to mind him expressing opinions about his homeland so long as the debate was always couched in respectful terms.

It was not always easy for him, however, to tolerate the opinions of others who did not understand the strong yearning to return home. He remembered one occasion when he and Elisabetta had attended a talk arranged by some left wing political debating society with whom Angela had links. The subject of the evening's discussion was the best way recolonisation of Britain could be undertaken and what kind of society should be created. Entitled "The opportunities provided by a recolonisation of Britain", it was intended that personal visions would be set forth and discussed in a frank atmosphere by individuals from different backgrounds. Five speakers, three gentlemen and two women, sat behind a long roughly constructed wooden table and took it in turns to speak.

A bearded man in a green T-shirt and jeans sitting at the extreme left of the table was the first to rise to his feet.

'My proposal, ladies and gentlemen, is I believe a radical one but one which will solve a lot of the problems Europe now faces.' He cleared his throat and looked around before continuing. 'We are all too familiar with the problems of global warning, deforestation, pollution and the threat posed to wild animals through loss of habitat. The forests of Europe bear little resemblance to how they were five or six hundred years ago and some species are bordering on extinction. Yes, there has been environmental damage in other parts of the world, but no part of the planet is more densely populated than Europe, nowhere else has systematically abused its surroundings more and for a longer period of time than this continent. It is time to redress the balance and give something back to the earth that we have mercilessly plundered for generations. I propose turning Britain into a large nature reserve, through a massive tree-planting programme and careful animal husbandry. As Britain is an island it is the perfect site for introducing endangered species and keeping out predators that would upset the natural order. I therefore recommend that no wholesale recolonisation of Britain takes place, although some ecotourism could be arranged. A limited amount of infrastructure would be required for this to succeed but the funds generated could go on to support further conservation projects.'

Ben had kept himself quiet with great difficulty during this speech. The idea of the country of his birth being turned into one huge wildlife park was just unbearable. Did this man have any idea that Britain wasn't just a piece of land but a dream that lived in the hearts of many of its citizens? He raised his hand to ask a question.

'What about all the historical monuments of Britain, how do you propose to deal with those?'

The speaker nodded. 'I admit that not all the details have yet been worked out and there is still much to discuss. Personally speaking I would favour some limited scheme to preserve the most important buildings for posterity.'

A limited scheme? Did he have any idea how many historic

buildings Britain possessed? Ben imagined some future ecotourist plodding through dense forest only to find Salisbury Cathedral amongst the undergrowth, as explorers of old would come across the ancient ruins of some great, lost civilisation in the jungles of Africa or South America.

'What about the feelings of the British people at not being allowed to live in their homeland?' asked Ben.

The man attempted to look sympathetic. 'I realise how hard it would be for the British people to accept this and of course we would have to listen carefully to what they have to say. At the same time I would urge us all to look beyond our own national interests and try to consider what is best for our world as a whole. We have a wonderful opportunity to do something for the planet if we can only take the larger view.'

Ben was even more infuriated now. If he was prepared to listen carefully to what the British people had to say he would realise his idea was a non-starter. He was the one being selfish by coming up with a plan that would benefit himself and turn what was left of a proud people into permanent refugees.

Ben had come to the conclusion that there had to be a middle way, one which would allow for the return of the British refugees without the delusions of grandeur that those in the British Refugee Society still clung to. It had begun to dawn on him that it would be impossible to recreate the Britain of old, but that a new society would have to be created to deal with the challenges of the new world and Britain's altered standing in it. He regarded it as sheer stupidity that Ken Louis advocated the readmission of the United Kingdom as a permanent member of the United Nations Security Council once recolonisation came about. To restore the monarchy would necessitate giving the crown to a relatively unknown member of the British aristocracy who had emigrated to South Africa, and then of course there were the claims to Gibraltar.

Chapter 15

I T HAD BEEN some time since the meeting with Dr Bolden, and Ben had often wondered what would come out of it. He had resisted the temptation to call him up at the United Nations, realising that this would be counter-productive. Dr Bolden had especially impressed upon him the need for confidentiality and such communication would only diminish his confidence in the ability of Ben to keep a closed mouth. It was thus with a considerable degree of excitement that one morning he received a letter from the United Nations Department for British Affairs, requesting a further meeting.

Ben was directed to a small conference room, where Dr Bolden sat behind a desk with two other men. He smiled on seeing Ben.

'Well, we've been following your progress with some interest and you seem to have been causing quite a stir.'

'I only did what I thought was right,' said Ben, reddening.

'Quite so,' agreed Dr Bolden. 'We need people like you, people who can analyse a situation fairly and rationally without getting carried away.'

A younger man to Dr Bolden's left with a genial yet perceptive bearing returned the meeting to the business in hand.

'Before we start our discussion we must have your assurance that whatever is talked about remains strictly confidential. As I am sure you will appreciate, our topic is a sensitive one and there are many who do not want us to succeed.'

Ben nodded. 'I fully understand and will not repeat any of our discussions outside this room.'

The one who had sought this assurance, whose name was Mr Stendahl, continued.

'We are proposing that a group of about one hundred British citizens return to Britain. Whilst all the indications are that the land is safe for human habitation we cannot guarantee this. Understand that if you do agree to take part in this trip it will be entirely at your own risk. A number of conditions will apply. You will not be permitted to travel beyond limits set by the United Nations once you return to Britain. Neither will you be permitted to return to the European mainland for a period of at least six months. You will be required to perform certain set tasks as set out by the United Nations and go for regular medical checks when requested. In return you will be provided with accommodation and food. As a British citizen you must renounce all claims to any land outside the British Isles formerly held by Britain. Do you have any questions?'

'What kind of work will I be required to do?'

'Simple jobs such as the growing of crops and rearing of animals. We basically wish to see whether life in Britain is feasible again.'

'I have a partner. Will she be able to come with me?'

'Is she British?'

'She's Austrian.'

'I'm afraid it's extremely unlikely, it would be very difficult to allow an Austrian to live in Britain whilst we deny Britons that right.'

'When are you proposing to do this?'

'Next month. There is no point hanging around until your friends in the British Refugee Society get wind of it.'

'When would you like my decision?'

'Within four days, there are a number of things we need to start working on.'

'When the Gods want to punish you they answer your

prayers.' Who was responsible for that quotation? Ben would have to look it up when he got home. He desperately wanted to return to Britain but what kind of life would he have? Rearing chickens and planting tomatoes on a restricted area of land away from Elisabetta was not exactly what he had envisaged. He could see, however, why it could not be otherwise; why the return had to be slow and planned. He would be back again on British soil but it was not only the land that mattered to him, it was the life, the culture and the history. It was walking through the park on a Sunday afternoon, whilst the brass band played, it was hot fish and chips soaked in salt and vinegar steaming up car windows on a November evening, it was a Sunday morning spent in bed reading *"The Observer"*. It was all this and more and he began to question his motives for returning. As he mulled over the situation again and again a simple truth occurred to him. His former life had gone and there was no point in trying to resurrect even a small part of it. He would not be going back to Britain to pick up the threads of an old life but to start a new one, completely different from what had gone before. Did he want to go, though? Why not let someone else put up with the hardship of being part of the advance team if that was what they wanted? What would he gain through six months away from France and Elisabetta? He really had no idea whether to go or not.

It was obvious to Elisabetta that Ben was in a preoccupied mood that evening. He hardly talked and seemed to be wrestling with some intractable problem. What made it worse for him was that the opportunity did not exist to talk about it. Not only would she have provided a useful sounding board for his thoughts, he would like to justify his decision to leave for Britain if ultimately it came to that. She could hardly be expected to understand if one day suddenly found him gone without a word of explanation. He did what he normally did at such difficult times and reached for the whisky bottle. As the first glass moistened his lips another problem occurred to him: he had only four days to make the decision. The clock was definitely ticking and from the look of the faces of the three men at the Department for British Affairs, there would be no going back once the decision had been made.

'Is there anything I can do?' asked Elisabetta in a concerned manner.

'I wish there was, my darling,' replied Ben with a half-hearted attempt at a smile.

'You can talk to me about anything that is troubling you, you know that.'

'Shortly after the attack I stopped a man travelling to Britain and a certain death. I reviled the senseless loss of life and thought it better to save both our lives for when we could return one day. Now I wonder if I have half the courage of that person.'

'You have courage because you chose to live, death would have been the easy way out. You have always spoken up for what is right, not like those sheep from the British Refugee Society.'

'I have a difficult choice to make in the next few days. I'm not sure if you'll agree with it, but always remember that I love you.'

'You know I know that.'

'It's easy to say but you must believe it in your heart,' said Ben earnestly, looking her in the face. 'No matter what happens I will return to you.'

'What are you talking about?' said Elisabetta in a concerned voice. 'You worry me when you talk like this.'

'There's nothing for you to worry about except the strength of your own feelings and how much you trust me.'

'Perhaps it is best if we go to sleep now, things might seem much clearer in the morning.'

It was a deserted area of moorland and the wind blew strongly. The rough hardy grasses offered more resistance to this invisible force than Ben's clothing, which flapped with a great vigour. He was standing motionless on the summit of a small flat-topped hill looking down at the ground with a mournful expression, holding a bunch of wild flowers. Two heavy stone rectangles were placed side by side amongst the shortened grass in perfect symmetry. Lichen and moss had begun to creep over the grey stone but it was still possible to make out the name 'Maureen'. Ben slowly placed his bouquet under this word that had once signified so many of his hopes for the future and the wind scattered the flowers evenly over the stone rectangle. He knelt down and felt the dampness of the earth seeping through the material of his trousers to his knees. The vegetation was coarse and prickly and the surface of the stone was rough to the touch. Moss flaked off in his hand and looked like little pieces of green velvet. He ran his fingers along the chiselled letters of his dead fiancée's name and thought of some of the dreams they had once had. Moisture collected in his eyes, though it wasn't clear whether this was from the sadness of the occasion or the cruel remorseless wind. Despite the discomfort of the situation he wanted to stay there.

There was a grating noise, which stirred Ben from his thoughts, and he looked across to see the word 'Michael' written on the neighbouring stone. The wind blew harder and the sky turned a darker shade of grey. He had never seen such a dark sky, though suddenly a jagged white streak of lightning lit up the landscape, temporarily creating light and shadows. The inevitably loud clap of thunder followed shortly afterwards and the air was alive with electricity and portents, though no rain threatened. The grating sound was repeated and the grey slab covering Michael's grave moved up then down. Silence followed, but there was no reduction in the atmosphere of expectation. Then all of a sudden the stone was thrown off, revealing a black rectangular emptiness in which no detail could be discerned. Ben strained to look inside but all he could see was blackness. There followed a pause, then suddenly two hands simultaneously grabbed tufts of grass either side of the rectangle. At any moment Ben expected to see his brother Michael as he had in so many dreams, but instead a taller, younger, more athletic frame came into view as the knuckles on the hands whitened from pulling on the coarse grass stalks. The face was not immediately recognisable, though there was something familiar about it. Where had he seen that face before? The young man started to talk and then he remembered him as the one he had beaten up on the beach at Calais.

'Thank you for saving my life,' he said, looking straight at Ben without the slightest trace of anger in his voice.

'Where is Michael?' asked Ben, perturbed at the absence of his brother.

'Michael is at rest. He will no longer appear in your dreams.'

'Who are you? Why are you here?'

'You know who I am. I am here to give you a message.'

'What have you come to tell me?'

'It is now time to go back to Britain.'

Ben woke up and looked at the sleeping Elisabetta. He would miss her very much whilst away but had no doubt any more what was the correct choice to make. It wasn't possible to decide on an issue like this by considering the inconvenience it would cause to one's lifestyle. Neither was there room for sentimentality in the resolution of this dilemma. At the end of the day it wasn't really a choice at all but a duty, a duty he had to fulfil to his ancestors and those who would come after him. A duty to reclaim the land that was his inheritance and live up to some of the nobler virtues exhibited by those who had once trod the same earth. Would Elisabetta understand, and just how much could he tell her?

'Good morning, my love,' she said slowly in a croaky voice, opening one eye.

'Good morning, Elisabetta.'

There was a pause as her body became used to the new state of wakefulness. Part of that transformation involved remembering what had been said the night before.

'How are you feeling now?' she asked.

'Oh, better I think, I've sorted out in my mind what needs to be done.'

'That's good, we can talk about it later.'

Ben got up and dressed for work. He felt much better now except for a slight throbbing in the head caused by last night's whisky drinking. Then he suddenly thought about his job: who would do it whilst he was away? Would he give notice or simply fail to turn up one day? What was the financial remuneration for his six-month stay in Britain? A number of problems presented themselves to him, which he determined to resolve at the next meeting to be held at the British Affairs Department. At least Elisabetta could be counted on to look after things at the flat.

There was one positive outcome of the proposed landing in Britain, which bought a smile to his face. It would surely annoy the British Refugee Society and their new leader Ken Louis. Annoy? They would be practically foaming at the mouth in outrage. To watch them discussing their latest plan for returning to Britain and how they would organise a new society, only to discover that somebody else was already doing it would be a priceless privilege. It would kill the lie that they were representative of British opinion and show up their petty posturing over Gibraltar as just that. With a bit of luck it might even kill off Ken Louis' political career, now that he could be seen as an irrelevance. The attack had brought fame to a number of undeserving characters who had played on and mercilessly profited off other people's prejudices and fears. To start to return to Britain would remove at least some of those fears.

On the way home Ben was still running through his mind what he would say to Elisabetta. She was expecting an explanation for the cryptic discussion the previous evening and no doubt she deserved one. He wanted to tell her everything but had promised confidentiality and was determined to honour that pledge. It was necessary to gain her unquestioned loyalty and he had something in his pocket that would help to achieve that. She would be waiting for him back at the flat and he resolved to sort out the issue straight away. In the lounge where he had first seduced her with such insincerity the two of them faced each other for a talk of the utmost seriousness.

'Trust is the key to a good relationship, we both must tell the truth and believe each other implicitly,' remarked Ben.

'I totally agree,' replied Elisabetta rapidly.

'I wish you wouldn't say that so easily. Trust, real trust, is believing in somebody when everybody else tells you not to. It is putting up with feelings of pain, because you know your partner will not let you down. Do you have that kind of trust in me?'

'I think so,' said Elisabetta in a more serious voice than before.

'Good, because something will happen next month and I won't see you for some time. I can't go into the details but I will be back for you, you must believe that.'

'I don't like this kind of talk at all. Are you in any trouble?'

'No.'

'Is somebody blackmailing you? Are you doing anything illegal?'

'The answer to both of those questions is no. As I said last night the only thing you have to be afraid of is your own feelings. Trust me and everything will work out OK.'

'But I am still worried …'

Ben held up a finger to his lips to silence her. 'Remember: trust, belief. There are good reasons why I can't discuss what's going to happen. Believe and trust in me.'

'How long will you be away for?'

'I think between six months and one year.'

Elisabetta let out a sigh.

'I do have something else I'd like to ask you,' said Ben, rummaging around in his pocket. 'I'd like to ask you to marry me,' and at that moment he held out a plain gold band for her to admire.

'You really do confuse a girl!' exclaimed Elisabetta. 'First you tell me you are leaving then you ask me to marry you.'

Ben felt it was a lot like the situation when they had first met: the cold shoulder followed by promises of love. It was probably best, however, not to remind her of that time.

'Can we marry before you leave?' she asked.

'Of course we can. We can even try to start a family.'

'The answer is yes. I would love to be your wife.'

'Now, about starting that family …'

Chapter 16

THERE HAD NOT been much time to arrange a flight to Salzburg and all the things that accompanied a marriage ceremony. In a way Ben thought that was good, so that it remained simple. He had in fact wished to hold it in Paris but quite understood Elisabetta's desire to have her family present at the ceremony. A registry office marriage was all that could be organised given the time factor, and that suited him just fine. It was raining heavily as the crowd of about twenty people, family and close friends, made their way to the small whitewashed building tucked away in a green quiet corner of Salzburg. Although its interior could not be compared to the grandeur of the city's churches, the authorities had made an attempt to make the main ceremonial room pleasant and welcoming. A large polished wooden table with a large vase of flowers in the centre added brightness and optimism to the occasion. The formalities were conducted in German and English, although Ben was the only person who did not understand the native language. There were smiles all round and Elisabetta's brothers hugged Ben repeatedly during the day, possibly in an attempt to compensate for the lack of family he had with him.

In his speech afterwards Ben made reference to the fact that he was going away for some time, though it was expressed in such an oblique manner it was questionable whether anyone caught on to it. Elisabetta used her few words to express her fulsome adoration of Ben and took the opportunity to embarrass him yet again with tales of how he had stood up for the oppressed despite all the suffering he had endured. The crowd cheered and Ben reddened as he tried unsuccessfully not to listen to the stories heard so many times before.

As Ben and Elisabetta were tying the knot in the rain of Salzburg, Robert and Mwamba were using an hour set aside for siesta to renew their vows to each other. They had never repeated these in the presence of another person and the form of them changed from one time to another. As well as being a rededication of their love it was an opportunity for each to tell the other what was on their mind, how they saw the relationship going and what new insights they had gained from it. It always ended with a period of love-making, which was made all the more special by the tender words that had gone before. Through Mwamba's gentle encouragement and a few carefully selected books, this aspect of their relationship was slowly improving and adding a new layer of intimacy to it.

Ken Louis was sitting in his office in Paris wondering what to do about an unpleasant rumour that had reached his ears. Someone had reported that the United Nations was going to start to recolonise Britain, though there had been no consultation with the British Refugee Society on this. The former Member of Parliament was trying to glean more details on this before making any representations, but little information was forthcoming. He had phoned Frank Oates, who knew no more than he did and of course the United Nations was remaining tight-lipped. Even if able to confirm the return was on the cards, he had no idea what day it was on or the port of departure. As with the widely anticipated D-Day landings, which heralded the end of the Second World War, only a few were privy to those details and plans were already afoot for a game of bluff and counter-bluff. Certainly none of the returning one hundred Britons had any idea where they would be leaving from or when.

Ben and Elisabetta returned to Paris as Mr and Mrs Collins. There would be no honeymoon as Elisabetta wished to remember the ordinary details of married life when Ben was away and cherish the experience of keeping house together. He had been told that he wasn't required to pack, nor say anything to anybody about what was going to take place. In short, no arrangements of any kind were to be made. The manner in which he was to leave home had been discussed by the two of them on numerous occasions. It was decided that there would be no date hanging over their heads to be dreaded for days beforehand. Elisabetta just wanted Ben to say goodbye one morning and hold her in his arms one last time. It was thus that on the morning of the 6th August the two of them were in a tearful embrace in the living room of their flat in Paris. Ben promised he would be faithful to her and would return, whilst Elisabetta promised to wait faithfully for that day. A black, unmarked Mercedes from the UN Department for British Affairs stood on the road outside waiting. Ben looked up at the window to see Elisabetta following his progress. He waved with an attempt at a smile then opened the heavy door of the car and entered it carrying no luggage.

Tallis sat in Pedro's living room, trying to appreciate some Spanish guitar music. Pedro raved about it and had practically forced his friend to listen but no matter how much he concentrated, Tallis could not understand what was so special about it.

'I think I'm just not familiar with your musical culture,' said Tallis apologetically.

'This musician is from Gibraltar, he is British just like you.'

Tallis raised his eyebrows, there was no way he was even going to start this conversation.

'What do you think about Gibraltar anyway?' asked Pedro.

'I've never really thought about it,' admitted Tallis. 'Now I suppose there seems to be no point in Britain trying to hang on to it.'

'What did you think before the attack?'

Tallis shrugged his shoulders and took a deep breath. 'I was never really into politics.'

'Let me tell you it was stupid, stupid for Britain to own a part of Spain.' Pedro thumped his hand on the table and Tallis was taken aback by the passion this subject seemed to provoke.

'Why do you say that, Pedro?' asked Tallis calmly.

'Look at the map. Look at where Britain is, look at where Spain is.'

'Look at those uninhabited islands off the African coast, which Spain lays claim to. Morocco sent soldiers to plant their nation's flag on it, then the Spanish navy threw them all off and raised the Spanish flag. Then all the soldiers disappeared and left it to the seagulls again. It makes one wonder sometimes what the animal inhabitants of the island make of this strange human behaviour.'

'What are you trying to say, Tallis?'

'I'm trying to say that all this nationalism is just daft. Who owns what piece of land is by and large irrelevant, since none of us owns anything in this world.'

'I see you have been talking to Robert and Mwamba.'

'No, I figured that out for myself, having seen the stupidity of war up close.'

'You have changed very much since the last time you were in Spain.'

'You're right, Pedro. I have changed very much.'

Chapter 17

A DISUSED PRISON BECAME Ben's new home after a two-hour drive in the Mercedes. Two others had been picked up en route though each had instructions not to talk about the fate that awaited them. The building could have been used to house asylum seekers heading for Britain in the days when that island was a desirable destination for so many. It had the obvious advantage of total security: nobody could get in or out and mobile phones or any form of communication with the outside world were prohibited. Each of the one hundred returnees had an individual cell with a toilet. They only met up for the daily conferences and even ate in solitude, so afraid were the authorities of any plan being cooked up other than the one they had in mind. Their 'captors' were most apologetic about the hardships they were forced to endure but assured them they were necessary and would only last a matter of days. A planned and intensive training programme was followed, which involved instructions on how to sink a borehole, plant crops, construct simple buildings and resolve any disputes that may arise. Whatever they did, they were required to meticulously record their actions. Certain people were assigned specialist tasks and it was stressed that in order for the entire enterprise to work everybody had to know the exact nature of their role.

Ben put up with the difficulties of his confinement stoically and even tried to be optimistic, realising there was no going back now. Thirty years down the line it would be a story to tell his grandchildren and he was indeed privileged to be participating in a slice of history-making. When he thought about it most of the famous people he had admired at some time in his life had been through a difficult patch. Indeed it could be said that their ability to survive was the reason for their greatness. When set against the adversity some of them had suffered his was no big deal. He had convinced himself that he would be OK, but still worried about Elisabetta. What state would she be in not knowing where he was and what had happened to him? He wished the day of the journey would come soon so at least she would be aware of his fate.

There was really no doubt about it any more, something was definitely being planned. Throughout Europe there were reports of British men and women who had left their families and workplaces. The British Refugee Society had demanded an explanation from the United Nations but so far had not received anything. Ken Louis was meeting with his most senior advisors to try to decide on the next course of action but each possibility seemed fraught with problems.

'If we go public,' said Frank Oates, thinking carefully and obviously weighing his words, 'on what grounds would we complain about this repatriation?'

'On the grounds that nobody has consulted the British Refugee Society,' bellowed Ken Louis.

Frank Oates exchanged glances with another member round the table. 'That won't look good. It won't look good at all. To be standing on ceremony when our most cherished objective is being fulfilled.'

'I am not standing on ceremony,' replied Ken Louis angrily. 'I am merely stating our democratic right as Britons to conduct our own affairs in the way that we see fit.'

'What do you suggest we do?' asked Frank Oates.

'We need to know where and when the journey will take place. I'm almost sure they'll go by boat. Check the ports, listen for any information, use all our resources to find out exactly what their plan is. Once we know that we can send people to demand to join the trip. Storm the ship, have some swimming out in the North Sea so that they're forced to take us. We will return to the United Kingdom but it will be on our own terms.'

'Do you think that everybody's life has a meaning?' asked Tallis.

'I'm convinced of it,' replied Robert without a moment's thought.

'How can it be then that fifty-eight million people's lives stopped having a meaning at precisely the same time?'

'Just because they're dead it doesn't follow that their lives have ceased to have any meaning. One can never say when a life will stop having any influence.'

'It seems such a waste when one considers what all those lives could have achieved.'

'It depends how you look at it. You could say that their deaths have taught the human race the most valuable lesson in history.'

'And yet our lives were saved. Do you ever wonder why and know what life has in store for us?'

'Yes and no is the answer to that question,' replied Robert with a smile. 'Somehow I don't think Spain will be our final destination, pleasant though it is.'

Their conversation stopped for them to admire the sun which was now a dark red, its colour reflected in the water of the Mediterranean. They were sitting on Robert and Mwamba's patio. Tallis had been invited round for the evening to see how well their new barbecue was working.

'I suppose I'd better be getting back home now,' said Tallis.

'Let me give you a lift,' offered Robert.

'No thanks, I enjoy walking the streets at this time in the cool night air. It gives me a chance to collect my thoughts, reflect on the day and wonder what tomorrow will bring.'

'What do you think tomorrow will bring?'

'Something extraordinary,' remarked Tallis.

Ben was alone in his cell, having just finished his evening meal. If he felt a little miffed at his voluntary imprisonment at least he could not complain about the food. They were offered a choice of two or three items for each of the three courses and even a modest amount of alcohol was permitted. It was as if the UN were trying to compensate the returnees for their lack of freedom by offering their stomachs the licence to consume whatever they wished. It was thus that Ben received his surprise visitors with a certain amount of good humour. Mr Stendahl arrived with two other men, probably security, whom he did not recognise.

'I have to apologise for these conditions,' said Mr. Stendahl, looking around the tiny space with a critical eye. 'I hope you understand their necessity.'

'I understand, just so long as I don't have to stay here for too long.'

'That's what I've come to talk to you about,' the UN representative said, lowering his voice. 'Tomorrow is the day when we are planning the voyage. The coastline is crawling with members of the British Refugee Society who know something is in the offing. The sooner we act, the better.'

'I bet they're mad as hell,' said Ben with a smile.

'I think that would be an accurate description.'

'So anyway, why are you telling this to me now?'

Mr Stendahl took a deep breath. 'We want your landing on the beaches of England to be publicised by the media. There will be TV cameras present to record the historic moment you set foot on its soil. We need one of the returnees to make a speech.'

'Surely you're not suggesting that I ...'

'That's precisely what I'm suggesting, we feel you would be

the most appropriate person to say a few words.'

'But I don't want to,' protested Ben. 'I'm not used to giving speeches.'

'Those are two of the reasons why we chose you.'

'But I can't, what would I say?'

'You will be able to do it when you think how it will smash the pretensions of the British Refugee Society and its odious leader Ken Louis once and for all. As for what to say, I have numerous quotes and ideas that may be of use when composing the speech. The final decision on what to include, however, is yours, we will not even require that you pass it by us first for approval.'

At this point a file was handed over with about thirty typed sheets inside.

'I'm afraid we can't allow you a computer, a pen and paper will have to suffice.'

'That's OK,' said Ben, still a little dazed from what was expected of him and the weight of responsibility that had suddenly been transferred to his shoulders.

Mr Stendahl rose to his feet, closely followed by the two guards. The metal bar door shut behind him and the lock made a clang of metal on metal as it was turned. The man from the UN stopped for a while outside then looked at Ben.

'Make it good, you're not the only person who hates Ken Louis.'

The pen stuck in Ben's hand and the blankness of the white sheet of paper seemed to mirror the blankness of his mind as he struggled to construct a few sentences. He attempted to ignore the fact that millions would be watching on television tomorrow as he played a leading role in an event of epic historical proportions. That realisation, however, kept forcing its way into his mind and contributed to the mental torpor. After all the careful planning of the United Nations it seemed so strange that he should be given a free hand to speak his mind. Thinking about it, it was probably the first time any of the returnees had been given any choice as to the manner of their return. Perhaps that was the point, perhaps his speech was intended to signal the start of British Independence. The views of an individual, however artlessly constructed, would at least accord the event some authenticity and give the lie to the British Refugee Society's inevitable allegation that they were all stooges of the United Nations. Ken Louis and his acolytes would be watching television tomorrow. How could he fix them once and for all? Certainly not through a message of hate and intolerance, nor through a game of point-scoring. His words would inhabit a plane of understanding above their own, which they could not reach. The pen started to move in his hand.

Chapter 18

THE LIGHTS WERE switched on at five a.m. Loud voices instructed the cell occupants to make ready to assemble in the dining room in half an hour's time. They ate their breakfast in silence, partly because many had not woken up properly, partly because it could be sensed that something important was in the air. Without explaining the reasons for the early morning wake-up call, they were shepherded outside to the parade ground where four windowless prison vans were already parked, their engines running. It was at that stage that it became obvious to all that this was the day they would be returning to Britain. There was no real sense of celebration, just a few apprehensive glances exchanged between the compatriots who had only just started to know each other. It wasn't possible to see where they were going but the journey lasted no more than twenty minutes. Upon disembarking they realised that the vans had driven onto a pier, which had an unmarked medium sized boat tethered alongside. The gangplank was already down and the UN officials who had travelled with them seemed obsessed with getting them all on board as quickly as possible. Ben looked towards land and saw a small settlement, which he did not recognise. He had thought all along that they would probably leave from one of the large ports, like Calais or Boulogne, not a little-known fishing village. A register was quickly taken of all the one hundred men and women, and immediately afterwards the instruction was given to set sail.

Ken Louis was convinced it was Calais. It had to be Calais: his scouts had scoured the coastline for signs of activity and it was the only port housing a UN frigate. Moreover there had been signs of activity there in recent days: officials coming and going, inspecting the premises and holding meetings. There was not a moment to lose, the return would occur any day soon, so a group of volunteers from the British Refugee Society was sent post-haste to attempt to disrupt the planned voyage and demand to return with them. It was a cold Saturday morning in Calais and they had maintained their vigil all night, aware that even an hour's loss of concentration would be sufficient for the ship to slip its moorings and sail away without them. It was now nine a.m and someone had been sent to a café for hot coffee and croissants. He did not return with the ordered breakfast but with some devastatingly bad news. French television was reporting that a ship with one hundred returning British residents had left France and was now nearing the coast of south-east England.

Tallis had just arrived at a supermarket in Nerja when he got the telephone call. Mwamba was on the other end.

'You must come round to the house quickly,' she urged him.

'Why, is there something the matter?' he enquired, rather concerned by the pressing nature of the invitation.

'No, everything is fine, but you must come straight away.'

As Tallis arrived the first television pictures were just coming through from a reporter on board the boat that was now stationed out at sea just near Dover. The docking facilities at Dover harbour were not to be used until they had been thoroughly inspected and declared safe both from viral material and any unforeseen circumstance that may have occurred during the three and a half years they had lain idle. Accordingly a number of lifeboats were being lowered whilst the main vessel dropped anchor some two kilometres off the coast. The television crews were happy about this. The return would be reminiscent of the Pilgrim Fathers landing in America or William the Conqueror leading his troops ashore in 1066. To see these British citizens climbing out of small craft as they ran aground on the beach, getting their trousers dirty and wet, would be one of the moments of the century.

'It's all so sudden,' said Mwamba. 'I never thought it would be like this.'

'It couldn't be otherwise,' replied Robert. 'It could never have been planned with everybody's knowledge and agreement. Well, Tallis, you said something extraordinary was going to happen today. Did you know about this?'

'Of course not, it's just that miracles seem to be happening every day this month. I thought, why should today be any different?'

'Miracles are natural and common if you know where to look,' said Mwamba.

Ben boarded a lifeboat and it was gently lowered down to the sea below. The proximity of the water excited him, he could smell the salt, feel the spray on his face and sense its power from the movement up and down. An engine was started which took the craft slowly towards the coast. As it came closer to the bay the land of England bordered him on both sides, like two arms giving an embrace to welcome him home. They all stepped out of the boat into the shallow water and for the first time in years felt the soil of Britain underneath their feet. The walk to dry land was slow as the rush of emotions that flooded him impeded his progress. The television and press also wanted them to stop along the way for photographs and film. It was only when he reached dry land that a feeling of great happiness and relief passed over his whole body and he knelt on the sand of Dover beach giving thanks to he did not know who. After a few minutes a small podium was brought ashore and an elementary sound system rigged up. Ben was guided towards it and shuffled in his pocket for the speech written the evening before. He looked at the assembled crowd of people: they were not numerous and looked a bit ragged, but it had probably been like this at some of Britain's most historic occasions. With no words of introduction he began to speak.

'Ladies and Gentlemen, we are privileged indeed to be participating in this historic event. I would like to start off by thanking the United Nations for making the return possible under the most difficult of circumstances. At the risk of paraphrasing Neil Armstrong, let me say that this morning was one short journey across the Channel but one long journey back to our homeland. Moreover the journey is not over, as the task to rebuild a nation has only just begun. For many of us, including myself, this journey has been more of an internal quest to discover ourselves, rather than covering a distance, and for that it has been all the more challenging. I have given some thought to what constitutes a nation during the last three and a half years in exile and have come to the conclusion that it cannot be solely defined by a geographical boundary. It is more about a sense of belonging to a society of which one is proud. In some ways Britain has never left me during my time away. Although I may not always have realised it, it was always there. Those British citizens around the world today, even if you never return to these shores, know this: that Britain lives in the hearts of each and every one of you. The challenge facing those of us returning is to rebuild that society and stay true to the values that made it so great. When I say rebuild I don't mean that we should slavishly seek to copy the institutions that once served us so well, the world has moved on since the fateful day three and a half years ago and new challenges await us. What I mean is that we should thoughtfully create a new society according to the principles of justice, freedom and the rule of law. To this end we will welcome people of different faiths and traditions.

We will show our strength to those who attacked us by building the most tolerant and fair society the world has ever seen. Our children will be taught the way of peace so that they may one day be as proud of us as we are of those who preceded us on this noble island.'

'Now I think I most definitely do believe in miracles,' said Tallis in amazement.

'I agree, it is a historic day for us all,' said Robert.

'That man who gave the speech …' Tallis paused as if he couldn't quite believe what he was about to say. 'That man was the one who attacked me on the beach at Calais.'

'Are you sure?' asked Robert.

'There's no doubt about it,' answered Tallis, still shaking his head in bewilderment. 'I wonder who he is.'

'I'm sure we'll find that out in the coming days,' said Robert.

Ken Louis was pacing his office rapidly, incandescent with rage. He had turned off his television set after Ben's speech and had a mind to throw a stone through the screen. Already, however, he was planning on how to exact his revenge. He would discredit this landing and arrange one of his own, by breaking through the UN blockade if necessary and, yes, using violence. He would not be so easily sidelined and exiled to the political wilderness.

Elisabetta could hardly contain her pride at seeing her new husband making the speech on the sand. It had not been an easy few days for her, not knowing where Ben was, but her faith in him had remained intact and now she was being rewarded for that. The phone had not stopped ringing from well-wishers, including her family, full of admiration for Ben and the speech he had delivered. Angela had come round to the flat in person to deliver an apology for all the mean words she had once said about

Ben. Elisabetta, however, was in no mood for recriminations and forgave her former housemate's words with a dismissive wave of the hand.

Robert looked at Tallis, who was still trying to make sense of what had happened. 'I sense the hand of fate in what has happened today. I think we are being told something.'

Tallis nodded slowly in agreement, thinking about what Robert was saying.

'The kind of society he talked about building,' remarked Mwamba, 'I think we could all play a useful part in its construction.'

'Who does he speak for, though?' asked Robert. 'And do you think he was serious?'

'He speaks for me and he was serious,' said Tallis.

'In that case we have found our home,' concluded Mwamba.

On a large ship it is best if there are no passengers. Everybody on board must play a full role if it is to keep afloat for any period of time and it needs to trade fairly at all ports of call. There is as much spiritual as manual work to be done and each person has to learn to be tolerant of and try to understand the other. At the end of the day there is nowhere to go to avoid those on board. If one hurts another everybody is adversely affected and an act of sabotage can result in the whole ship going down.